FORTUNE LIMITED

A. R. Kingon-Daniels

First published by Moira Publishing House 2025

This novel is entirely a work of fiction. The names, characters and incidents portrayed in it are the work of the author's imagination. Any resemblance to actual persons, living or dead, events or localities is entirely coincidental.

First edition
ISBN: 978-0-7961-8815-1

A. R. Kingon-Daniels asserts the moral right to be identified as the author of this work.

To my family for believing in me.

To Sean, for your encouragement, and for constantly reminding me to write these words and sentences.

"Democracy cannot survive over-population. Human dignity cannot survive it. Convenience and decency cannot survive it. As you put more and more people into the world, the value of life not only declines, it disappears. It doesn't matter if someone dies. The more people there are, the less one individual matters."

-Isaac Asimov

Prologue

Dr. Marlowe gripped the armrest as his car came to a sudden halt. Shooting his driver a look, he composed himself: tie straight, blazer smoothed.

"Another stop like that and you'll be finding employment elsewhere," he said. Cold and curt.

He ran his fingers through his slick black hair and allowed the bellboy of his hotel to open the door for him. The driver could be heard sighing in relief as his master removed himself from the vehicle.

Dr. Marlowe strolled into the opulently adorned hotel entrance without so much as an acknowledgement to any of the staff he passed. Reception was straight ahead. When Dr. Marlowe entered the lobby, the two receptionists immediately stood at attention. He motioned with his hand behind him, indicating to the two bellboys (who he knew were behind him with his luggage) to take his belongings to his personal suite. The bellboys were all too familiar with the cue.

They nervously mumbled a pathetic, "Yessir," as if their master had bothered to lower himself enough to give them a direct, verbal order. They retreated in embarrassment; Dr. Marlowe hadn't cared enough to hear them. He laid his forearm on the front desk, as if he owned the place. Despite his age, he in fact did own the place. It was his hotel.

"I trust I won't find any issues with my suite this time?" he queried in a tone that could chill ice. "If I find another stain in the basin..." he trailed off, faux-perplexed as he lifted his arm to find some dust that had attached itself.

The receptionist closest to imminent danger began shaking uncontrollably. She was a young girl, likely from one of the outer suburbs, barely seventeen years old. She looked to her senior, who quickly made eye contact with the floor.

"Well," began Marlowe, "this is a bad start, isn't it," he glanced briefly at the trembling receptionist's tag and pronounced her name with icy accuracy, "Caoimhe?"

"S- sir I-" stammered Caoimhe.

"You're not from around here, are you? With an Irish name like that, I imagine you came down here to try to make something of your life? Correct?"

Caoimhe was too stunned to respond. Too scared to assume a response was required.

"Correct?" Dr. Marlowe reiterated, a tinge of annoyance in his voice.

"Uh, ye- yessir!" she responded, "My family thought it best that I-"

"So why, then, is your station dirty? It seems to me that this is a very simple responsibility to perform. How can I trust you to perform adequately in my hotels if you can't even do this correctly?"

"I'm so sorry sir, I-"

Marlowe turned around and began to move towards the elevator, "I would expect more from an employee who travelled all this way. Perhaps you can reflect on that on your travels back home."

Caoimhe began to whimper audibly.

"Sasha, begin the search for her replacement," Marlowe turned around briefly to indicate nonchalantly towards the densely populated street outside. "There are plenty of fish in the sea."

Sasha froze the minute her name was uttered. She chose then to shoot a "help me" glance to her former colleague, who was by now in tears. How did he know her name? He barely looked at her. In her stupor, she managed to let out a feeble, "Yessir."

"Good," replied Marlowe as he entered the gold-encrusted elevator. He gave a sweeping glance over the front desk, "Let that be a lesson, everyone is expendable. My usual dinner at six, if it is not too much of an inconvenience, Sasha."

With that, the elevator doors closed on Dr. Marlowe, and Sasha noted a small grin just beginning to appear on his face.

Marlowe grinned to himself. Not a grin you might get from hearing a mildly funny joke, but one of those maniacal grins that only select evil persons can perfect.

And perfect it he had.

Marlowe glanced at his state-of-the-art watch to check the time and to see if he had missed any important calls.

Five-thirty in the afternoon and no calls. Good, his people knew when not to bother him. Tapping his wrist, he impatiently waited for the elevator to stop on the top floor. The pent-house suite, of course. He was not a patient man by nature, and he needed to perfect tonight's speech, which would require him to double-check his portfolio and make sure the evidence was there. This was an important night for him. The elevator slowed to a halt and the bell ring announced Marlowe's arrival.

The doors opened directly into his living room; he stepped out to survey the area.

Everything as it should be so far, he thought to himself.

He noted his luggage beside the door. He clicked his tongue and grabbed the two large bags. The standard of his employees was slipping; the bags should be brought directly into the bedrooms, especially if the patron was of his station. He wheeled his luggage into his bedroom and took out his device, punching in a memo for himself to revisit staff hiring procedures once he has done what he came to do on his business trip.

Marlowe made certain there was liquor available in every corner of every room. He set his course for the bedroom tray and poured himself a stiff tumbler of whiskey. Swirling it around, he looked out at the view. He could have gone onto the balcony, but he had work to do. Instead, he took a moment to gaze into the haze of the horizon, Table Mountain barely visible through the smog. He took a big swig of his drink and set the glass back on the tray.

He turned back to his luggage and opened the smaller of the two suitcases. He quickly retrieved an even smaller briefcase from inside it and brought it with him to the living room. After seating himself on the couch, he opened the smaller container with exceptional ease. The clasps flicked open and Marlowe ruffled through various graphs and write-ups.

Briefly, he thought to himself, *Why on earth isn't this all just on a tablet?*

From the same case, he retrieved a thin black leather folder and flipped it open.

That was why he chose not to use them: for effect. There was nothing like holding a detailed dossier in his hand while in a meeting: no possibility of malfunctioning screens, login errors, or the like. All his audience would need to do is page through with him, hold the important documents with him and close the file decidedly, with him. No chance of Delegate Kalitz playing some juvenile dash game during the meeting: the meeting that could change the world and the future of one's empire, and more importantly, one's legacy.

No, Marlowe would have the full attention of the table. The particularly large table. What he lacked in traits such as kindness and empathy, he made up for in persuasion and showmanship. He could convince anyone to do anything – with the correct materials in front of them. Marlowe paged through the file; he finally had the correct materials this time. The name 'FORTUNE LIMITED' flashed from a page in front of him.

Too on the nose? he thought, then decided, *No.*

A car crash outside broke his attention and he grunted. Something needed to be done about this. No one knew about peace and quiet anymore. Not unless they were privileged enough to live in a mansion in some remote part of the world. Which, of course, the Marlowe family did.

There was a knock at the door; Marlowe called for them

to enter. It was his dinner.

Right on time, at least they got that right, he ruminated.

As Sasha entered feebly with a tray of Marlowe's dinner, the doctor waved for the TV to turn on. He beckoned her to set the tray on the dining table in the adjoining room.

"And the world is poised to hold its breath tonight," spoke the reporter on the news channel as the TV booted up, "as country leaders and influential businessmen and women from around the globe gather tonight in Cape Town for the first-ever World Population Summit."

"Will that be all, sir?" queried Sasha, hoping that there was nothing else needed.

"Yes yes, leave me"

"Of course, sir," Sasha gave an odd curtsy and backed away to the elevator.

"Though the first ever, this summit is met with a great amount of anticipation and hope! Having been in unofficial talks for the past few years, this evening marks the night that members will hear arguments and ultimately decide on a policy that will help curb the encroaching danger of overpopulation," the reporter carried on, but Marlowe was no longer interested.

He flipped the TV off. He still had to eat, then prep and rehearse his speech. This was his one chance. But all he needed to do is what he did best: convince.

***

The noise outside the vehicle was staggering. Marlowe's car sidled slowly up to the entrance of the convention centre amongst the traffic. Camera lights were flashing; a crazed mob of reporters and bystanders flooded the bridge-covered entrance. Dr. Marlowe could just make out the chopping of three separate helicopters hovering above, hoping to angle their cameras underneath the bridge to get footage of the esteemed guests. The more savvy reporters were present virtually, their humming drones hovering mere inches from the general population. Marlowe cared little for the people's safety, but noted their proximity with the intention of mentioning the drone regulations to the relevant authorities, should his solution be dismissed. Or even if it was passed.

An individual dressed in a rented tuxedo rushed up to Marlowe's side and opened his door for him. The lights themselves seemed to become louder as the silo of the vehicle was breached. Nevertheless, Dr. Marlowe exited with finesse, buttoning his freshly pressed suit jacket. He gave obligatory nods towards various individuals with brief, miniscule smiles. This was out of character for him, yet it was necessary. The world, and the guests already inside, were watching. He was on the job, charm turned up to maximum.

He began a slow stride towards the entrance. Occasionally lifting a hand to wave. One or two reporters managed to make themselves heard and he briefly entertained their questions with the most complex, nothing-answers he could muster. He was in his element. They received no information, yet left his side thinking they had a scoop.

These idiots are nothing compared to what's to come, he thought, they're just the warm-up.

The glass doors opened in front of him. He'd made it past the gauntlet and now a challenge that required a little more skill approached him. Mingling. He greeted the doorman, making himself seem approachable and within seconds, the delegates from India, Russia and SearchMe were almost upon him. Smiles were wide and fake pleasantries were exchanged.

"So this is your neck of the woods, is it, Dr. Marlowe?" enquired Russia.

"Beautiful, isn't it?" Marlowe replied.

India chimed in with a little spite on her tongue, "I enjoyed it back when you could actually see the mountain."

SearchMe's representative attempted to join in, "And the harbour, am I right?"

"Now now, Pooja, this is why we are here, no?" Marlowe said, ignoring the spry, young SearchMe rep. Just because you represent the new hot search engine of the last few decades, does not warrant you an immediate 'in' with the likes of nations – or Marlowe.

But they are here, I suppose.

India nodded in agreement, "One must be positive. Hopefully, we will leave this summit with a solution."

"I bet you hope it's yours, hm, Doctor?" Russia chimed in.

"I have my own solution, that's true, but really, I just want to fix this."

"Don't lie, Marlowe, the contract would be life-changing, wouldn't it?" interjected SearchMe with a childish laugh; his champagne sloshed dangerously close to the edge of his glass. Marlowe allowed the outburst and the familiar tone only because it gave him social credit. This night would end in a vote, after all.

"Well, of course money is always nice to have, but let's not pretend like any of us are starving at the moment, Lawrence," Marlowe played, "no, I am really only here to do my part. Offer my plan of action and hope for the best. I am not such a fool to believe there won't be a better option presented," he locked eyes with Pooja and gave a friendly chuckle, "I mean, it's practically like a lottery, how many solutions are going to be tabled? No, I have an idea and I feel obligated to present it."

"Ten, doctor," said Pooja, "there are only ten solutions being presented."

Of course Marlowe was well aware of his odds. He was merely playing to the crowd.

"Oh really?" he exclaimed. "That's interesting news. In any case, ten is still a large number."

"True," said Russia, "I hear the U.S. has something involving Mars."

Mars again?

That had been tried a few years prior. Short of terraforming Mars, it was not a viable short-term solution. It would take at least decades to get the first batch of colonists settled. One rejected, eight more to beat.

"Mars is an interesting option, I look forward to their proposal." Marlowe lied.

"Bullshit," interjected Lawrence.

"Anyway, what does *your* plan revolve around?" probed Russia.

Marlowe couldn't help himself, he smiled and, with a flick of his index finger, he said, "Choice."

The three faces before him were intrigued.

"But we shall see what happens," he quickly tacked on.

He didn't want to give away any more; he'd already planted the seed of human choice. Something that everyone cherished; the free will to do something. He began backing away, wanting this thought to marinate in these chatterboxes and disperse amongst the other delegates. He needed to give them time to do some guesswork before his speech. Plant the seed in more minds.

Looking over his shoulder, he muttered, "Did I hear something about a one-child policy?"

***

The room was dark, lit up by pinpointed lights that lined the long, oval, mahogany, United Nations-type table, which took up most of the large conference hall. Each delegate had a column of light upon them and the summit's unique crest lay plastered on the floor in the middle. It created something to look at when the talks got boring. At the head of the crest, in a break of the gargantuan table, stood a podium, also adorned with the summit crest.

Marlowe and the rest of the delegates had just completed a rather lack-lustre round of applause when he noticed the chairperson (one of his own, South African President Ndlovu) take the stand.

Within moments, her strong voice boomed, "Thank you to the esteemed delegate of Brazil. We move now to the last proposal on our agenda for the evening. I would like to remind everyone of the confidentiality agreement we all signed, as we break for a short recess on the tail end of this last presentation. You are required to please make your way to your own isolated pods to make use of the time to consider for yourself, your vote."

Marlowe stiffened, hoping his pregaming had paid off. At the beginning of the proceedings, the delegates were aware of the tidbits of information he'd shared. And he would be last to present, therefore creating a cathartic reveal at the end of the proceedings.

He'd be on their minds the whole evening.

Marlowe searched the corners of the room for his people with the dossiers ready for handout. He was the only delegate presenting tactile proofs; something the delegates could take to their isolation pods.

"Please give a warm welcome to Marlowe Enterprises's founder and CEO: Dr. Klaus Marlowe."

With that, the president returned to her seat, clapping politely. The hall buzzed with a healthy applause as Marlowe made his way to the podium. He nodded to his people to begin dispersing the maroon files as he readied himself. Before long, almost all delegates had a dossier.

"Please refrain from opening the dossier until everyone has had the opportunity to receive one. We will begin momentarily."

Marlowe opened his own file. 'FORTUNE LIMITED' once again came into vision, beautifully embossed in gold. He put on a confident smile, looked up and proudly stated, "You may open your dossiers."

There was a mumbling of voices, but Marlowe quickly regained their attention, "Fortune Limited!" he exclaimed, "The Solution!"

Everyone's attention was transfixed on the showman. Marlowe's smile turned slightly more sinister.

Game.

Set.

Match.

40
Years Later

Chapter 1

Lance

Fumes fogged the air as the lively suburb, recently renamed 'Outer Suburb Sixteen', began readying itself for the evening. Not much would change except the lighting. Many factories would carry on operating, which meant that there would still be a steady stream of shift workers moving to and from work. The local bars would pick up a bit, though not much more than in the day. In a twenty-four-hour work day, the need for alcohol for off-shift workers heightened extraordinarily. The evenings would be only a little busier due to the younger crowd sneaking out after curfew.

A halo of warm yellow light extended from the ill-fitted front door of the Mason residence. Such light was not uncommon on their street, yet to many members of the community it symbolised something very unique: a warm, happy family. Despite the countless issues the Masons faced on a day-to-day basis (not unlike anyone else), they were resilient. Like most other families, they engaged in a cycle: work, get paid, provide and repeat. Despite the monotony, they always seemed like an anomaly in a particularly dystopian science experiment. There were always smiles on their faces and love in their eyes.

Even for the strangers across the road.

The residents of their street were nearly jealous of their positivity. They had very few prospects, yet ever-filled glasses of optimism. Lance was in his early twenties, but he had the wits about him to know that that outlook on life – the one that many would cringe over, the one that protested to the outsider that 'everything was fine' – was really the only way to keep him from curling up on the floor of his small, cramped bedroom and cry into the void about life's unfairness. Lance contemplated the same act many times, only to stop himself and ask: what would a Mason do when confronted with seemingly insurmountable odds? The answer was almost always: get your ass up and do something about it. So he did.

Tonight was a special night in the Mason home. Lance's younger brother, and designated middle child, Marc, was turning nineteen. For as long as Lance could remember, birthdays were always celebrated in the best way possible in the Mason residence. Usually, they involved special family meals topped off with secret (though not so secret) birthday cakes. His parents, Anita and Grant, had done a great job of raising their little family. Lance was proud to be their son. This birthday evening was no different; all members were in attendance, seated around a small dining table tucked away in their small kitchen. Hanging from the ceiling, just above the birthday boy, was a homemade sign that read: Happy Birthday Marcy! Its creator, Lance's twelve-year-old sister Jan, sat proudly next to Marc. And Lance occupied his other side.

"Jan, I don't mean to question your work but," Lance said, playfully tapping Marc's shoulder, pointing at the sign, "who is Marcy?"

The table laughed, Jan included.

"*I* didn't choose to spell his name like that," Jan defended herself.

"Well, it's beautiful, dear and *I* read it correctly: Mar-K-y," chuckled their mother.

"I would hope so, mom. The 'c' was your choice, after all," said Lance as he got up to dish his parents some food.

He had taken his elder sibling role to heart as of late. He wasn't trying to win brownie points or anything, he just wanted to show them that they could trust him to have their backs. He knew his father and mother worked tirelessly to provide for them and he also knew that his siblings depended on him. Jan was still in school, so that was obvious, but Marc was another thing entirely. He, like Lance, worked. He gave what he could to help, but even so, Lance felt a parental obligation to him. And so he would do the small things, like serve food to everyone at dinner to show his commitment to them. On this particular evening, however, he was intercepted by his mother, slapping his hands. Anita took the reins and relocated the food to Marc's plate first.

Lance held up his hands and smiled, "Sorry, I forgot."

"How could you forget! You were just making fun of my name!" piped in Marc. "This is my day, I will have you know."

"Oh is it? I had no idea."

Grant, who had been watching the show quietly, let out a hearty chuckle, "Come guys, dish up or it will get cold, your mother spent all her free time today cooking this, let's not waste it."

Marc dove into his plate and through a full mouth, exclaimed, "I'dth never dream ov'it."

"Marc, manners!" said Anita through a smile as she dished her husband some, "Is it good?" A thumbs-up from Marc brought another smile to her face.

The family enjoyed their dinner. Unsurprisingly, not a scrap of food was left on the table by the end. The family all sat back in contented silence as they let their mouths take a break and their digestive systems some time to do their jobs. After a decent pause, Lance glanced at the vintage clock on the wall. It was a bit worse for wear, but it showed the time all the same. He made eye contact with his mother and she looked over as well. Her expression told him that she knew it was getting late, but not too late.

"Jan, dear, it's getting late and it is a school night," Anita began, giving her daughter an inconspicuous wink, "we don't want you falling asleep at your desk, do we?"

"But you said I could do online school tomorrow-" began Jan before she remembered the ruse she and Lance had agreed to earlier that day.

"I don't think we have much data left this week, Jannie."

"Uh, yes oh… ah- awww! Fine, I'll clean up then," Jan struggled to recover. She stood up and collected the plates. Marc remarked about how out of character this was for her as the others pushed out their chairs, ready to get on with their evenings.

"Marcy dear, are you working tomorrow?" asked Anita.

"Yes and no, they gave me the morning off, I just have to come in for half a shift."

"How nice of them!" Anita responded, beckoning to the living area, "How about a movie tonight then?" Marc smiled.

Lance knew he would rather go to his room and rehearse some side for some audition of his coming up, but his mother's face looked so hopeful. Lance put his hand on Marc's shoulders. They rarely all had time to watch a movie together. Marc nodded as his father passed him with a pat on the back, headed to his favourite tattered leather armchair.

"What movie do you have in mind, Mom?" asked Lance as he bounded to the couch. Anita walked over and lifted up a Movie Card, inserting it into the TV.

Lance smiled, "Looks like we are going old-school again, Russian roulette!"

The TV booted up. It was not a top-of-the-range TV, in fact, it was quite dated. But it still had a functional card reader.

"When do we not?" chuckled Marc as he plonked himself next to Lance.

The four of them stared at the TV, waiting to see which movie the card decided to play. Movie Cards were almost a novelty, but in their heyday they were all the rage. You bought a Movie Card and it would have a free connection to a curated film storage cloud, any film that had been uploaded to the cloud could be accessed, but the fun of it was that the owner had no control over what it chose. You could have either an Oscar-worthy production or a terrible, C-rated horror. Each time was different. Eventually, they lost popularity and the company went under a number of years ago. Now, the cloud was still accessible, but the library had not been updated in almost nine years. Most people threw their cards away, though a few – like the

Masons – hung on to theirs. A free movie in this economy was nothing to turn your nose at! The luck of the draw was a fate they were willing to take. In any case, the family would typically comment on the film as it played, giving their scores for acting, cinematography and so on. It was less about the story and more about the analysis. An activity for the whole family.

Just as the film started, Jan burst from the kitchen in a loud, off-key rendition of 'Happy Birthday', carrying a modestly-sized homemade cake. Anita and Grant joined in the choir followed quickly (after hitting pause) by Lance. A wide smile spread across Marc's face as his family chanted to his health and birth. Jan set down the cake on the coffee table in front of him. Lance noted that not only was there cake, but there was a candle atop it and five cups of coffee on the tray. Coffee was scarce and he knew it fuelled their happiness that night.

"Mom, Dad, coffee too?" Marc blurted out, hugging his mother and then his father.

"Yes, my boy, " said Grant proudly, "I had a little extra money this week, so I thought, why not!"

"Thanks, Dad, and Mom, this cake looks amazing! Is it-"

"Chocolate? It sure is!" anticipated Anita, clearly happy to see her son and family in such high spirits, "Now come come, blow out your candle."

"Wait!" Jan shouted just before Marc could blow, "You need to make a wish first!"

"I know that, silly!" Marc closed his eyes, took a moment and then opened and blew.

"What did you wish for!?"

"Jan, telling you defeats the magic of the wish," replied Marc with a smile. He picked up the knife and began slicing his cake.

"If I had a guess, it would be to become a famous actor!" joked Lance, jabbing Marc in the side lightly.

"Shush!" said Marc.

"Well, you know there's always Fortune," said Lance, who immediately regretted his words.

The atmosphere in the room went cold. Smiles left the faces of his family members. Marc stopped mid-cut, staring into his cake. The cold silence seemed to go on for an eternity, though in reality was probably only a few seconds.

Anita broke the silence, uttering gravely, "I told you not to joke about that company, Lance." Lance nodded his apology.

As he wished he could turn back time, Anita attempted to bring the cheer back, quickly changing the subject back to Marc, "Where's my slice, darling?"

Grant put his hand on Marc's shoulder as he was handed his slice of cake, "You know, we will do everything we can to help you with your dream, my boy. Any way we can."

Marc tapped his father's hand and replied warmly with a tender smile, "I know Dad, thanks." Marc plated a piece of cake for his mother and then himself.

He leant back in his seat, acknowledging the drop in festivities with a loud, "Well! I hope the card has decided on a goodie, last time we got 'Alien 10' and you know how that went!"

The rest of the family snapped back to themselves: hearty, happy. They nodded, laughed and commented on the atrocious acting and camera angles from their last movie night.

If one was a fly on the wall of the Masons' lounge, and not interested in seeing what movie the Movie Card ended up choosing, it would have noticed, like Lance did, a tiny glimmer of sober thought that crossed the face of Marc Mason. But before it was completely visible, a smile flared up and he, once again, existed in the present.

The lounge was filled with laughter and frivolity that night as the family enjoyed their unusual-usual birthday evening together.

Chapter 2
The Masons

Grant Mason yawned himself awake. Turning over in his bed, careful not to wake his wife, he checked the time on his device; it was seven o'clock. His heart raced a bit as he momentarily forgot that he opted for the later shift that day, since he knew his previous evening would be a late one. Stilling his beating heart, he slowly edged his body to an upright position and rubbed his eyes. Anita sleepily turned over with a morning grumble. Grant smiled as he checked for messages on the side of his bed. Eventually, he stood and made for the bathroom – still half asleep.

The shower's rusty pipes moaned to life as he turned the tap. Water burst out and soon ran warm enough to climb in.

After a few minutes, Grant stood by the foggy mirror

in his towel. It was more an act of autopilot and ritual than necessity to stand in front of a mirror at this point in his life when shaving; it did not bother him too much that he could not see his middle-aged reflection. With the aftershave firmly applied, Grant grabbed his overalls from the back of a dining room chair that just happened to be in the bedroom. He put it on as he did every day and made sure to flush out the pockets; he hated when the material was bunched up. His hand moved to flatten his left breast pocket when he felt a harder clump. Not pocket material, something papery. He reached in and removed a crumpled up twenty-credit note. He smiled and nodded to himself, proud of his find. He folded the note and moved to the kitchen.

He flung open a scarcely occupied cupboard and fished out an energy bar for breakfast. He opened the cupboard above the stovetop next. Inside were three jars, each with a clear name written on masking tape that had been slapped onto them: Lance, Marc, Jan.

Grant hummed as his fingers slowly caressed each jar.

Which one?

Eventually, he decided on Marc's, given that it was his birthday the day before and all. Happy with his decision, he grabbed the jar and unscrewed the top. Inside was a modest amount of credits, some holding more value than others. He dropped the twenty credit note into the jar and screwed the top back on, shoving the jar back into the cupboard.

Grant and Anita knew they couldn't give their children much, but they did all that they could. These jars were emptied yearly into a savings account in each of their children's names. Grant was the superstitious one, insisting on a yearly deposit in case something happened, or the banks lost their money. In that terrible scenario, at least there would be something left in the jars.

So far, they had amassed a large enough sum for Lance, whose biggest ambition was to become a lawyer. Not a famous, world-renowned lawyer, just a small town lawyer who could live a comfortable life fighting for the everyday person. Lance was like that, a bit cheeky with his siblings, but he had a big heart. He cared for everyone he met. Grant remembered when Lance was having trouble deciding on medical school or law school. Grant would never admit it, but he was glad Lance had chosen law. With his ambitions modest but not high, he could afford a decent school (even if it wasn't top of the range). Med school would have been another story. Grant calculated that they had accumulated enough money for only one year's tuition. Lance was a smart boy and Grant was sure that he could get a scholarship for the rest of his studies if he kept his grades up. Grant would help out where he could, but as far as the big haul was concerned, his eldest was 'done and dusted,' as he liked to say. He would be beginning law school next year.

Jan was the youngest and still had a ways to go, but, so far, her ambitions were that of education. She loved people and was always teaching the Masons something or other. She had not said anything about it yet, but Grant and Anita were both putting their money on her going to a teacher training college. They were happy with that option. Teachers were in demand; she would be sure to get a job. Luckily, they still had some time to save, but by their estimates, they would be on track by her nineteenth birthday.

Marc was the special case, but Anita and Grant made no show of disappointment about his aspirations. They had instilled a dreamer mentality in all their children and they were happy that their offspring had passions. They believed Marc had talent so they supported him in every way that they could. The issue was that the life and path of an actor was not as cut and dry as finding an institution and paying a first year tuition. There were location factors to consider, and with that, a certain amount of budget for accommodation. They had no family car so he would have to commute quite far for auditions and roles, if he even booked them. Not to mention the factors that he and Anita could not comprehend; they'd never been in the industry themselves. Marc's dream was a challenge, but they took it in their stride, making sure to budget as best they could. By their estimates, they needed another two years before Marc would be able to happily pursue his dream for a year, unencumbered by the worry of everyday life and those unforeseen industry expenses. Grant smiled; Marc was now twenty credits closer to that goal.

Just then, Anita sidled into the small kitchen (really, a kitchenette).

"Morning, dear," she yawned as she moved towards the kettle.

Coffee. There was still some left over. She needed it if she was to get through her own working day. Anita's eyes met her husband's as his hand dropped from the handle of the kids' cupboard.

She grinned as she effortlessly fished a mug from the dish rack while keeping Grant in her sights, "What was the haul this time?"

Grant chuckled, "Twenty, my personal best."

"You lie!" Anita slapped Grant's arm playfully, "Where?" Grant tapped his breast pocket and moved towards the door, Anita nodded, "That's a lot to suddenly find in your pocket."

"I suppose," Grant agreed as he slowly backed towards the front of the house, "but you know the drill: if I don't know what it's for-"

"-then I know what it's for," Anita chimed along as her husband disappeared out the front door with a 'love you!'

That was their rule in life, well, one of them in any case: if they found money and didn't know what it was originally meant for, then it was to go directly into their children's future. Anita chuckled and returned to her coffee as Jan burst into the kitchen, eager for breakfast. She was likely after the rare coffee.

***

Grant's commute to work was not entirely unpleasant. Yes, the streets were always crowded, and yes, the beautiful South African morning sunrise was blocked by tall exhaust chimneys and the smoke they pumped out, but despite that, the route was pleasant. People on the streets greeted him kindly every day. Occasionally, Mrs. Smith would offer him a coffee on the go since, for some reason, she often had some to spare. There was even a nature reserve that Grant liked to cut across instead of taking the road up to the official entrance. He would always show face at the main entrance, of course, he just liked the walk. Today was no different. Grant entered the nature reserve, strolling through the plant life. Upon entering the factory premises, he turned down the fence line towards the main entrance, where he always met his co-worker.

"Morning," greeted Alec, "how was your night?"

"Great, thanks, and yours? Stella doing good?"

"Oh yeah, she's great, false alarm though. No little Alec

just yet!" Alec joked with a slight annoyance in his eyes.

He had taken the late shift today because he thought he would be helping his wife through childbirth the night before. To his dismay, it had been just a cramp.

"You can't take chances, Alec, and in any case, I'm glad you'll be keeping me company."

"You're great and all, but I'd prefer a cold one at a decent hour on a Friday night. No offence."

Grant laughed as he held his employee badge up to the scanner. The scanner beeped once and the turnstyle clicked, ready for him to enter. On the other side, he waited patiently for Alec. After a hurried ruffle through his overall pockets, eventually Alec came through.

"So chivalrous!" Alec joked as he patted Grant's back, angling him towards their work station for the day, "And your boy? Had a good dinner?"

***

Though Anita Mason worked, her job was not shift work, like her husband's. This arrangement was for the best, they had decided, given that it would allow Anita to be at home at a regular time each week day. This way, she could help the kids with whatever they needed. From a young age, Anita had wanted to lead a household. She adored her family in her younger days and had always wanted a decent sized one of her own. She liked to feel needed by her children. In her mind they (her whole family, really) were her real career.

She worked at a local school during the day, allowing her close proximity to her children. Bookkeeping was never her top priority, but she still took great pride in everything she did. She was not shy of standing up for herself in the staffroom and had enjoyed many well deserved promotions. She was recently appointed to the Head of Office Staff at the school. She was like a manager, only paid the equivalent of a first year teacher's salary. She did not mind that all too much. After all, her *real* job was all the more rewarding.

The clock struck three-thirty in the afternoon and Anita let out a sigh of relief. She sat behind her desk in her tiny, personal office; it was personalised with digital frames, an old diffuser with an intermittent supply of essential oils that made her workplace smell fresh and friendly. The office was the only perk she received from her promotion and even if she couldn't afford a constant supply of office accessories and refills, she'd be damned if she didn't try and make it her home away from home.

Anita cracked her fingers before the urge to stretch took over her whole body. A yawn slipped out as well. She soon stood up and packed a few of her belongings into her handbag. She seldom had work to take home with her, but, at this time of the month, she had to review some staff changes before they made official terminations.

Grant can help me with this, she mused, *he always knows how to go about these types of things.* Then with a sigh, *Either way, Janet's going to be devastated.*

Zipping up her bag, she grabbed her cardigan, employee badge and headed out.

The hallway to the entrance of the school was long and narrow from the admin block, where she was stationed. It was an old building with face-brick walls inside and a two-toned, smoothed concrete style flooring that ran throughout the entire school. Her heels clacked her passage down the corridor. The sound reverberated rather ominously that day. Anita finally reached the entrance and pushed the door open while simultaneously scanning her badge to clock out. With one last half-hearted wave goodbye to her colleagues, she disappeared.

The sun had decided to momentarily poke its head out from behind the clouds. Anita's eyes lit up as her vision adjusted to the yellow-grey light and sudden greenery that juxtaposed oddly against the backdrop. Despite the disgusting architecture of the school, they kept the grounds tidy. Many schools in the country attempted to maintain their plots of land, trying their best to keep the grounds as green as possible. With population levels on the rise, more and more land was being consumed by apartment buildings, houses, and factories. If the school grounds weren't well-kept, Anita knew plenty of businessmen could argue that the land surrounding the school could be used more effectively. So, they did their best to keep it tidy and maintained. It was one of the reasons Anita enjoyed her job; she could stroll through the beautiful garden. She playfully lorded the ease of her career over Grant, who was painfully jealous.

***

There was a clanking sound that shook Alec's work device off of the handrail it had been so precariously placed upon. He and Grant had been scheduled to do maintenance on a generator – it was in dire need of help.

Grant looked up from the underside of the massive machine, face blackened by oil and smoke, "What did you do?! It was working just fine."

Alec held up his hands in protest, "I did nothing! What did you do?!"

Grant took a deep breath and exhaled, choosing as

always to keep his frustrations to a minimum. What good would getting angry do? He grabbed a spanner from his toolbelt. Alec was a great friend and co-worker, but he lacked an array of technical skills. Grant, being older, had become somewhat of a mentor to the young man. He tried to teach him the tricks of the trade, but most often felt that the info was going in one ear and out the other. He peered around again as he tightened a bolt to see Alec muttering to himself and picking his device off the floor. Just after placing it back on the rail, he twitched slightly and the device went flying again.

"Shit!" shouted Alec.

Grant just chuckled, "Relax, these things are practically indestructible."

He was already suspended next to the generator, so he flicked the tether clamp and began his descent, "I got it, if you managed to tighten the loose bolt, then why not give it a whirr so long? Use the embedded panel on top!"

"Sure, yeah, thanks," Alec looked around for the generator's ladder.

In truth, he had only barely tightened the bolt. He was too scared to mention that to Grant now, after just making a fool of himself twice. He hurried over to the generator's ladder; there was a groan of metal as he hopped on. He shrugged it off and proceeded to climb the machine.

Grant placed his feet on the ground, unclipping himself to pick the device off the floor under the gangway. He held his breath before flipping it over. Alec's expletive was right. It was cracked and glitching in places. He could make out the generator's schematics and systems, but they were buzzing in and out of vision.

"Oh, Alec," he muttered to himself as he attempted to salvage the device as best he could, ambling slowly back towards his tether.

Alec had now reached the top of the generator. Panting, as he was not the athletic type, he fumbled open the embedded panel. He shifted his weight slightly and the generator shuddered with another metallic groan. Alec muttered to himself something about the company not investing in the newer models.

He couldn't see Grant from his position no matter how far he leaned, so he called out, "G, got my panel?!"

Grant was too focused to properly listen to Alec, so he just replied, "Yeah!"

He was busy rebooting the system, hoping that would sort out the glitching so that they could at least work with the cracked screen. Mindlessly, Grant used his free hand to clip his tether back on.

"Alright!" shouted Alec, "Flipping the switch!"

He pressed the 'power on' button. Instantly, the machine roared to life, but the loose bolt shot off and the generator's other clamps, under the weight of Alec, buckled dangerously. Alec barely had a second to comprehend what was happening as the generator vibrated to life. The other bolts came free and the power wires fell from the ceiling.

Rapt in thought, Grant Mason didn't notice the chaos around him. Too focused on helping his co-worker, he barely made out the reflection of the generator in the glitching screen as it hurtled towards him.

***

Anita reached home at four o'clock, just like she did every other day. She entered the cold house just as it began to drizzle outside. She hung her coat on the little rack by the door and headed over to the kitchen to fetch a glass of water.

Perhaps there's some coffee left?

Jan rushed into the kitchen to greet her with a hug, and to mention the maths homework she needed help with. Sighing, Anita agreed to help her daughter on condition she helped prep dinner first. Jan agreed.

Lance and Marc had only just arrived home and settled into their evening routines of doing little other than relaxing on the couch, when there was a knock on the door.

It was an unsettling knock that seemed very out of place in the neighbourhood. It seemed rehearsed and formal. Not one inhabitant of Thirty-Five Cellar Road moved a muscle. Then the knock came again, louder this time. More forceful.

Lance broke the silence, "Mom, someone's at the door, must I get it?!"

"No, darling, you relax, I'm up already," came the reply, "Jannie, please watch the pot."

Anita set her wooden spoon on the counter and wiped her hands on her apron as she moved towards the front door. As she walked, each step seemed to feel off to her. They rarely received any houseguests on weekdays. And any of them would call out before they knocked, or at least message her first. She passed the lounge, her steps growing heavier; she twirled her wedding ring out of nervous habit. The knocks sounded through the house once again, this time they were greater in number and faster. With a lump in her throat, Anita suddenly thought of the small list of bills they had yet to pay.

Have we gone too far past due? Her mind raced, *I'm sure Grant paid just last week.*

Her steps stopped as she reached the front door. She told

herself it was probably nothing.

If anything, it's a girl scout selling biscuits.

But, then again, when was the last time girl scouts went door to door instead of online?

She was, however, uncharacteristically wrapped in fear and she entertained these thoughts purely as a way to ready herself for the news that she did not know she was getting, but *felt* nevertheless.

She drew a breath as she pulled down the ice-cold door handle, opening her home to two sullen men in damp overalls. Anita took note of the emblem embossed on the front of both of their front pockets. She knew immediately where they were from: Grant's work. In fact, one of them looked familiar.

Alex? No, Alec.

More thoughts rushed through her mind, though none as tragic as the truth she was about to receive.

Alec seemed too distraught to speak. He probably should not have been there, he should be sitting at the back of an emergency van in a blanket being talked to by an EMT, but there he was. Although he was a joker, he was a principled man. Perhaps the reason Grant had taken a liking to him in the first place. He looked as though he should be the one delivering the news, but he seemed too distraught to speak.

The man accompanying him was the one to say it. He knew Grant's family, though only through peripheral encounters. In that way, he was the right one to speak. With soft, mournful words that sounded both kind and despicable to Anita, he relayed the events of the afternoon. He then recounted how Grant had been a good, honourable and helpful man. How he had known the risks. He spoke of how Grant's loss was a blow to the whole crew and that they would miss his friendly, fatherly presence on the workfloor.

No one could fault his words or even why they were said (as they had a tinge of self-preservation – likely words enforced by the company). What someone could fault him on was the timing of the sentiments. Though Grant's buddies at the factory had known and at least had a little time to mourn their loss, Anita had not had such a luxury. She was bombarded, unprovoked by a barrage of terrible facts. Her husband was dead, the one responsible was standing in front of her, it was acknowledged as a loss to the company – but what about *her*? What did it mean to *her*?

The hand she had on the doorframe suddenly dislodged itself and Anita had no energy to replace it. It slumped to her side as the two ex-colleagues looked at her in awkward silence. For some reason, Anita's first thought was about dinner and how she had prepared enough for five, though now it would go to waste. One cannot judge someone for their mind processing information, but she did. Suddenly, a wail erupted from deep within her and tears started pouring out. Her knees buckled and she fell forward, caught carefully – awkwardly by Alec, who brought her gently into a sitting position on the small front porch. It was still raining. Anita cried. She cried for her husband and she cried for her thoughts, she cried for the loss of her best friend and she cried for her children, but most of all, she cried for her life that had suddenly been ripped apart at the seams.

***

The news of the accident spread like shockwaves through

the tight-knit community. A larger population usually meant people were less likely to know each other (big cities where everyone is just focussed on their immediate life and family because there are simply too many people to really care about). In the case of Outer Suburb Sixteen, this was not true. Outer Suburb Sixteen was an anomaly, while its population was one of the most rapidly rising of the suburbs, it still retained its small town feel of yesteryear. Everyone knew just about everyone... or at least the family as a group. Everyone was friendly with everyone, for the most part.

Though they liked the family feel, they kept their issues to themselves. They enjoyed friends and company, but if there was an issue, they preferred sorting it out before anyone could add their own opinions on the matter. Unfortunately this was not a matter the Masons could easily hide, nor would they want to pretend like everything was alright, because it wasn't. It was also particularly difficult to hide the solemn scene in the doorway of Thirty-Five Cellar Road from the people passing on the street and the fortunate stay-at-home neighbours watching with shocked faces and bated breath from their windows.

Luckily, the Willemses from across the road took matters into their own hands. They were long time family friends, in the truest sense, and Tracey Willemse – the matriarch of the family – decided to take all the funeral arrangements upon herself. She did not ask Anita. From knowing her through twenty years of friendship, she already knew her actions would be appreciated. She made the calls and within a day she had a whole plan ready to present to Anita and the rest of the Masons.

With her handbag under her arm, Tracey crossed the street in a pencil skirt and blazer look that was iconically

'Tracey'. Usually, she preferred the louder colours to accompany her larger-than-life personality, but today and for the next few weeks, she felt tasteful greys and blacks were prudent. She reached the front door and her slender arm rose to knock. The door opened before she had the chance.

For a moment, Tracey was slightly confused by who stood before her. She looked at the familiar face, wondering if it was the same person, the expression was one she never saw him wear. The same age, but suddenly wise beyond his years, Lance's eyes were red and, though clearly distraught, he had on the smallest of genuine smiles.

All he could muster was a feeble, "Aunty Tracey."

"Hello my dear," replied Tracey with a warm, sympathetic smile as she leaned in for a hug.

It was more just a customary embrace, the kind one does when meeting anyone they generally liked after a little while apart, though Lance reciprocated with something deeper.

Tracey was taken by surprise, but indulged in the longer embrace and patted his back, "There there," she reassured, "come, let me inside and let me help."

Lance wiped newly formed tears from his eyes and nodded, ushering her into the house. Tracey followed Lance to the living room, along the way she greeted Jan and Marc, who were sitting together in the small passageway. Marc had his arms around his sobbing sister. You could see he too had been crying, though Tracey noted a very strange expression on his face; an expression of determination, with a hint of defiance.

But he was still young, still a teen.

She let that thought pass through her mind.

Tracey entered the living room to see Anita seated on

the couch, staring out the window into the distance. In one hand she held her device, the other hand's finger tips were slowly getting lost between her lips as she mindlessly bit them. All around her lay plates of barely touched food and many overly used tissues. Tracey found an open spot on the couch and seated herself.

"Can I offer you some tea, Aunty?" asked Lance politely, as if his father were still around to insist he offered.

"No thank you my dear, I just came to speak with your mother quickly."

Anita only now moved her head to acknowledge her best friend. Tracey smiled at her and shifted herself a little closer.

"Oh Tray," began Anita before she was stopped by Tracey's hand carefully grabbing her head and bringing it in for an embrace.

This time, it was meant to be like the one Lance had taken earlier. Anita sobbed again.

"Shh Anni, shhh. I'm here, we all are. Me, Alan, everyone," Tracey pushed Anita back to look into her eyes, "we are here for you and your kids. In fact, you know me, I came with a plan. All you need to do is nod and I will get the ball rolling."

Anita mouthed the words 'thank you' as Tracey pulled out her device.

"Now Anni, I know this is going to be difficult, I have done most of the funeral arrangements already- " Anita gasped a little, not because of the fact that Tracey had taken it upon herself, but by the fact that she hadn't even thought of it, "Anni, most of it is done, I just need your opinion on these two things and I can get it done. You'll just need to show up."

Anita sniffed, wiped her tears and nodded for Tracey to

bring the device closer. As she did, a web page of coffins came into view. More tears started to form, but she held them back, until she saw the prices. She let out another gasp, which let loose the flood gates again.

"Tray I, I can't- I- I-" she motioned to the bills scattered around her, "I can't even- I- Grant, he's-"

"Anni, listen to me," came Tracey's stern yet kind voice, "I said all I need is your opinion."

"But- But I can't, Tray," continued Anita through her sobs, "I can't give my husband a- a- funeral, I have to- I need to-"

"Anni, Grant will have a funeral. We are going to say goodbye to him. You don't need to worry about that."

Tracey wiped Anita's tears and held her face in her free hand, "I told you, Anni, we are here for you. Now, this mahogany looks very nice, don't you think?"

Anita took a second to acknowledge what her best friend was doing for her and then, without even looking at the device again, she sniffed and nodded, "Yes, thank you."

***

The funeral was short and meaningful in all the right ways. Tracey had done a good job and everyone present (which was a lot of people) paid their respects to the family, and to Grant.

Anita and her children were dressed in black. While Anita stood there, she hated the fact that her mind wandered. Wandered to silly things. Like to the likelihood that others in attendance would notice that the black they wore was faded on certain pieces of clothing. That they would also notice that the Masons wore very similar mourning clothes as they did a few years ago for their cousin's funeral.

Eventually, Anita's mind wandered into more dangerous territory: numbness.

Before Anita lost herself – perhaps forever – she noticed that one of her children had a peculiar look on his face. Marc had been shifting around throughout the proceedings and occasionally looked her and his siblings up and down, feeling the cuffs of his old jacket. Someone not losing herself to grief would have identified his expression as that of determination, but also of duty.

9
Years Later

Chapter 3
Lance

It was getting dark. Lance stood in front of an old-school pinup board, staring at it with desperation. He begged for it to offer up some new clue or unexplored avenue. But it gave him nothing.

Red string and blue pins still connected photographs to logos to people, explaining both what he knew and what he wanted to know. Lance placed a cautious two fingers and traced the red string, breathing out through his nose as he did so. The red string could have been any of the others. He needed there to be something.

There has to be something.

The board remained silent.

What he knew: Fortune Limited was a company that was founded, and still run, by a man named Klaus Marlowe.

Had he any desire to show this man the same respect he usually showed superiors, he would have written Doctor Marlowe next to his printed image. This man, however, Lance would not give the satisfaction of rank, even in private. Rank and respect were earned, and by Lance's standards this man had not achieved either.

Lance tapped the image. Marlowe was the CEO, Fortune Limited was built upon the promise of creating a solution for the overpopulation problem. Despite nearly four decades in the game, the statisticians so far could not yet agree if the company's methods had actually had a significant impact, but the nations who invested were in way too deep to pull funding at this point. Populations showed no sign of slowing their birth rates and even given that millions of contracts were ended per year, the knock-on effects were still through the roof. In the minds of the wealthy investors, Fortune Limited was a baby that still needed to grow up.

A single red string leapt out from an image of Klaus Marlowe, a man with sharp features and almost snow white hair, and made its way to a post-it that read: investors. The post-it itself was a jumping point for a number of other red strings all pointing to various countries: China, India, USA, EU, and others. And then to large businesses, LazerTech, FetchIT and the like.

The investors' offshoot seemed to hover like a dark cloud above the head of Dr. Marlowe, ready to sentence him to death at any moment. It was a coincidentally apt image, given the power they held over his brainchild. And the nature of Fortune.

Next to the doctor was a man whose face seemed friendly, but whose eyes spoke evil: Arrigo Meyer, Corporate Communications Officer. Strings linked him to the news and media networks. Various articles took up space on the board: praise from the bought media, damnation from the alternative media. The bought media, though, still had the cultural power. Meyer knew that. However, despite his importance in being the media face of the company, he was not that important to Lance's investigation. And that was it. There were a few other tidbits pinned up, but nothing that amounted to much, just professional guesses.

Lance peeled himself away from the board with a sigh. He knew there had to be a way to get at some dirt, but at that point in time he had no leads.

He walked back around to his desk. Lance's study was moderately sized, though relatively grand in design. He had thick block-out curtains and a selection of restored furniture from the early nineteen hundreds. His desk was large, dark oak; solid and built to stand the test of time. Lance sat himself in his leather swivel chair and fell into his usual position: elbow on the side of the desk, hand cradling his chin. He sat there deep in thought, staring at his desk top.

Though his desk and surrounding furniture were old-timey, his appliances were top of the line. He had a slim LazerTech device with a variety of wireless accessories dotted around. Cluttered, but not a mess. Lance mindlessly pulled himself into the desk, straightening up his back, and with his free hand, caressed his headphones. His mind was wandering, he didn't like that all too much. It made his chest feel weighted, sad. Sad was not an emotion he liked to feel very often, especially when it pertained to Marc. But even so, he couldn't help feeling that all too familiar feeling of annoyance, sadness and, though it hurt to admit, gratitude.

Marc had sacrificed himself, sure some might not see it

that way, but Lance did. His family did. Lance had arrived home one day nine years ago to a sight unfortunately all too common those days.

***

On the street in front of the short path that led up to the Masons' front door was a black limousine. It was immaculately clean: buffed and polished so that it appeared to be right off the showroom floor. A stark contrast to the dilapidation that surrounded it. The driver's door was open and, upon inspection, Lance noticed that the person (who must have been the driver) was in the doorway of his home. And the doorway was wide open.

Anita stood in the doorway. An arch that seemed to her to have become less of a portal from the harsh country to the warmth of family and more of a harbinger of bad news. She stood, hand in front of her mouth, eyes glassy with tears. Her unwashed and uncombed auburn hair spoke to the state she was in. As did her choice of clothing: a nightgown and slippers.

Lance slowly edged towards the door. As he did, he started to hear part of the conversation taking place inside. The driver's cold tone was failing in trying to console his mother. He kept on mentioning something about it being 'his choice', that he was 'doing it for his family', and that she 'should be proud of him.' Lance was still confused when he found himself standing next to the driver. He took his mother around the shoulders, and shot a quizzical look at the man. He had slick black hair and such thin lips that Lance struggled to imagine any positive words could ever come out of them. If a cog in a machine was a person, this was him.

"Ah, Mr. Mason, please, will you calm your mother down?" implored the driver, with an air that was the wrong amount of familiar, "I must go help your brother pack."

"Pack? For what? Where are we going?" Lance asked, shooting a confused look at his mother. She simply shook her head in defeat.

"Not you, Mr. Mason," came the curt reply, "just your brother, Marc Mason. I am correct, this is the Mason residence of a one Mr. Marc Mason?"

"Uh, yes, but-"

"Fantastic, here is the paperwork for your records, Mr. Mason will receive his own digital copy once we process the original he has just signed. As protocol, we ask that you keep your copy safe. Better to have everything safe in triplicate. Better for everyone involved to be on the same page."

The driver shoved a thick, leather bound file into Lance's hands as he entered the Mason residence. Lance looked down at the file and the first thing he saw made his blood run cold. In icy gold letters the words 'Fortune Limited' ran across the cover. Lance took a few moments to adjust.

Is this really happening?

He flicked open the file and scanned the pages. There was not much processing during the scan. He noticed the checked boxes, but what he really needed to see were the signatures. And he saw them. Lance slammed the file shut and threw it down, rushing inside after the suited man.

The driver was still making himself accustomed to the living situation of the Masons, inspecting, with visible pity and disdain, the small interior trying to figure out which way to go to find his mark.

Lance raced past him straight to Marc's room, which was really a reconstituted small study barely big enough for a bed and a chest of drawers. The Masons didn't have much, but they made sure their children would live as individuals. Own rooms and all. This was a fact that Lance now regretted on his parents' behalf as he whipped inside. Perhaps if he and Marc had shared a room, and been less individual, he wouldn't have had the space to make this monumental mistake.

Marc was busy packing his bag. 'His' bag was not quite how Lance would describe it; it was clearly provided by Fortune Limited. It was brand new, jet black, with signature gold detailing. And it was big.

"What the f-" began Lance.

"No!" said Marc, cutting his brother off, "I don't want to hear it!"

"Marc, Marc please, what have you done?"

Marc flippantly gestured with his hand around the room. He wasn't just referring to the room.

"I did what needed to happen, Lance," Lance knew what he meant, but he was going to ask anyway.

Before he could, Marc interrupted again, "Look at us, we have been flailing about. You and I *can't* support this family on our own. You know it, I know it. Shit, even Mom knows it."

The Masons were still reeling from the loss of Grant, and while Lance knew that his brother spoke the truth, he just couldn't accept it. He knew that, since his father's death, his mother hadn't been the same. She'd become secluded in her own world. She was in a state of shock. A state that no one could blame her for being in, but life around her carried on, and Anita hadn't been able to keep up. She'd lost her position at school. As a result, her two working-age children had to step in and take more shifts. Lance and Marc had been working previously, but more on a part-time basis. They earned some money that helped with the household, but their parent's made sure they knew that they could keep most of their earnings for themselves. However, they'd always taken small cuts from their wages and put them into the family funds against their father's wishes, or knowledge. With the loss of both their parents' income streams, though, the boys couldn't support their family for much longer. At least not on their student-level jobs.

These were the facts Lance knew, but it was a reality that he couldn't quite accept. He knew what the only real solution was; Marc knew it too. As he stood there watching Marc stare into his soul, one hand holding a neatly folded shirt, Lance suddenly felt an uncomfortable tingling at the base of his neck. He looked down, trying to find the words he needed to convince Marc of his error. But he had nothing. He closed his eyes briefly. He couldn't accept what was happening, because, deep down, he was ashamed that he had not had the courage to make the decision himself. Lance opened his eyes again and looked at his brother, who had resumed packing. An unwelcome sense of admiration, yet steeped in anger, poured over him. This was his job. He should have stepped up. He was the eldest. And now he was standing in front of his younger brother who had quite literally just signed his life away.

"Marc," began Lance, "there must be another way."

"I've already signed, Lance. There's nothing more to do," Marc placed his last item of clothing into the suitcase and glanced over Lance's shoulder. Lance could feel the smugness of the driver hovering behind him in the small passage.

"Please, just five minutes?"

This plea seemed to serve its purpose because Lance felt

the drone of bureaucracy retreat down the passage. Marc tried to zip his bag closed, but couldn't quite get it to shut. Lance walked over to help and Marc stood back.

"I'm going to be an actor, Lance, at least-"

"Closed, now you can leave," Lance snapped as the zip pulled closed, immediately he felt terrible.

There was a long pause and both brothers stood in the small room. The walls felt closer than they had a few minutes ago.

"I'm sorry," Lance said, "you're going to be the best."

Marc smiled weakly, "You know, I'm not going forever, we'll see each other, quite a lot in fact. They just prefer their clients to stay in their client apartments is all. And I know you all wouldn't want to mo- anyway you get the point I'm just trying to say that I'm not..." his voice trailed away as he realised that he hadn't caught himself.

I'm not dying? Is that right? Lance thought and fought the urge to reply with a heartbroken 'yet', but decided against it. His brother was doing what he thought he had to. On top of it, he was getting to live out his dream. Lance took a deep breath and decided that, though he wouldn't be happy for his brother, he could at least be civil. Lance grabbed the suitcase handle and jerked it up off the bed and onto the floor. Pulling the handle out smoothly, he motioned with his head for his brother to walk ahead of him. Marc headed out the door, down the short passage, out into the yard and into the limousine. Lance watched. He knew that Marc was doing it for his family, and knew the fame to come was purely secondary, even if it had been his dream since he was a little boy.

The limousine pulled away while Lance held his mother up and made a silent vow to himself: I will find a way to stop this.

After Marc was taken, Lance's life went by relatively fast. In fact, all the Masons experienced the same sort of time jump. One minute, they were mourning the loss of their father or husband; next they were mourning the departure of their sibling or son; then Lance was joining the military to pay for his studies; Jan graduated high school and started down her own career path and Anita, slowly but surely, began to live again.

Lance served two tours and saved up all he could to make his way through law school. He, of course, had the benefits of Marc's deal that he could have enjoyed. However, he felt it was blood money and wanted nothing to do with it. He loved his brother, and eventually became happy for his success, but he was less thrilled about the method Marc took to get there. No matter the heroic intentions.

Jan was less concerned about the idea of blood money and guilt. Her take on the whole ordeal was that it was happening, and she may as well make the most of a tough situation, as Marc had intended. She decided to use the money from Marc to pay her way through university. She soon changed her tune of becoming a regular teacher and found a love of linguistics. She was a lifelong student working towards her PhD on the connection (if any) between the Proto-Indo-European and Proto-Afroasiatic languages. These were words that flew over Lance's head, but he was proud of her nevertheless.

Anita took longer to come around than Jan, but quicker than Lance. With a lot of conversations that went around in circles, she eventually accepted Marc's help. She would not admit the reason to him, she had confided in her eldest that it was mainly so that his sacrifice would not be in vain. Her heart ached for her son, but eventually she accepted his decision and decided to put on a brave face.

Marc (with the eventual help of Lance and Jan) focused most of his earnings on his mother. He made sure that she wanted for nothing. Lance knew that Anita had learned to appreciate that. She moved out of their old home with their old, painful memories, to an upper-class suburb. Closer to the city. She lived comfortably and happily, for the most part. She made new friends, never forgetting her old ones and regularly entertained both in her home. What was most telling about his mother's character, as Lance noted to himself during his many visits, was that she remained grounded. She kept a job working at a legal firm as an administrator that specialised in workplace deaths. She knew she didn't effect much change, nor did she need the money, but still, she knew she had to remain connected to reality in some way. That was her way. Lance admired her for that.

Lance had made something of himself, by himself. He was very proud of his achievement. He was a lawyer at the very same firm his mother worked at. It was he who managed to get her the job; he preferred her to be close to him. He would never let another tragedy befall his family. Not while he could help it.

**

An ancient clock in the corner of his study chimed eight o'clock and startled Lance out of his trance. He had gone on another one of his binges. Somewhere along the line of his wandering thoughts he had picked up his device and begun another hunt.

When he was bored, he hunted Fortune Limited. He would comb through articles, chat forums and the like to find anything and everything he could to build his case.

The case he had been building for nine years. The case that was all pinned up on the wall opposite him. The case that had so many leads, but no direction. The case that was still just a dead end.

Lance looked back at the board as if to challenge it to a fight. His eyes moved slowly towards a post-it note that had a number on it. He stared at the post-it for what seemed like eternity. His heart raced. He found himself needing air after a few moments, as he had apparently forgotten to breathe.

Lance looked back at his device and noticed his thumb was hovering over an article. It was about a hacker's attempt to breach Fortune Limited's data centre in one of the local offices in the outer suburbs. He was not very interested, but still stared at the subpar CCTV camera footage of the suspect in question. It was quite blurry, but he could vaguely make out a face. The figure's hand was outstretched in front of them, and their head was angled slightly to the side, as if looking over their shoulder while they made their hasty escape.

Then, his device rang.

Chapter 4

Lance

Lance glanced at his device; it was vibrating on the desk beside him. It was his mother. He sighed. Anita Mason had become a helicopter parent. She felt as though she'd lost her son because she hadn't paid enough attention to her children's lives, so now, she was trying to compensate. She kept tabs on them all, and went beyond the call of duty if needed, no questions asked – mostly. It was beautifully perfect: a mother who would literally do anything and everything to make sure her children were alright. It was also very annoying.

Lance sighed and prepared himself, saying a pretend prayer, hoping for a quick call. He gestured with his hand for the device to answer and initiated the loudspeaker function. He was more interested in browsing the web than listening to her.

"Lance, it's your mother," came Anita's voice, so perfectly relayed that it sounded like she was in the room with him. Her voice was caring with a twinge of worry in it, as if she worried, but didn't want her son to worry with her. Years of practise meant that Lance picked up on it instantly.

"Yes Mom, I know. What's wrong?"

"Oh uh-" was the reply, realising her ruse had failed, "well, dear it's just about Jan."

"She's on a flight isn't she?"

"Well that's the thing, she was on a flight but she must have landed an hour ago. That's what the flight details say. She hasn't checked in with me. You know she always does. This time she didn't."

That last part was a blatant lie, and both Lance and Anita knew it. Jan was notorious for not picking up her device, or really conveying any relevant information about her whereabouts or state of mind to anyone of her own volition. Information always needed to be teased out, though most times it could be inferred from past experience. Anita was speaking more in a generalistic sense. She had made it a family rule for everyone to update her when travelling long distances; Marc and Lance were good at it, Jan not so much. On this occasion, Jan had come back from a semester abroad in the European Union.

"I don't know where she is and I am getting worried. It's getting late," continued Anita.

"I'm sure wherever she is, she is fine. You know Jan, she can hold her own."

"So you don't know where she could be?"

"No, mom," replied Lance. This time it was his turn to lie – well, kind of. He did not know where she was exactly, but if he was under oath, he could probably guess with ninety percent accuracy. Jan was a free spirit and loved to socialise. When studies called, she focused. She had just been rigorously doing a thesis or something else of similar academic nature. Also, she has just spent six months in the EU doing this without her best friends. She would want to party and to see them, more so than she'd want to have dinner with her overbearing mother. Where could someone go out and do that in the evening? A club. The fact that Anita had not cottoned on to that idea proved to Lance that she still thought of them as young children. Children she needed to keep tabs on; children she needed to protect.

"Oh dear, I hope she's not in trouble."

"She will be fine, she is probably out with friends. Listen, if she calls me first I will direct her to you, alright?"

There was an uncomfortable pause and then, "Alright dear, please do."

"Anything else you need, mom?" asked Lance, hoping the answer was a 'no'.

"No dear, just checking in," her voice drenched in resignation and sadness.

Unnecessarily or not, she was worried about her daughter. Lance couldn't help himself.

"Look mom, if she doesn't call you or me in an hour, I will call her myself, and if that fails, I will go look in her usual spots. I'll bring her here for the night, she'll be fine."

This seemed to reassure her. Slightly.

"Thank you, dear. Please let me know."

The line disconnected and Lance let out another pent up sigh. Really, it was a sigh of resentful frustration. His mother wasn't always like this. She used to trust them to do their own thing, he and Marc – even Jan – could go out or to friends whenever they wanted without being interrogated about it. And it wasn't just a one way street. His parents' trust fostered a responsible air amongst the children. They would, for the most part, let someone know where they were or at least jump at the opportunity to correct a misconception of their whereabouts – without provocation or fear of punishment. That all changed nine years ago.

Just another loss thanks to Marc, thought Lance, then quickly he corrected his own runaway thought: *Just another loss thanks to Fortune Limited.*

He stared at his device and decided to do the brotherly thing and check on his sister. Just in case. With a swipe up hand gesture, Lance activated his device's call functions. His hand did a circular motion, another unique gesture that he had programmed as a shortcut and the device dialled Jan. As it rang, he continued his Fortune hunt. Suddenly, the club entered his study and Jan's strong yet still remarkably childlike voice shouted out, "Lance?!"

Lance took a moment to compose himself and acclimate to the loud music of the club, "Yeah, listen, Mom-"

"Hold on, I can't hear you," Jan cut him off.

Lance could hear a chair loudly scraping the floor and voices of one or two of the friends he knew asking Jan the usual 'what's wrong' and 'where are you going' phrases that are typical of a person in the background of an unexpected call.

He heard one mention something about shots being on their way.

Lance was a watcher, he knew how people were, and given time, could read them like a book. He preferred cataloguing his siblings' friends based on their actions. He didn't need much other than the background noise and the cadence of the other voices to know where Jan was and who she was with. This ability to categorise and catalogue people was partially what made him such a good lawyer. Suddenly, the club atmosphere dulled slightly, only to be replaced by the hoots of cars on the street and people chatting on their way to and from work.

"That's better, I think," said Jan's voice again.

"Jan, mom just called. She's worried. Give her a call, will you?"

"Urgh, why?"

Exactly the response Lance expected.

"I get it, Jan, but you know how she is."

"But she's going to make me come home!"

"Aren't you tired?"

"I slept on the flight, Lance."

Unlikely, thought Lance, before he said, "Fine, whatever, still call her, please. And where are you?"

"Stanley's," came Jan's short reply.

Lance braced himself for the request he knew was coming: "Look, can I just tell mom that I'm staying with you tonight? Come fetch me in a few hours?"

Jan was lucky that he had already anticipated this scenario, mentioning as much to their mother. To be fair, Jan's request was not all unreasonable. Lance lived relatively close to the club, at least considerably closer than Anita did, so it made sense for her to take the shorter trip home.

"Jan, you know I have work tomorrow-" began Lance, he wasn't going to let her off that easily. She'd have to work for his help. She knew this.

"Look, Lance," she began with the authority Lance imagined she would speak with to an undergrad at one of her lectures, "when last did you go out, huh? I haven't seen my friends in like eight months! We're catching up and you need to let loose a bit."

The eight months was a stretch, but Lance gave it to her. She might've been concentrating on her thesis before her semester abroad. Possible, but unlikely.

"Look, fine, two hours? Just two hours? Then you can rock up and snatch me away and I won't complain," there was a self-imposed pause, "well, okay I will, but I will try not complain too much."

Lance could hear the pulsing music of the club grow louder, as if Jan was already moving back inside. He allowed a small smile to cross his lips as he imagined Jan edging slowly but surely back inside in anticipation of a positive response. It was this image of a young woman acting like a young, naughty child and only this image that made Lance agree to her terms.

"Fine, Jan. But two hours, and nothing more, hear me?"

"Thank you, you're the best!" was Jan's response, and then, "You know, I meant what I said, go out for once, square. Isn't that bar you like just down the road? Why wait the two hours in boredom in your study? Anyway, bye!"

The club left his study as abruptly as it entered.

How did she know? Was he also that predictable? His quest to release his brother from his contract was no secret, but was it such a cornerstone of his character nowadays? Lance surveyed his study, and found his answer. A modestly sized room with all the bells and whistles of a lawyer's home office with the added feature of looking like a nineteen-fifties detective's office. It was replete with the large board filling most of the opposite wall, the countless hard copy files of various Fortune Limited leads, and the obligatory dart board that had a printed picture of Klaus Marlowe unceremoniously dotted with darts and dart holes. All this, plus the fact that it was Friday and he was scrolling through old Fortune Limited related news reports on his device made him take stock of his life. He was obsessed. Of course he was not so affected by this realisation that he would stop his search. He had made a promise to his brother and himself, and he never broke his promises. What bothered him was that he had become predictable. And he hated that. Practical upshot: Jan was right. He wasn't living – even though she didn't say it in those words, it is what she meant.

Lance placed his device face down and sat a while in his thoughts. Then he retrieved it from his desk and headed for the door.

Chapter 5
Lance

Lance was never a regular at the clubs like Jan or Marc. Unlike them, he usually preferred the quiet of a night in. He would watch films or series, read, or – inevitably – do more research on his near decade-long nemesis with the occasional trusty bottle of whiskey. However, he did like to pop his head out for a drink with an old friend at the local bar: Gretchen's. On occasion. If not with a friend, then he would go and drink alone. Sometimes, he would use the time to wind down after long courtroom proceedings, but usually he'd be brooding about one of many dead ends in his investigation over the crappy beer.

To change his routine up too much would be too much of a shock to his system, so he decided on this night to uphold the latter tradition. He would find his usual spot at

Gretchen's, order a beer and sit in contemplative silence until it was time to collect Jan. Everyone would get what they wanted, without major character alterations in the process. Jan would get a night out, stunted a few hours, and Lance would get a night out in his own way. All metaphorical bells and whistles left at home in a box in the attic. In Lance's mind, it was the perfect compromise.

It did not take him long to arrive at his destination. Gretchen's Bar stood out like a sore thumb amongst the dreary office buildings that surrounded it. There was no mistake to be made, however. Gretchen's looked dreary too, but it had bright green neon lights that spelt out most of the letters in its name and its facebrick wall completed the old school aesthetic that it was not originally going for, but maintained nevertheless. Gretchen's was a staple in the city's nightlife. It had stood the test of time, even managing to stay in (questionable) operation during and after the great party strip shift of twenty-seven. It was hard to believe for the casual tourist now, but a few years ago, this street was the place to be for nightlife. In the twenties of the twenty-second century, various clubs and bars had decided to move two streets down. This made it the new hotspot for all things reckless abandon. Gretchen's remained resolute in its heritage and refused to budge. It retained its regulars, however, to Lance's knowledge, had not since managed to build its clientele. The only new faces to the establishment were faces no one had ever seen before, or the faces that didn't want to be seen. All too often, Lance had laid eyes on a defendant or two looking for a drink in peace. To date, none of his own, luckily.

Lance greeted the bouncer like an old friend who reciprocated, then opened the door for him. The warm glow of the bar lights flooded Lance's person. As he entered, he noted that it always felt like he was travelling backwards through time as he stepped over the threshold of the establishment. Perhaps that was its appeal? Lance was himself an old soul, and this bar certainly was old.

The night was not unusual for Gretchen's in terms of patron turn out. Lance's eyes wandered the medium-sized room. Smoke hung in the air, but he could still make out the regulars at the pool table, the one or two at the gambling machine, and the obligatory lost soul hunched over at the bar. He actively chose not to judge this person, as he knew others would slap the same attributes on himself in a minute or two.

As he walked over to the bar, he scanned for his usual booth. It was his favourite because it was almost hidden in a corner, if you didn't know it was there, you wouldn't see it. He could be left alone.

Ah, perfect, it's open.

As he approached the bar, the bartender smiled in recognition.

"Well I never! Lance Percival Mason?!" boomed the jovial man. As if he was in a movie he added, "In the flesh, as I live and breathe!"

Lance smiled, he was familiar with the bartender, they had gone to school together. His name was Gary, but everyone called him Gaz, and he was as carefree a person as anyone could be. His beer belly wobbled as he chuckled, and if a sad soul were unlucky enough when ordering a drink on a quiet night, he would happily regale them with a tall tale that almost certainly did not happen to him, despite his insistence that it did.

"What's up, Gaz?" greeted Lance, "And you know that's not my middle name."

"One day I'll get it and then won't you be impressed!"

replied Gaz reaching for a beer glass, "It has been a minute, man, can I assume it's the usual?"

"'Usual' implies I am here more often than I really am, Gaz."

"Yeah, well, every time you're here, you order the same thing, and seeing you is a rarity – sort of like a unicorn," replied Gaz, "so when you are here, people tend to remember, and a bartender of such calibre as myself would remember your order. So, usual?"

Lance chuckled and nodded; Gaz had already started pouring.

"So, to what does Gretchen owe the pleasure of your patronage?" asked Gaz in a faux british accent.

"No real reason, Jan's back from the EU and partying it up at Stanley's up the road-"

"And you're on pick-up duty?"

Lance nodded, "She suggested I live a little and-" Lance spread his arms in a gesture that said 'here I am'.

"You know you're at Gretchen's, right?" Gaz joked, "I'm sure this is not what she meant."

"On the contrary. And in any case, baby steps Gaz, baby steps," said Lance as he smoothly swiped his device over the payment receiver on the bar. He grabbed his drink and casually turned to head towards his spot, "Cheers, Gaz."

Lance could hear Gaz mutter a goodbye through a chuckle.

With his gaze focused on sliding his device back into his pocket whilst balancing an overflowing beer in his other hand, he slowly moved towards his booth. With a few steps to go he looked up, only to find it occupied. He was sure it was empty a second ago. Lance stopped in his tracks. He studied the person in his booth. She appeared to be about his age, wearing a baggy hoodie that clearly masked a slender figure. Her smooth, dark complexion took Lance by surprise. Lance was good with faces, he was good with people in general – perhaps less so socialising with them, and more so their features and general habits. This woman, though, whom he knew he had never met before, looked extremely familiar. Very, *very* familiar.

The woman noticed Lance staring, and shuffled uncomfortably. Her brown eyes darted around and she flipped her hood over her braids. Clearly, she did not like being watched.

Lance soon realised his staring and decided to leave his thoughts behind him, he looked away and spotted another empty booth. Not *his* booth, but it would do. Just as he was about to move towards that one instead, perhaps it was his initial staring or his later indecision of what to do, but the woman abruptly stood up. It wasn't a physically rushed movement that she made, but the intention was clearly one of necessity on her part. She moved past Lance, pulling her hood over her face more and moved towards the exit.

Lance was perplexed, but his booth was now free, so he headed towards his original destination and sat down, his beer sloshing to the rims of the glass.

It was just in casual interest that he turned his head to glance again at the woman.

She was almost outside, now. But just before she crossed underneath the doorway, she looked back. Worry ran across her face.

Then it hit him like an anvil.

That face. That stance: back facing, hand outstretched, head looking over her shoulder. He *had* seen her before. He had seen her tonight. On the news. She was the Fortune Limited hacker.

Lance's eyes widened as he stared at his drink. He

couldn't believe his luck. What were the odds? If she was the hacker, then she could know something about Fortune that he didn't. She could help him in his own investigation. She could be the first strong lead to something – anything – he'd had in a long time.

But she'd just left the building.

His mind raced.

What should I do?

In the few seconds that followed, he weighed his options: go home safe, stuck with the same leads as before, or follow her and risk becoming a criminal by association.

A criminal with a lead.

He took the second option.

He pushed himself up and out of the booth, spilling some of his untouched beer as he bolted after her.

The city street was already slick with a layer of night-time dew mixed with the hovering imposition of a premature storm cloud. Lance stepped onto the street, which was still filled with people, despite the dampness. Most sported overcoats and rain jackets and held unfolded umbrellas over their heads, making Lance regret his decision not to grab something to fight against the drizzle himself.

He looked left and right a couple of times, trying to decipher in which direction she'd gone. He thought back quickly, making use of his lawyer brain.

What was she wearing? A hoodie, yes – what colour?

Navy flashed across his mind. His shoulders immediately slumped. Discerning black from navy in a sea of people wearing black or darkly coloured rain apparel at night? Nearly impossible. He needed something else to go on.

He searched his brain.

What else? He thought quickly, *What other discerning characteristic did she have?*

Fear. That was it. Unlike all the other city walkers, his lead had more than a tinge of paranoia about her. She did not want to be seen, while the rest couldn't give a rat's ass. With this in mind, he scanned the throngs again and noticed a figure – unmistakably in a hoodie, though the colour was indiscernible – turn and look over her shoulder. He grinned. He'd now seen variations of that look three times in one night.

The woman noticed her stalker almost instantly, and began to speed up, shoving past her fellow pedestrians. When Lance saw this, he sped up himself. What if he lost her? What if she outran him? He hadn't realized until this desperate moment how important she was to him, or at least how important she could be. He had to talk to her. He had exhausted all of his other options, she was also the first, proper, new path of inquiry he had had in years. His heart started to race as he followed her.

The woman darted down a side alleyway, out of sight, and when Lance eventually reached it, she'd broken out into a full-blown sprint. She was scared; Lance did feel sorry for her. Nevertheless, he met her pace.

His stint in the military, although not the best time in his life (he was not a fan of some of the military practises. They seemed a bit archaic to him), did provide him with a unique physique and athleticism only attainable after years of service. It had been a while since he had been put to the test like this: with a full-on chase through the dank and slippery back alleys of the city, but he was confident that he would be able to catch up, despite her head start.

The woman showed remarkable agility, too. She didn't go around the crates, boxes and jutted piping; she soared over them with the grace and flare of a parkour enthusiast. Lance was less graceful. He took the obstacles in standard run-of-the-mill hurdle jumps. Crude and definitely less pleasing to the eye to the casual onlooker, but it worked.

They continued running, passing windows displaying city residents' bedrooms. Some lights were on and a few silhouetted figures gazed down upon what was probably the most interesting thing they had seen in a while. Lance hoped that, rather than call the police, they would appreciate the show.

The woman darted to the right, and Lance did the equivalent of a handbrake turn, hot on her pursuit. He was getting closer now. She turned her head back, frantically checking the distance between her and her assailant. The alley had a dead end that was approaching rapidly. Lance saw the tall wired fence that split the alley into two, and silently mouthed a 'thank you' through gasped breaths. However, the woman didn't seem to think she was going to stop. Without giving Lance time to comprehend what was happening, she launched herself up against the cold, hard, mesh wiring, and began scrambling up. Her booted feet struggled to find a home amongst the just-too-small gaps in the wiring. But her grit, determination and apparent brute upper body strength allowed her to scale the fence.

Lance reached the base and caught his breath. The panging and chinkling of her body against the mesh and metal support poles sounded frantic. He looked up to see that she was slowing down. Losing her momentum.

"Wait, please!" yelled Lance, "I just want to talk!"

His message seemed to renew the woman's vigour, and she began climbing at her original pace.

Lance decided to follow suit, "Please, I'm not going to hurt you," he began through his panting as he followed her. She was almost over the top. Not slowing down.

"I just want some information. I'm not-" more

exasperated grunts escaped his lips as he lost his footing slightly, "I'm not… whoever… you think I am… "

The woman was at the top, ready to jump, when she paused.

Is she starting to listen to me?

She looked at him, then at the ground below her, and back again. With that same renewed grace, she grabbed the fence bar and swung herself so that she was hanging on the opposite side.

Nope.

With the intensity of a precision strike, her one boot collided with Lance's left knuckles. He let go out of shock. This gave the woman an advantage, and she took it. She used her body to shake the thin fence, already groaning with their weight. Lance, already one hand down and out of breath, couldn't help but topple to the ground with a thud. As he fell, the world seemed as if it was in slow motion. He felt like he could've counted to a hundred before he hit the ground. When he looked up again, he noticed the slightest of a smile on his target's face.

The woman delicately dismounted the fence, offered him no more than a glance, and turned to bolt away. She was about to take off when Lance threw out one last, desperate grunt, "Please, I need help."

He winced at the desperation in his own voice. Was this how it ended? Begging to a complete stranger for something he wasn't even sure she had?

But, to his shock, she didn't run away. He watched as she stood there, fidgeting with her fingernails. Did she feel bad for him?

At some point during the chase, her hoodie had blown off her head, and now, her long braids laid down the length of her back. Her back – really, her whole body – was heaving from sprinting and scaling. As Lance watched her in the dusty, evening-light, shifting the weight between her feet nervously, he couldn't help but wonder about her age.

How old can she possibly be? My age? A little younger?

Suddenly, he didn't see a wanted criminal, or a thief on the run. He saw a girl. A girl who must have somehow been completely screwed over by Fortune's promises. A girl who had lost something, or someone important to her. Why else had she done what she did?

Lance shook his head. When he looked at this girl, he saw Jan.

"Look," he started, sitting up from the ground, "Fortune ruined my family's life."

Her back straightened.

"We lost my father when I was young, and my brother signed with Fortune so the rest of us would be taken care of. For ten fucking years, I've tried finding him a way to get him out of it. Looked into exposing Fortune, even in the most miniscule ways possible," he looked down and sighed, "his expiration date is approaching. I can't – I don't-" he trailed off, unready for the amount of emotion encompassing his voice.

He swallowed and continued, "if you can't tell me anything, I don't have any more options."

He watched as her head bent down slightly, and she shook it, as if she knew that listening to him was a bad idea. Still, she turned around, and walked closer to the fence, to Lance.

Her dark brown eyes pierced his soul. She took the time to assess him the way he'd been assessing her. Her eyes roamed him, surely checking for weapons… for obvious lies. Lance rose, a newfound determination and understanding washing over him.

"What makes you think I know anything?" her voice was abrupt, blunt, and the question would've startled him, if he hadn't been prepared.

He leaned in confidently, "Because people who aren't guilty don't run."

She stared at Lance, and let out a huff that resembled a half-chuckle.

"You've got me there, man," she said.

Lance smiled in the silence that followed. He did have her.

For the first time, he really looked at her face. Desperation. All over it.

Her head turned, and her eyes darted around. Lance began to hear the mumbles of groups of people coming around the corner. She returned her focus to Lance, and the fence. She sighed and hopped back onto the fence, scaled it with ease, and dropped down in front of him.

"Not here," she panted, motioning towards the alley walls, "too many eyes and ears," she brushed past Lance and motioned for him to follow.

"The name's Grace, by the way. Don't make me regret this."

Chapter 6

Grace

Grace did not know how to feel as she began leading a complete stranger back to the dingy back-alley bar she'd found only the week before.

Why did I agree to this? He could be a spy for all I know.

She scoffed. 'Spy'. Had it come to that? Scratch that, yes it had. This stranger could definitely be using her to tease out vital information about her most recent cyber attack, and then arrest her. Or worse.

Grace clocked a side alley as they passed it. She could still make a break for it. She could hear the man still breathing, behind her. He was tired, whereas she had a few minutes of sprinting left in her. Especially if the sprinting was to safety, and away from the possibility of corporate-sanctioned abduction.

But something still stopped her from running.

Perhaps it was the way he had pleaded with her? He certainly sounded like a man down on his luck, just trying to save his brother.

Grace had no idea what to say.

The pair walked silently back to the bar. She looked over to him. Whereas she was keeping her mouth shut out of fear, his eyes looked like his mind was racing, searching for the right questions to ask. She took the time to brace herself. How much was he going to ask? How much of herself should she present to him? Would he just want specifics about Fortune, or her motives as well? Eventually, the neon lights appeared through the hazy evening mist. Grace could make out the 'G' and the 'etch', but that was all.

They approached the front, and the bouncer ignored her, but greeted the man.

"You're back!"

"Huh, yeah," replied her stranger awkwardly, and then added, almost as a joke: "just had to run out for a minute, Jay."

The interaction's cringe-iness was palpable, but at least she could then discredit this man as a spy; he was friends with the bouncer. Somehow a spy bouncer combination did not match well with her. It made her feel a bit calmer.

As Grace sat across from the stranger, he let out another of his, by now, signature awkward expulsions of breath. It was neither a sigh nor a deliberate blow, but something in between. He rasped his fingers on the grimy table top, occasionally looking up at her expectedly. Grace knew she was torturing him by remaining silent, but, at the same time, she didn't want to speak.

Couldn't speak.

On their way in, she'd motioned at the bartender for a drink. She hoped whatever he gave her was strong.

"Uh, well, I'm Lance, by the way," Lance managed to conjure up a start to the conversation. Grace looked him up and down and made a subtle nod to herself. He seemed like a Lance, though what made a 'Lance,' she didn't know.

Lance continued, "You said your name was Gwen-"

"Grace."

"Yes, yes, Grace, that's it," chuckled Lance uneasily, "I was close."

Grace's shots were delivered to their booth, cutting the tension a bit. Lance seemed bewildered by the hard liquor finding a home next to his beer.

But it was obviously short lived. He raised an eyebrow and pursed his lips, as if saying, 'ah, it's an I-don't-want-to-be-fully-sober-for-this-explanation' kind of explanation.

His hands moved towards the first shot. Grace, however, did not wait. She swiftly dispatched both of her shots. They were indeed strong enough. She looked back at Lance, who hadn't had his *first*.

"Drink up, you'll need it."

Lance drew in a breath, cocked his head slightly. He looked like he was going to regret this before the end of the night. He threw back both shots in almost as smooth a succession as Grace. She could see a faint sparkle in his eyes as the fire of the alcohol ran down his throat, then dissipated throughout his body. He shuddered.

"So," breathed Lance, "you gonna tell me what you know, or not?"

"Buckle up, man."

***

The date was irrelevant, other than the fact that it was a while ago. Grace was living her best childhood life, or at least she thought she was, until the hard hand of reality hit her square in the face. Sibu Makeba, her father, and a gifted man of engineering, met with a tragic car accident on one of his everyday walks around the block. An accident which had left him confined to a wheelchair. Though optimistic, Grace's father could not manage to continue his engineering work at the plant in his new condition. Grace remembered numerous times when she would arrive home from school to find her father sitting in the living room. This was odd because, before the accident, he always came home around seven and ten every other day. While she obviously enjoyed spending more time with her father, she did feel it was very odd.

Of course, being so young, she didn't know that he had attempted to go into work those days and been sent home because he couldn't complete the tasks. To spend more hours at the plant, unable to complete the other tasks meant that the company would have had to pay him for effectively nothing. So they sent him home. To his credit, Grace remembers that her father never once appeared despondent or unhappy with his situation. At least not to her or her brother's faces. Thinking back, Grace could admit to hearing one or two minor arguments between her mother and her father with words like "bills" and "we will make it work".

Despite those minor spats, her parents were the best specimens a daughter and younger brother could hope for. They took everything in their stride, and always with a steady, calculated hand. The children knew very little of any issues the family might have been facing.

For this, Grace – and her brother, Thabo – were grateful. Their attitude towards life was infectious, and made their childhood pleasant, despite the battles of a family growing up in the twenty-second century's social and economic world. Their life was pleasant, despite growing up in an era where Fortune Limited was growing in popularity. And power.

Tragedy shot through the recovering family once again in the latter part of that same year. This time, the victim was Grace's mother. During one of her routine trips to the store, she had been in the wrong place at the wrong time. As she was leaving the corner shop with a bag laden with milk, bread, water, and a chocolate for each of her kids, she had not taken two steps before a bullet passed through her brain. She felt nothing; she was gone in an instant. Merciful. The assailant had mistaken her for the other woman who had entered the store moments before her and who was by then cowering behind the nearest self-service paystation. Something about a wild affair and messy divorce. Grace's mother, Thandi, had simply not known to not wear her grey jogging hoodie that day; a mistake the assailant would attest to in order to lessen his sentence. Almost as if, *had* he murdered his *actual* target, it would be more of a reason for a court case. On more than one occasion, Grace would look back and realise that her mother clearly meant less to a court than the random adulterer that was his original target. He got off with manslaughter. A technicality, yes, but to Grace: a gross miscarriage of justice.

Grace's father's facade of eternal steadfastness broke that day. Grace could tell the exact moment her father became a changed man: they were sitting in the living room watching a feel-good movie from the olden days on their old Movie Card, when her father's device rang. He ignored it at first, though eventually, after the fourth attempt, he accepted the call. Grace saw his face change from irritable to deadpan. He said nothing and his arm dropped to the side of his wheelchair. Grace and her brother spent the rest of the night trying to get through to their father while a steady and silent stream of tears trickled down his face.

It wasn't until the police came by the house the next day to ask questions that the two children were informed of their mother's passing.

Grace's father was changed from that day forward. The funeral came and went. The court case came and went. The condolences came and went, and by the end of it all, Grace's father was a new man. After the inability to get justice for his love, he turned his attention to his family – what was left of it. Grace noticed that now he was less jovial and more pragmatic. Of course, he still loved his children and showed them as much, but there was a sense of innocence lost in her father's eyes that young Grace mourned.

Times were tough. For nearly one year, the family barely managed to make ends meet. They were short on one income – a harsh reality, for the time. Gone were the days of single income streams in families; inflation and general cost of living in this overcrowded world made that kind of life virtually impossible, unless a family was part of the one percent, of course. And even then, most trophy husbands and wives had their own sponsorship deals, sports or beauty ranges that undoubtedly ensured they had an income stream of their own. Grace's family was no exception. Her father was struggling to work jobs that he could manage in a wheelchair. At one point, he was working four different jobs. Grace knows this because she had to babysit her brother nearly every day and night for days on end.

Another blow would come to the Makeba family, this time in the insidious form of Fortune Limited. At his wit's end, Sibu had signed a contract with Fortune Limited that ensured financial stability for himself and his children and allowed him the opportunity to work at the most prestigious engineering firm in the country. He would be able to work on the next missions to Mars and thus be able to ensure that his children received the very best education money could buy. At the time, Grace did not register the dire nature of the trade her father had made. Future Grace, however, saw it for what it was: rich people giving out money at a terrible, government-sanctioned price. All in the name of prosperity and 'looking to the future'.

Fortune Limited's public aim was to help curb overpopulation. There had been a summit a number of years ago, when overpopulation had been at its peak, and numerous world leaders and big corporations had met to find a solution. They had heard many plans, but most of them either amounted to removing freedoms from the public, or being too long-term to help with the crisis at that point in time. Dr. Marlowe of Fortune Limited (which, at that time, was nothing more than a well-detailed and planned dream in his twinkle-less black eyes) had stepped up to offer his plan. He would offer any person ten years of anything they could possibly imagine. You could become a famous actor, singer, surgeon, astronaut, or even provide a stable income for your family without fame and glamour. All this was provided to anyone who would want to sign up. The only caveat was their lives. Fortune Limited effectively promoted business-level, government-sanctioned euthanasia. Once your ten years were up, you were recalled and humanely euthanised. Marlowe had ended off his presentation stressing the fact that his solution both offered a relatively short-term solution to the overpopulation question, as well as it did it in a way that allowed no freedoms to be affected – legally. No one was forced to sign-up, they did so of their own free will, knowing all the risks.

Participants willingly signed up, knowing they had just started their own death row.

The glory and practicality of the death row is what made it so alluring. Hundreds of thousands across the world signed up in the first few years after the infrastructure had been put into place. Grace would often think that those with nothing, struggling to live a simple life would end up taking the Fortune Limited option out of necessity to help their families. Sure, it was all voluntary, but what about the circumstances surrounding the *voluntary* act? Are they simply negligible? When her father made the decision and signed on the proverbial dotted line, she remembered thinking to herself: *This is the only solution for our family.*

What else was her father meant to do to survive? To keep them surviving? Sure, there were other long-term solutions, but their family did not have a lot of time ahead of them. He had no other viable, quick, solution. He knew the risks and he took them. He just didn't consult his children.

Grace held a modicum of anger at her father for that last part: the lack of consultation. She did understand why, though. She was the eldest, and at the time was only around thirteen or fourteen. Sure, she could read, and did pretty well at school, but understanding the nuances of a decision that grave; when your whole life you had been raised to think that when things were bad, there was always a way

to make them better – and with a smile! Sibu knew that
Fortune Limited was the only way he could ensure their
continued path to success and stability. It took him just
over the better part of an hour to choose his children over
himself. What Grace loved most about her father was his
selflessness, though, at times, what she hated most about
her father was his selflessness.

The paperwork was done in such a speedy manner that
the Makebas barely had much time to process. Within
days, a long fancy, sleek, black car pulled up to their home.
It was closely followed by a Fortune Limited cargo truck
that quickly dispensed workers that entered their house
with boxes, packing their life away. Thabo and Grace were
then told by their father that they were moving houses, and
that they would love it in their new home. Grace had asked
where it was going to be, but her father did not seem to
have an answer for that. He had patted her gently on the
shoulder and rolled out the house to discuss logistics with
a tall man dressed in a crisp black suit.

The move was over almost before it began. They were
taken away from one of the outer suburbs and placed in
a prime position closer to Table Mountain with beautiful
views of the harbour and the bustling city. Their new house
– no, mansion – was atop a hill and had all the furnishings
they could have ever asked for: coffee machines, huge
couches, bathrooms for each family member, a pool, a
scullery, the latest TV monitors. Thabo pointed out the
Fortune Limited logo to Grace; it adorned every appliance
in their home. And, despite it practically haunting
everything in their new home, she couldn't help but feel
grateful.

In hindsight, Grace shuddered at her thinking that. She
shuddered at the idea that Fortune Limited banked on that

exact kind of mentality.

Before Thabo and Grace were able to go pick out a room for themselves, their father rolled up to them and motioned for them to come closer to him, out of the way of the movers, just to the side of their new entrance hallway.

"Now listen very carefully," began Sibu, sternly, "we might be living here, but this is not our house. You are not yet old enough to understand everything, but Gracey, you at least must know that by the time-" Sibu faltered slightly. They had talked about this, but, coming out of his mouth, it just felt so wrong, "by the time my contract is… up, you two will have to move out. Which means that for the next ten years, we need to be on our best behaviour. These people are doing a lot for us, but they are still a business, and I have a contract." Sibu let the message sink in. He eyed his children lovingly and added, "Understand?"

"Yes, dad," muttered young Grace. She had been doing economics at school, and she thought she understood her father's overall gist: don't break anything, because it's his contract and not theirs and if she wanted her and her brother to be living their best lives after all of it, then they needed to keep their wits about them.

Thabo just mumbled something about the latest gaming station he spied in the adjoining family lounge. He raced off towards it, and her father chuckled. Grace's eye fell on something that was lying on the floor, just behind the door to what she imagined led to the garage. As her father wheeled away, she started towards the door. Before she had time to properly see what it was, a Fortune Limited mover in black overalls burst through the door and swiftly picked up the item on his way back out the front door. He passed Grace and she could make out the form of a little girl's doll being stuffed into his overall pocket.

Time passed. Sibu loved his work. He helped plan and build a newer, more streamlined landing system for the Mars program. He'd been appointed to lead engineer on the jet propulsion system overhaul project as a result of his good work on the landing system. Thabo was being his usual self, though Grace noted more and more annoying boy tendencies finding their way into his personality. Despite that, Thabo seemed to have developed a knack for tinkering with technology, not unlike his father, and had great aspirations to continue in the field his father worked in. Grace grew up with an interest in medicine, thanks to Fortune Limited, she was able to go to the best school in the province, which was conveniently located near her *temporary* home. She had made good friends with a few other Fortune Limited children in her grade, though she found the constant reminder of their temporary nature and situation somewhat depressing – especially given what was at stake.

Over the years, Grace finally truly understood what her father was trying to say to her that first day they moved in. *You are getting this because of him. When he is gone, it all goes away.*

She cottoned on to this realisation, and after a few difficult conversations with her father, she and him had set up private bank accounts for her and Thabo. Every month, they deposited a generous amount of Sibu's earnings into each account. Most Fortune Limiters only thought about short-term goals, and didn't plan for the aftermath of their contracts. While legally everything they bought and earned was theirs, everything they received from Fortune was taken away from any dependents. The only things they could keep were what was in savings, and what was bought by the salary earned during their ten years of prosperity.

Cold, but fair, Grace had to admit.

And so, to combat this issue, Sibu and Grace set up trust funds for Grace and Thabo for The Aftermath, when they suddenly found themselves homeless and without a parent figure to support them financially. Grace was lucky that, by that time, she would be an adult, just finishing med school. Finding a job would be relatively easy. Sibu was not a fool, and he confided in Grace early into his contract that this was all something he had calculated. They would live well for ten years, but unless they prepared, they would sink back to where they started afterwards.

***

Lance leaned back into the booth. Grace could see all the emotions fluttering around and across his face.

She knew that everyone had a story when it came to Fortune Limited; hardly anyone would be reckless enough to sign up if their life was going well. Losing the financial stability that two parents could afford within a year and a half, added on the fact that she actually lost one of them… it was enough to make strangers weep for her. She didn't mind. She'd weep with them. But there had been no alternative; there was only one way her and her brother could lead successful lives, and that was the sacrifice her father had made.

But as she looked into Lance's eyes, she saw something she didn't usually see in the faces of strangers: understanding.

Lance took a while to respond to anything Grace had said. During her story, she'd noticed moments where a flick of the hand (which usually indicated a sudden interruption) would be left hanging before dropping back to the table in defeat. She also noticed the occasional opening of the mouth to utter condolences. Through all of it, she had pressed on with her story. Now that the meat of it was done, she took the time to gather her thoughts, because she was not quite finished.

"That shit sucks, I'm sorry," was Lance's reply. Grace could tell it was a calculated, but a genuine response. He did not know her well enough to hug her or pretend he had known the family, but he had likely had a similar experience. His response was perfect: friendly and sympathetic, but also to the point. Grace continued.

"Yeah, it does. Want to hear the bad part?"

Lance choked on his beer, "What?"

"Yeah, so, I don't know if you recall, but a few years ago there was this huge policy change. New contracts were altered to suit this new addition. Remember what it was?" Grace was asking the question rhetorically, "They started offering open executions-"

"Please don't use that word," piped Lance, which threw Grace off her guard.

"Executions? What are they then, Lance? Are we putting them to sleep?"

"I know what they are," Lance insisted, Grace could hear a level of anxiety in his voice. He repeated, "I know what they are."

"Whatever, fine. They started offering open... 'expiration services with the option of becoming a donor', if you want to use official jargon," said Grace, semi-sarcastically. It really was the official jargon. Those who signed up and who came to the end of their contract were referred to as 'The Expired,' and the company was the entity that provided the 'expiration services' required to terminate the contracts.

"Yeah, my brother opted for the closed option. Said he didn't want us to see him… well, die," said Lance into his drink and then took a swig. "What's your point?"

"My point is that yeah, it's all fine and well that people get the option to actually donate their organs to science after they… expire… you know, at least they get that final choice now. And I am sure it helps those in need-"

"Your point?"

"My father didn't have that option," came Grace's response, "My father's body was shipped back to us, all dolled up and ready for burial."

Lance looked somewhat perplexed, "And so now you're what? You're wanting to bring the company down because they performed the service their business model is based on?"

Grace shot Lance a look.

Stupid idiot, must I spell it out for him?

"No, Lancy," the 'y' rolled off her tongue before she could stop it. The shock on his face made her pause briefly, but she shook it off and continued, "you didn't let me finish."

"What did you just call me?"

She ignored him. If he didn't want to be babied, he shouldn't act like one, "They shipped his body back all dolled up for a funeral. Only I didn't like the generic suit they put on him, so I went to find his favourite party suit and dressed him in that – and let me tell you, getting authorisation to change his suit was a mission in itself, but that's when I noticed the autopsy marks."

"Ok?" Lance was still not on the same page.

"Lance, why would he need an autopsy?"

"To determine cause-" Lance trailed off, Grace could see his brain finally starting to function.

"To determine cause of death. Yes, correct. But, how

did he die? Oh, that's right, Fortune Limited. used their patented go 'sleepy-night-night juice' on him on the night of December the twelfth. Specific, I know, but some things are hard to forget."

Grace could feel the anger and drive swelling within her again as she made it to the punchline: "why in the world would you need to do an autopsy on a euthenasia case that you carried out? Please Lance, enlighten me."

Lance was staring into his drink again. He picked it up and downed it before uttering under his breath, "It wasn't an autopsy."

"Ding, ding, ding! We have a winner!" cheered Grace loudly in a mocking tone. She could feel in her bones that she was being unnecessarily harsh to this stranger, but she was too worked up at this point. He would just have to forgive her. "Now, Lance, add the sudden policy change that happened literally overnight and what does that smell like to you?"

"Cover up."

"That's what I thought, so I did some digging. I didn't bother Thabo with it, though I probably should have, look at me now. He's the tech genius and I'm not so much – but I know a thing or two. So I did some digging, hacked a few terminals, the ones I could get to anyway, and got nothing from them, really. What I did find was a lot of dark web anonymous posts about human experimentation," Grace let that sink in for a moment, but only a moment, "I even found a post that outlined – admittedly without evidence – everything. The fact that the company was using the bodies of the deceased to harvest organs from before shipping them back to their families. The public started to suspect, so in an effort to quash those theories, they made up stories about how some clients opted for cremation, while others were asked by the families themselves to perform an autopsy to determine some medical information – or for inter familial transplants-"

"Hence the autopsy. Hang on, cremation?"

"Cremation, yup, you heard me. I saw reports of Expireds requesting them at the last minute to 'save their family the heartbreak of seeing them like this'. Bullshit, right? Anyway, so the post basically outlined that the policy change was to throw people off their scent. Making a donor option available, plus all the other lies they have been telling would just make a whole heap of hearsay and not amount to anything. Covering their tracks. Like it never happened."

Lance groaned. Maybe because she had just spilled a metric tonne of previously unknown information on Fortune Limited – the reason for which he chased her through the streets.

Perhaps it wasn't really useful information.

Grace took a second to contemplate the thought properly. It was pretty useless, unless you had evidence. Which she didn't have.

"Yeah," she said, "and so, as to why I am public enemy number one, well, that's because I then tried to use my know-how to hack into a peripheral Fortune Limited office's database mainframe, and well… came up short. You saw the news."

"So you have nothing but a hunch that Fortune Limited was organ harvesting dead people, and has since stopped, a few years ago?"

"That about sums it up," was Grace's response. Defeated in tone though it was. She had motioned for a glass of dry white during her story telling, and since it had arrived, she had just been shifting it around in her hands. The icy coldness of the condensation on the glass mimicked the sensation she was now feeling in her heart.

"They're good, Lance," she said finally after taking a sip, "they know how to cover their tracks. Socially, digitally, and legally. I tried to do what I could to get hard evidence, but there was nothing. Like not even a hint of a shady transaction – nothing." Grace faltered slightly, "My father would have wanted me to focus on my life, but instead it feels..." she trailed off. She had forgotten about her brother's needs, her own livelihood.

"I don't quite know what I was hoping for from you, Grace," said Lance leaning back in the booth again, "that evidence would have been great, but to be honest, would it do much? In any case, at least Marc had the option. At least people now have the option."

Grace could see where Lance was coming from; she was there too: hopeless defeat. Hopeless defeat that led to the bitter realisation that nothing they could do could stop a multi-billion credit company. At least not a company, that by their own deduction, no longer did anything unlawful. There was a feeling of misused time in the air. Lance's device pinged and he gave it a glance.

"Yeah, dude," sighed Grace, "At least there's that."

Chapter 7
Lance

Lance was silent on his short journey to fetch Jan. She had called just as Grace had finished telling her story and who had slumped into an apparent withdrawal from the high she had been on while recounting her situation. Lance was glad for the call. There was an awkward silence between the two at Gretchen's. Neither of them knew how to put into words the futility of their desires to destroy Fortune Limited.

Lance was silent on his journey back to his home with Jan slurring in the backseat about The EU, and how otherworldly it was on that side of the world. For a moment, he remembered Grace's story, particularly the part about setting up a trust fund.

He didn't need to worry about his own finances after

Marc's contract expired, and neither did his mother. Jan, on the other hand – She'd been surviving off of Marc's money… from Fortune.

For a moment, Lance wondered what would happen to her.

She needs to get a job, he thought, and chuckled at his own late-night, morbid joke.

They pulled up in the driveway of Lance's house, and for a moment, Lance allowed himself to marvel at his achievement. A house – a standalone house – in an economy and world like this. The only reason the Masons had had a house in Outer Suburb Sixteen was because it was an ancestral home; it had been in his father's family since the late twenty-fifties. Lance's smile faded. They had had to give that home up. The ancestral lineage would soon be down to just himself and Jan to continue.

Now and then Lance found himself thinking, *Perhaps* his *home will become the new Mason ancestral home?*

Then, he took a second and appreciated the irony of that thought: the same Mason ancestral home brought about almost entirely because of the death of one of its family members? Not the best start to a home's life.

Lance got out of his car and for the first time that night realised, due to the wobble of the world around him, that he was not quite sober enough to drive. Luckily, he had made it home. Jan clambered out the back, stumbled, and fell comically up the one or two steps that led to the modest entrance. She reached the door and realised with disgust that she did not have keys.

"Lllllance!" she roared, though in a whisper, so as not to wake the neighbours, "Mh keys, gimme key!"

"Hold your horses, I'm coming, I'm just getting your bag."

Jan slumped down the side of the wall, "Who needs bags?"

Getting Jan to bed was an easier process. She was out like a light the minute her head touched the pillow. Lance exited her room, and stood motionless in the passageway. Was he tired? Yes. Was he feeling tired? No. Lance headed towards his study for the second time that night.

Upon entering, he went straight to the whiskey bar he had set up for himself. He was not a big drinker, but when his mind was stumped or his dreams shattered, he would indulge in a good aged whiskey. Tonight, he felt that, because both reasons applied to his current state, he deserved a double. Neat.

Striding to his desk, he groaned and plonked himself down in the leather bound chair. As if by magic, it swivelled to land him facing his Fortune Limited board. There he sat for the rest of the night, drinking his whiskey, and wishing for something to jump out at him. Preferably something useful.

***

The sun glistened through the used, crystal whiskey tumbler that sat precariously on the edge of the desk. Sleep had eventually found Lance, and he lay in his desk chair, mouth agape. Anyone within a ten metre radius would have also heard a snore erupting every so often. He was awakened from his slumber by both the warm creeping sunlight and his own loud rumbles. Lance sat upright, groggy at his desk. Beneath him on the desk top were two devices, one his smaller, travel-sized device and the other his larger, office-bound one. Both were still active on different websites that – as far as he could remember –

showed why Fortune Limited had been doing experiments on the cadavers of their Expireds.

One site was claiming that the experiments had something to do with Luna University. Due to the scope of experiments that could be done on Luna, there was some sort of shortage of cadavers. That many people wanted them. There was some merit to it on the research side. It was true that some of the newest and frontier pushing experiments and research was being done on Luna. They had been for quite some time now.

What was once called the Moon was now dubbed 'Luna'. And it had very recently been afflicted with the most terrible parasite evolution ever created: humans. Around the year twenty-fourty, NASA teamed up with the Chinese National Space Administration to create what was first called "The NASA and CNSA Coalition Lunar Research Base". There were long reports of negotiations being bogged down over which agency would be credited first in the name. Eventually, NASA forked out a few extra billion to the investment, and bought their way to first place. Of course, this was all for nothing, as very soon the laborious name was truncated by the Americans, the Chinese and virtually everyone on Earth to be simply: Lunar Base.

Over the years the idea for an outpost on the Moon became too good to pass up and aside from your privately owned space companies like LazerTech other countries such as: Russia, India and the newly established European Union started to funnel money into their own bases. Even a South African and Namibian coalition research centre was set up. Of course they all had to rely on Lunar Base for on the ground support and thus they all essentially became a nation of many. As time moved on, those on the Moon felt strange calling themselves the Moon when the Earth was the body above them in the sky every day. Though supplies had to be run up and down from earth, usually staff who came to work on the Moon came to stay. Along with state of the art labs, most countries shovelled out a little bit extra to make half decent living quarters. The residents of the moon eventually began talking about how you had to be a lunatic to come and live on the Lunar Base. It was a joke at first, one that eventually stuck. A few years went by and the name truncated to: Luna.

At the turn of the twenty-second century, Luna had almost octupled in size. It was veering very close to small nation status as all its component nations and companies were sending people up there to live, indefinitely. And as people do on an island alone from their superiors, the whispers of independance start to float. Since most inhabitants of Luna are educated, they began setting up their own governing systems, makeshift schools, courts and so on until it culminated with Luna's pride and joy, the thing that set them apart from any nation on Earth: Luna University.

It had complete accreditations, and specialised in the sciences as they pertained to astronomy – with a few exceptions. The kind of experiments the students and faculty members could perform in true non-atmosphere, low gravity circumstances was unprecedented in humanity. Luna U was Luna's claim to fame.

Travel and cargo shipment to Luna was expensive, but not too astronomical for Fortune Limited to bear, what with (as the article he had been reading claimed) the 'blood money' from the scientific elite on Luna.

Lance had serious doubts about this theory. For starters, surely there would be more evidence of this type of cargo being sent. Luna shipments were the most heavily regulated shipments humanity had ever had. And they needed to be.

If something were to go wrong on Luna, Earth would not be able to respond quickly. As such, certain items were deemed contraband, including weapons. Not even the security forces stationed at Luna had firearms – of course, Earth security sent with certain important payloads to Luna *did* have the luxury of firearms. Lance always mused that that was how they ensured Luna's dependence. That and the withholding of resources. There was only one official shipment channel recognised by the countries of Earth. Luna had, as of yet, not managed to deal with that impediment.

Lance doubted very much that they would be able to get the cadavers up to Luna, do their experiments (without causing extreme harm to the bodies) and ship them back to Earth through the one channel in a one-week turnaround time. It was just not possible. No matter how smooth the operation, with all that bureaucracy, and the amount of clients that they had at the height of their illegal experimentations, it was impossible. Even if there were some cremations.

The other device had an article about Fortune Limited using the cadavers to test the effects of the venom of spiders unique to the Amazon Rainforest, and specified that this was happening in a four by four metre research prefab situated south by southeast of the Madeira river and just before the fork that becomes the Machado. Lance gave this theory even less credit, as the specificity was just too high.

With a jolt, Lance realised he had just been sucked back into his sleuthing. He jumped out of his chair, and wobbled a bit from a mixture of head rush and nausea from his hangover.

Shower, he thought, *I need a shower and then breakfast*

– what's the time?

Lance glanced at his antique clock, and the hands read ten to nine. After a mini heart attack, Lance remembered a late night work message had been sent to him stating that his client had accepted a settlement and so instead of a hurried court hearing they would fine tune specific conditions on the next business day. He did not have work that day, which made his waking from his Fortune deep dive stupor make sense. He proceeded to have a long, hot shower.

Lance left his room feeling much more refreshed and ready for the day. He strode downstairs to where he had left his sister the night before: the guest bedroom. Lance hardly had many overnight visitors, except his sister, so he affectionately called the room: "Jan's room", but never to her. She'd get a big head and think that she could move in. He tapped on the door with his knuckles and gently called Jan to wake her up.

"I'll be in the kitchen, I feel like pancakes, don't miss out." Lance heard a groan that was a mixture of delight and pissed off. He smiled, left the door slightly ajar, and made his way down the passage to the kitchen.

It was a generously-sized kitchen for a family of four, and so it was quite grand for a family of one – at times, two. It had all the luxuries wanted in a kitchen: polished, stainless steel finishes and machines of various kinds and functions. He entered and started straight away, grabbing the mixer, the flour, and sugar in well-rehearsed movements. Soon, music was playing through the household system. Clearly, Jan was up, and getting ready herself. Lance recognised the song as one of her favourites, obviously she thought the place needed some ambiance.

There was a knock at the door.

Lance heard it, but over the music it just sounded like something in the kitchen had shifted or moved into place. So he ignored it. He carried on with his frying. His first two attempts at perfectly thin pancakes had been unsuccessful, he was about to flip his third-

There was another knock at the door, this time louder and unmistakable.

Lance put down his spatula and switched off the gas. He took a second to think who would be calling at his home at such an odd time on a Saturday. His first instinct was his mother, she often did pop in unannounced, and what with Jan staying here…

Lance, confident he had tagged the correct person with the knocking at the door, left his kitchen and started down the hall to the front door. The door was glass, but frosted and with a sepia tone colour. He could not make out the features of the person's face, but he definitely could discern between his mother and someone else.

This was not his mother. The person was taller, almost two heads taller. Now, Lance was nervous. His mind raced, parsing through everyone who might have wanted to visit, but not let him know. He came up blank. Everyone he knew would at least call while on the road. That meant that this individual was not someone he knew. That scared him, but he told himself it was a postman or someone delivering old-school mail – or something like that.

Lance reached the door, and held out his hand towards the door knob. He hesitated for a second, but then put on his lawyer face and grabbed the handle, twisting and confidently pulling the door open. His stern face faded as fast as it appeared.

"Hi, Lance."

It was Marc. There he stood in his usual dark, tailor

made suit. While he usually dressed to impress, this outfit seemed... impersonal. In the background, Lance made out the top of the line Mercedes parked next to his own wheels. Despite the impersonal clothing, Marc stood tall, just above Lance, with a general presence that exuded warmth and friendliness. Lance smiled before he could greet his brother. It had been a while.

"Marc! What an awesome surprise!" came Lance's response, "Uh- come in, come in!" he said, and shifted back to allow Marc to enter. Marc proceeded to remove his jacket, revealing another tailor-fitted button up garment, pale green in hue. He hung his jacket on the nearby coat rack, and started to unbutton and roll up his sleeves. He acted as if he had just come back from a trip to the shops for milk. Lance watched him, with a smile on his face.

"Well, one thing's for sure, you could have let us know!"

"Us?" said Marc, "Is mom here?"

"Nah, just me and Jan," replied Lance as he passed Marc and gave him a shoulder tap, "I'm just making pancakes, what a lucky time to drop by unannounced!"

"If you're cooking, I wouldn't characterise it as 'luck'."

Lance chuckled as he walked and Marc followed, eventually finding himself a spot at the kitchen's island. Lance returned to his stove and reignited the flame. The sizzling of batter once again filled the room, still accompanied by Jan's playlist.

"I should have guessed," Marc pointed into the ether, "this is not your music. Unless you are branching out?"

"Well just maybe I am."

"Artist and song title," challenged Marc. Lance chuckled again and waved his free hand in a dismissive gesture.

"Yeah, don't try me, Mason."

"Noted, *Mason*," said Lance with a grin. He was just

about finished with the pancakes. Some looked a little worse for wear, but he figured they would taste just the same.

"Lance, I hope there's a vegan friendly option!" Jan yelled from her room.

"There would be as soon as there's a vegan over for breakfast!" was Lance's reply.

Jan came out of her room and walked down the passageway, "How do you know I haven't seen the light? Hmm?"

"You asked for a beef burger on the way home last night. You specified beef."

Jan entered the kitchen, ready to line up a suitable retort, but stopped in her tracks when she saw Marc. Her expression was not unlike Lance's: pure happiness. With Marc's job, with all his shoots and press tours, he barely had time to spend with the people he loved: his family. So, when he was able to see them, he usually arrived in a fashion that was very over-the-top and planned. Not like this. Lance saw the look of uncertainty flash briefly over Jan's face, as it had admittedly done to him the past few minutes. There was a question stirring in the back of their minds: why was Marc here?

There were no words exchanged, just a frantic hug and a few squeals from Jan.

There was hearty chatter around the breakfast table that morning. Marc regaled them with tales from his time on set of his most recent film: 'The Owner 2'. He claims it was a half decent follow up to the first instalment, bungled a bit by the script and the overall editing. Jan listened with eagerness while Lance, not uninterested, thought about other things. Things he would rather not think about. Fortune Limited related things and the eventual demise of his brother at their hands.

The room went quiet eventually, and Marc's features became less jovial. The air of warmth suddenly became palpably tense. Marc was about to say something that he knew would not go over well with his siblings. Lance could tell. Marc took a deep breath seemingly to gather up the courage.

"So," he began carefully, "while this has been fun just catching up, I must confess that there is a reason I came over today. While you being here, Jan, was a surprise; I was planning on stopping by mom's after here. I assumed you would be there."

Lance and Jan sat quietly, they had words to say, but did not say them.

"Fortune Limited-"

Lance let out an audible breath of disgust.

"Fortune Limited," repeated Marc, "came to me earlier this week to suggest that I start, well, start making my rounds."

"Rounds?" said Jan, "What do you mean 'rounds'?"

"You know what he means, Jan," snapped Lance, uncharacteristically snappy. His sister was a linguist, she knew what he meant, she was just playing dumb. For what reason, Lance could not fathom.

"They suggested I start seeing… people," clarified Marc, "uhm, say goodbye to some people, confirm who would be, um… attending. You know, the usual stuff."

"There's nothing "usual" about this, Marc," said Lance as he stood. He had to busy himself somehow. He didn't want to talk about this, he didn't need to talk about this. Why was Marc talking about this? Marc had already 'seen' to his close family in terms of financial inheritance; he had set up a fund for them on top of insisting on giving back over the years. Lance of course would take not one credit of it – and he hoped the others would follow suit. In any case, Marc sure as hell wasn't saying goodbye that morning and getting murdered later that day. So then what was the need to ruin a perfectly happy breakfast?

"Lance, please," was Marc's response, "I've done most of the paperwork and all that, the reason for me coming is to let you know – in person – the um… the details."

"The details?" chimed both Jan and Lance.

"The when, and where," said Marc as he looked down at his plate, which was very quickly snatched up by Lance as he busied himself with clearing the table, "they suggest that the participants extend the information in person. Helps with the eventuality, or something."

"'Participant', 'information'," muttered Lance under his breath, though loud enough for them both to hear.

"Yes, I have the details written here," he tapped his left pants pocket, "you don't know, but I recently received the chance to change my, uh, service choice, and I have now opted for an open service. I would, um, I would very much like it if you came-"

"To your corporate and government sanctioned execution?" Lance pounded cutlery onto his tower of dirty kitchenware, "Would I like first row tickets to your murder? What happened to the closed one?"

"Lance, please. I know it's hard, but this is what is happening. I made the deal, I did it of sound mind-"

Lance made a face.

"I know that you said you would find a way to stop it, and I know you have tried. We don't talk much about it, but mom and Jan have filled me in. I know you tried, and I am grateful-"

"No, what you are is a coward, and what you're doing is

giving up!" shouted Lance. Jan jumped at his outburst and Marc simply sat in his chair.

"What, you can't even face your death alone, you need us to see you die? You want me to hold your hand and give you that little bit of hope even as they stick the needle in? Tell you that it will all be okay? Well, newsflash Marc, it's not going to be okay, you are going to die!"

Lance both did and didn't mean what he just said. Jan moved over to him as he slumped into his own seat again. She held his arm and shoulder. He was angry, lashing out. Of course he would be at the service, he would never abandon his brother out of spite like that. But it didn't mean he had to be okay with Marc being okay with the whole thing!

"Marc, you're our brother, of course we'll be there," she reassured Marc. She looked at Lance, "We may not like it. We may not think it is right, but what we are not going to do is let Marc... go alone."

Lance knew what Jan was saying was the truth and logical given the circumstances, but even so, he could not help it.

He wanted to say, *But why must we let him go at all?*

Marc stood up, solemnly. He had a different air about him now. The kind of air a scared soldier has before going into battle for the first time: duty mixed with apprehension, yet layered on strongly with acceptance. As he stood, he took the invitation out of his pocket and placed it decidedly next to Lance on the table.

"You did your best, Lance, but this was always going to happen. I have made peace with it," said Marc calculatedly. He did not want to get into any more of a fight with his brother. Then he added, "I have to go to mom now. We'll see each other again soon, I promise. I'd love a family bring and share?" The last sentence was a request, Lance could hear the hope in his voice at the thought of spending more time with his family before it was too late. He did not wait for a response though. Marc appeared to think it best that he left. Breakfast ruined, he exchanged a shoulder clutch with Lance and a side hug with Jan before heading to the hall to gather his jacket and make his exit.

The door shut and the house felt cold. Lance could not stop staring at the stack of breakfast plates and cutlery in front of him. He thought back to his pin board. To the leads that led nowhere. To the random number scrawled on a piece of paper. It was happening, and he didn't know what to do.

After what seemed an eternity staring at his dishes, Lance said, "*I* won't give up."

Chapter 8
Grace

The door to Grace's apartment was not the type of door to adorn the hallways of the Ritz, in fact it was a little worse for wear. Nevertheless it opened and locked as it should. She had not yet upgraded her system to the digital locking systems. Apparently, they were meant to be super effective. Grace, however, saw a fatal flaw in that all her privacy and access needs were in the palm of her hand… or rather: one device. Though she could not deny technology had seen wonderous advances over the years, there was just something about putting all your eggs into one basket that didn't sit right with her. That and she notoriously lost small objects. On this particular day arriving home she regretted her decision to remain manual.

Grace made it to her floor and was walking to her door

when she noticed something unusual: sunlight. Sunlight burning the stained carpet in the hallway outside her apartment. As she neared it, her brain put the pieces together before she saw the door that was swung open. The handle looked as though it had been yanked off and was lying uselessly on the floor. Grace stood for a second, unable to say anything, as she stared into her home.

She looked through the doorway and saw broken lamps, pages from notes and books (some of which were priceless antiques), scuff marks on the white walls, and glass littering the modest entrance hall.

Grace snapped out of her stupor. No time for standing around, mouth agape. She dropped her shopping bags and bolted inside, only one thing on her mind: Thabo. She sidestepped the broken pieces of her home lying strewn across the floor, dodged a toppled cabinet, and then darted towards his room.

"Thabs!" she shrieked, "Thabs, are you there!?"

There was a murmur, and Grace's heart skipped a beat: he was alive, at least for now. She reached his door which was closed, but not locked, and threw it open. Thabo's room was in a state of its own, but Grace noticed that nothing was broken. Puzzled briefly, she took a moment before seeing her brother huddled on the floor next to his bed. Grace rushed to his side.

"Thabs, Thabs are you okay? What happened? Are you hurt?"

Thabo, clearly in some sort of daze, shook his head and mumbled something unintelligible. Grace proceeded to inspect every inch of him, remembering to be very gentle.

"There doesn't seem to be any cuts or bruises on the outside. Please tell me, are you hurt?"

"F-fine," expelled Thabo as he looked up to his sister. He

had been crying.

"Thabs, what happened?"

"The- they came after you left-"

"Who?"

"I don't know, I didn't see them… I was in here… as usual," Thabo nodded with some effort around his room, "I- I thought they were going to come in here, but… they didn't. They just trashed the lounge and I think… the kitchen? And then they left."

Grace stared at her brother; her helpless, defenceless brother. The dried tears became pathways for the fresh tears that began running down his face. Grace drew him in gently, hugging him as tight as she could.

"I was so scared, G," sobbed Thabo, "I was so scared, I couldn't do anything. I'm useless!"

Grace shoved him back a bit too forcefully to look him in the eyes, "You are not useless, you hear me?" She embraced him again, and then slowly stood, helping Thabo carefully back into his bed.

"You just get some rest, Thabs," said Grace, tucking him in carefully. She dove her hand into her pocket and retrieved a chocolate bar, opened it, and gave it to him, "I'll deal with this."

Grace headed towards the door. Towards the mess. She looked back at her brother and let out a sigh of both relief and sadness. He had been lucky this time, but what if the burglars had wanted to search the rest of the apartment? What would they have done when they saw him?

Thabo had a very rare disease: *Skelatis Morsus*. It affected the bones in its victim's body, not rendering them weaker or stronger, only inflaming the nerve tissues to such an extent that doing almost anything was painful. As far as anyone was aware, it was not a fatal disease, and it did nothing to affect brain function, it just stopped you from doing anything physical in the long run. Eventually its victims would be wheelchair or bed ridden, not unable to move, but preferring not to because the pain would be too much. It was not a transmissible disease, but one that came from a certain gene that only a small percentage of an already huge population had. Until recently, not much had been known about it. There was no cure, and Thabo had only recently been diagnosed.

Grace's mind went to the worst. There was a sub-faction of terrible people who thought that people living with *Skelatis Morsus* were a burden to society. In a world barely able to contain its current population, of which most were in poverty, why should those with *Skelatis Morsus* be allowed to live off the dole? It was just pain. They could suck it up and get to work like the rest of them. Grace shuddered to think of what the assailants might have done had they found her brother.

As she stepped out of her brother's room, she was greeted once again with the chaos that was left in the wake of the burglary. She let out another sigh – this one out of frustration – and began slowly to pick up the pieces of her life. She took her time, deciding to look at the circumstances as a way of taking mental stock of her life. As she packed away the digital photo frames (broken now) onto the shelves and rearranged the couch's cushions that weren't ripped, her mind wandered. Had she been too focused on seeking justice for her father? Afterall, he had entered into the program willingly and knowingly. Had she been neglecting the only family that she had left? She mulled that thought over as she picked up the broken pieces of a vase that once belonged to her mother. Both her mother and father had been only children, and her grandparents had all long since passed on. There was no one else Grace could truly call family other than Thabo – thump! – the armchair she had been putting back upright thudded into place.

Grace leaned on the back of the chair for a while. Her brother was fighting an illness that she could barely fathom, and here she was trying to hack into a company's servers to find, what? A smoking gun? For what? No amount of hacking or exposition would change the fact that her father was gone. Grace grunted silently as a thought that often crossed her mind rose to the surface again: it was his fault he died. He chose this, and now she had been wasting her life trying to avenge him. Avenge what? Fortune Limited didn't kill her mother and injure her father.

Grace pushed away from the armchair and pushed that thought out of her mind again. What she had been doing wasn't a waste. He shouldn't have had to make that choice, and Fortune Limited *had* been doing some shady things with their 'Expireds'. That mattered. It wasn't a waste, but perhaps it was over now. She had been working this angle for long enough, and had come up with nothing. She had an ailing brother, and needed to prioritise the family she had left, before she was the only one. She had to think about other, more important things, like moving to a less crime-ridden neighbourhood. She had some money saved up she could-

That's when she noticed it.

Lying inconspicuously enough on the floor just next to a side table was a small golden object. Grace's eyes caught it in the light. She moved to pick it up. Whatever it was, was not hers. She didn't own anything gold. Gold was tacky. Gold was for rich people. She brought the object up to her eyes, and as she turned it over, it became clear it was a cufflink. It was round, and had the initials 'F' and 'L' engraved on it. Gold was tacky, gold was for rich people, gold was the colour of Fortune Limited.

Suddenly, Grace's thoughts went racing, they tore through everything she had just been thinking. This changed everything. There had not been a burglary in her apartment, Fortune Limited was sending a message. Grace looked around again. She had found this cufflink by chance, but if Fortune Limited had wanted to send a message, they would have left something obvious. An *actual* calling card – otherwise what would be the point? Her eyes fell on the small, dark, laminate wooden table that served as a sort of TV unit. She hadn't noticed before, but there was something black laying on it. On closer inspection, she saw that it was an actual business card in matte black with golden lettering. On the side facing Grace, it read: 'FORTUNE LIMITED', Grace picked it up and turned it over. It was a normal business card; there was no special inscription, just one of Fortune Limited's many cryptic slogans: 'A BETTER TODAY, FOR A BETTER TOMORROW.'

Grace knew what they meant by that slogan. They made people's lives better in the short term to make humanity's collective life better in the long term. It's how they sold their product. Appealing to peoples' senses of greed and wanting to do something honourable that would make them seem selfless. The reality of course was that most of The Expireds applied because they had no other choice.

Grace also knew what the slogan meant for her; what Fortune Limited wanted her to know. They had stopped themselves from destroying her entire home, in the hopes that she would decide to let her vendetta go. Today was some sick way of them saying that what they did was better than what they could have done to her. It was like they were reminding her at least she had a tomorrow.

Grace threw the card back down on the table. Now, she was even more conflicted. Fortune Limited knew who she was and had not gone to the police, which meant that they were toying with her. At any minute, they could turn her in. It would be easy, it was widely understood that Fortune Limited had an in with the police. But they hadn't given her up yet, which meant they thought their little scare tactic would work.

Well I'm certainly scared. So, that's mission accomplished, assholes.

Grace turned on the TV. She wanted something to listen to as she began the cleaning process. The TV auto tuned to the news channel that Grace found most reliable. She began the arduous work of cleaning the kitchen floor, which had more broken shards of plate and glass than the lounge. As she worked, she tried not to think about her conundrum. Her attempt failed.

Should she roll over and drop everything she had against Fortune in favour of focusing on her family, or go head on back into the fray with renewed vigour and a sense of righteousness? The latter sounded more enticing.

The news anchor mentioned something about failing negotiations between China and QuarkZoid Enterprises. Nothing important to Grace, but some lovely background jabber to keep her mind off of what she didn't want to think about. Unfortunately though, trade deals and treaties were not enough to distract her. While stacking the remaining intact plates, Grace again fell back into her thoughts.

Fortune Limited was bad. It was an *evil* corporation. She wouldn't just be getting justice for her father, she would be getting justice for all the people who had been wrongfully experimented on after their deaths. She would be exposing them, and the families of those who had 'expired' to date would be grateful.

Grace nodded to herself, it was true that most people believed that Fortune Limited had definitely been doing experiments – even though the company vehemently denied it. If she could get proof of their past mistakes…

There was an annoying jingle for an advertisement that Grace had seen and heard many times before. It broke her concentration. She continued cleaning, now piling the debris into waste bags.

Grace's mind could not help but to go back to Thabo: her family. Shouldn't she just focus on him? So what if Fortune Limited had done experiments on their Expireds? Sure, they denied it, but now one opted into it. Nothing to expose there, just another free will choice. *Donating their bodies to science at the end of a social experiment probably gets them some massive perks while still alive*, she thought ruefully. Besides, even if she wanted to continue, she had nothing. Her mind was made up.

The TV let out a low beep and a cold voice filled the apartment. The voice sent shivers down Grace's spine. She knew that voice. It was Arrigo Meyer, Chief Communications Officer for Fortune Limited. Grace thought about the date, and realised that this broadcast was the yearly reminder of the next batch of Expireds' last remaining months.

"Good afternoon to everyone in the Southern African Sector," began the spokesperson, "this is a friendly reminder to all clients, and families of clients, expiring early next year. Please remember to make sure all your affairs are in order well before your expiration date, as late-minute scrambling slows the legal river terribly."

Grace scoffed at the man while tying a knot in the waste bag. She lifted the bag and began to move it towards the front door that was still wide open.

"This includes any complicated funeral arrangements and personal wills," continued Meyer, "please keep in mind that there are local Fortune Limited Offices all over your respective countries, should you require any assistance with your affairs. Remember to keep healthy, and have a wonderful rest of your twilight year. Thank you."

Grace halted. She looked toward the lounge – towards the TV.

"What was that?" she muttered to herself. She dropped the bag, definitely shattering the contents more, and moved swiftly towards the TV. With a gesture, she rewinded the broadcast.

"Remember to keep healthy and have a wonderful rest of your twilight year. Thank you," repeated the cool voice. Grace frowned and flicked her hand again, "Remember to keep healthy and-" flick, "Remember to keep healthy-" flick, "keep healthy and have a wonderful rest of your twilight year. Thank you."

Grace stared at the screen, and the frozen beady eyes of Arrigo Meyer stared back at her. After a while, she broke eye contact, and mind racing, pulled out her device. She had made her decision. For good, this time.

Chapter 9
Wolf

Wolfgang Ashley Goode felt the intense pain of a military grade fifty calibre rifle round sear through his arm. It wasn't until the deafening explosion of a nearby, all-terrain transport vehicle that he burst back into the realm of the waking world – with a tearful cry for it to stop. He felt shivers running down his spine, and his breathing was in overdrive. Slowly, he positioned himself until he was seated upright in his single bed. Alone in the dark of his characteristically dreary bachelor's pad, his hand instinctively rubbed the bullet wound, but found nothing but a long-since healed scar. Even so, Wolf caressed his arm as an all-to-usual tear ran down his cheek.

This was beginning to be a habit for him. Always the same dream, forcing him to relive a memory that crippled his psyche enough to induce crying in his sleep. While the sleep crying was beginning to become an expected occurrence, it was very out of the ordinary for Wolf to cry about anything when awake.

He found it a strange feeling, crying. A practical man such as himself found very little use for it. He knew people would say that it helps the grieving process and with letting out your emotions and that, but for Wolf, he found it utterly superfluous... annoying, even.

Once Wolf had settled down, and his lone tear's track had dried, he let out a little, wobbly chuckle to himself. Some people would say he was internalising the negative effects of the patriarchy. Not allowing himself to let his emotions out. To that, he would reply that there were a myriad of ways to let his emotions out. He was a shouter, a curser, a sulker – a sometimes-quick-to-anger. But a crier? That just wasn't his usual modus operandi. Practicality guided most of his daily life, and leaking out of his fucking eyeballs until he had a massive unwanted and fucking *unhelpful* headache was not, in Wolf's mind, a practical way to go about grief. He'd much rather shout, sulk, think alone or even chat heartfeltly to someone. He'd rather tell his feelings than have them represented by salty water and an ugly cry-face. He was not against emotion, he just preferred to do it in his own, logical way.

However, Wolf's body and aeons of evolutionary hardwiring couldn't be stopped on account of it being a slight pain in the ass. Go figure. And so there he was, wiping annoying tears from his face almost every morning at three o'clock.

Wolf glanced at his device that lay at his bedside displaying the time.

Four-thirty? Not too bad this time, he thought as he

swung the duvet off of him.

A sudden image flashed across his mind: a vehicle door flying past him with a disembodied hand still clutching the inner door handle. Wolf took a breath, steadied himself. This too was now a normal occurrence: seeing images of his platoon, who eventually had become his friends, in varying degrees of disembodiment. He felt a pang in his chest. Evolution wasn't done with him just yet.

"Fuck," he breathed, and sat up on the edge of his bed, eyes welling slightly. He blinked his tears away and began his morning ritual.

He knew well enough that he had to confront what he had experienced back in Europe. Somehow. It wouldn't do him well to ignore his feelings and the painful memories. Because of this, he had devised a ritual for when his mind wanted to remind him of what was definitely the single most terrible day of his life.

First, he would get up: he refused to allow himself to be put down. He would go to his tiny bathroom, and stare at himself in the mirror.

He would breathe, "You survived," he would tell himself, "You survived and that is alright. It is not your fault."

Then, he would close his eyes and try to reconstitute the mess caused by the bullets and explosions to reassemble his platoon. He would see their faces, he would remember the good times they had had. He'd remember how stubborn he was to make friends and the fact that they persevered. Then, he would open his eyes and sometimes, though he knew they weren't there, he could see his buddies next to him in the mirror.

He would smile, as best a pessimist could, and say something along the lines of, "It happened, and I miss you." And then he would turn around and deal with his life.

It wasn't a cure for his PTSD and even he would be the first to admit that imagining his friends in the mirror wasn't the most logical way of dealing with trauma. But it helped him. He allowed himself this one bit of airy-fairy-nonsense because it seemed to help him concretely. And no one saw him doing it, so he felt like it was his little secret method. It wasn't a cure, but it was a bandage. One that he had to redress everyday to keep the infection from spreading.

After showering and combing his thick black hair to an appropriate style, he clothed himself for the day in his blue jeans and neutral coloured t-shirt, and made himself some coffee. One of the few commodities he allowed himself to break the bank over. That and the occasional, nightly beer.

Shit. He was practically out of coffee. At least he had some for that morning.

He walked the two metres from his kitchenette to his desk where his desktop device was stationed. He waved the computer on and waited a few seconds for startup; sipping his coffee sparingly. He motioned for the internet browser, and it opened on his homepage: Jobzunlimited. He took another sip and hovered his pointer finger over the 'search' button. He hovered because he knew what was going to come up: nothing. He pressed the screen, and the site searched far and wide, all over the available internet, and sure enough, found nothing.

Wolf sighed a sigh that knew the result he just received was not unexpected. He had a job, a low-paying call service job working on troubleshooting devices for LazerTech. It was a job, sure, but not one that utilised his actual skillset... or that he liked... or that paid enough. He was a programmer, a tinkerer: a techie. Give him any device, and he would know how it operated and fit together within a day. But jobs requiring his skillset were few and far between. All the good tech jobs were filled. No one wanted to leave such lucrative positions, and the age of retirement was going up so often that positions barely opened up. The only tech jobs people could get were with startups, and aside from the lucky job seeker who landed a job at a startup that actually went somewhere, most techies were likely to be earning a similar wage to what Wolf currently was. Established tech jobs paid well, but with everyone wanting to study something tech related, a starting position paid next to nothing. People had to earn their spots. Wolf's practical brain would not let him move laterally. It was up or not at all. He could *just* survive, most of the time, where he was. There was no telling what could happen to a startup, and in the worst case scenario, he would have no job. And he had debt to pay.

Wolf leaned back and closed his eyes. He wanted quiet so that he could get his thoughts in order before he started his day, but that was impossible. Even at five o'clock in the morning, the city was a hive of activity outside his window. New York was no longer the only city in the world to never sleep. He could hear street vendors shouting out their morning deals, and he could hear the constant hum and horns of traffic.

Wolf opened his eyes, sighed, and grabbed his earpiece and microphone. He waved the browser minimised, and started up the LazerTechSupport app.

***

The sun's rays were starting to spread across the sky; Wolf let out a loud yawn and an overexaggerated stretch. As his arms flopped down onto the arms of his desk chair, he turned to look outside his window. He was high enough in his apartment building to see the sea; it had crept in on the coastline over the decades. Rather than pump billions into reducing gas emissions, many cities had ceded land: real estate, now part of the sea. They had built either little dam walls further inland, or chosen to develop older buildings and unfinished motorways to account for the lack of… well, dry ground. A large part of the Waterfront and surrounding areas had their higher buildings renovated to appear to live on stilts. It wasn't an issue for some buildings whose architecture already had the buildings on stilts, for them it just meant the construction of above water parking areas – and a modest fee for maintaining this new development from the tenants, of course. New roads had to be bridged to get to the buildings and that had cost a veritable fortune.

Wolf chuckled to himself, still staring at the glimmering water. The water was rising, and the solution was to put things on stilts. Mass migration still happened to more inland areas, but not too much. And only for the poorer of the citizens. But all was well, at least the fortune five hundred companies could still make bank from inflated fuel prices and oil.

The rich can keep on fucking riching, Wolf broke his gaze away, *eventually, this planet is going to do something that the Powers that Be won't be able to fix by throwing money at.*

He pushed himself from his chair only to hear his email notification ping loudly in his earpiece.

If this is another f-

Not a client, he realised as he leaned over his screen to read the subject line: RENT OVERDUE.

Fuck, it's worse.

Groaning, Wolf grabbed his device from his pocket as he slung his laptop bag over his shoulder, and sauntered to his door, logging into his banking app. He continued out his apartment, down the many, many flights of stairs and through the lobby, desperately trying to make the numbers on his device work for him. Perhaps he could call to reduce his internet package? Save a few credits? Unlikely, he was already on the lowest tier. It was the middle of the month, and Wolf had to make a choice: groceries or rent. His bank account was telling him he couldn't do both. As he stood outside on the busy street on the city's outer limits, he made his decision: he needed a drink.

He turned ninety degrees to the left and set off at a pace to match the foot traffic he was merging with. Being a taller man, he could easily see above the sea of bobbing heads. He knew where he was going, but it was an added luxury that he could see the street names as they passed by. After a short while, he happened upon a newly renovated cafe and bar, and decided that it would be his stop. He had another place in mind, but it was further down the road, and his curiosity got the better of him. Also, he needed the drink.

He made sure to check the fancy holographic sign indicating there was network access as he entered the bar section of the cafe. As a techie, he was never without his laptop. Sure, he could do almost anything on his mobile device, but nothing beat the feel of an almost-outdated metal rig in his satchel. He found the barman and ordered a pint of the cheapest beer he could find on the menu, deposited his rent money into the bar's pay machine, and walked to an empty table. He found one nicely situated next to a window. It would almost be a pretty view if it weren't for the sea of people constantly ruining the city sidewalk.

Flicking open his laptop's lid caused his last-used applications to pop up onscreen. A video played loudly, and Wolf quickly moved to shut it off. He looked around; no one even turned a head. He booted up the web browser, and his mouse finger instinctively moved towards the classifieds bookmark he had saved.

It wasn't Jobzunlimited, that was what he had saved on his desktop at home. The one perk from LazerTech was that each employee received a fancy LazerTech desktop with the job. The only problem was that, naturally, LazerTech monitored the web searches on them. Sure, he had Jobzunlimited open as his homepage, but it was the only one he had. He liked the idea of making LazerTech think he was looking elsewhere, however, he did not do all of his searching on that machine. He wanted LazerTech to notice. He wanted them to know that their job was kind of shitty, long hours for bad pay, but not notice so much activity that they could see that he was not doing his work. If that happened, they might just cut their losses and fire him. Employment contracts had changed in the last few years. No, he wanted them to notice, out of some strange sense of morality from his side, but not enough that his livelihood was in peril. He needed the money to make rent and buy groceries.

He sipped again on his beer.

These classifieds were not anything better than Jobzunlimited, though. All a bunch of unrelated jobs. Some were scams, some were relocation jobs to Luna or China; nothing that required his skills.

Wolf sighed his usual sigh, and gazed onto the street. He groaned and flicked his eyes back to his laptop. He opened up the browser and an accompanying command console. He made magic happen with his fingers. He changed firewall settings and adjusted his IP to mask his actual location. He bounced himself a few times around the world's satellite, just in case, and eventually logged on to the dark web. The act of getting onto the dark web was relatively simple. Anyone could watch a tutorial video online and figure it out. It was the act of not being traced that was a bit more difficult. Wolf knew the hoops to jump through, though. The last thing he needed was his employer finding out he visited the dark web occasionally. For jobs. Because only a very few people visited the dark web for jobs for good reasons. Wolf knew that him making money to survive was a good reason, however, the authorities might not see it that way.

Looking at the dark web browser, Wolf punched in the address of a site he had tried to vet well enough to ensure that, at the very least, he would not be seeing any hit jobs popping up. Though, with the dark web, one can never be too sure. What he found was a list of petty crime jobs. Hack into banks, hack into people's personal information to attain blackmail, change personal government records and the like. All *largely* victimless crimes, but crimes nonetheless. It was surprising just how many jobs there were on this site. Wolf sat there scrolling, imagining how he would execute some of these operations. He liked to look but not touch. Again, he was a practical man, and the thought of not being in control of a situation, plus it being illegal, just screamed to him: bad idea! Still, it was fun to imagine.

He could sit there for ages and plot. He sipped his beer again.

Chapter 10
Lance

Lance sat up straight in the dingy booth. He had his 'usual' beer, though it was untouched. He looked around the old bar, scanning for Grace; she was not here yet. On his tenth scan, he noticed two elderly women cackling loudly in the booth on the opposite side of the bar from him, a small group of seemingly disgruntled middle-class desk workers, and a lone ranger in dark clothing sipping his beer, and occasionally flicking through his device. Lance would think it an odd image, had he not been wearing a similar outfit and doing the same exact thing. Except he was looking around very nervously every two minutes.

A light tap on his shoulder jolted him from his scanning. It was Grace, a little out of breath, but still calm and collected. She slid into the seat opposite him.

"No drink?" asked Lance. Grace's reply was a hand wave as her beer was delivered to the table.

Grace took a big swig of her drink. She scrunched up her nose, as if to question why she chose a beer in the first place. Even so, she went at it again. Lance simply waited. His beer remained untouched. Eventually, it became too much for him, and he tapped the table lightly with his palm.

"Well? Why am I here?"

Grace finished her fourth swig, wiped her mouth, and breathed calmly, "No need to stress, Lancy," she said, "we're just two mates having a beer."

The tone of her voice told Lance that she clearly wanted him to act natural. Which he was finding very difficult at this point. Lance took a swig of his own beer.

"So," began Lance again, "what can you tell me?" he was attempting to sound as conversational as he possibly could.

"I was watching TV last night," stated Grace.

"Okay?"

"Saw something very interesting on a channel I don't usually like to watch," continued Grace, barely cryptically.

"Okay?" came Lance's response again.

"It's funny what you pick up from a few lines in a show, you know-"

"For god's sake this is a tiny, old bar that hardly anyone knows about," burst out Lance, "No one is spying on us. Just tell me why I'm here."

Grace did not seem amused at this turn of events. She simply lifted her eyebrows, pushed her drink away and looked Lance dead in the eyes.

"You tell that to the men who broke into my apartment last night," Lance looked shocked, "go ahead, tell them

I'm being paranoid, tell them."

"They broke into your place?"

"Broke in, terrorized my brother, destroyed my shit. Yeah."

Lance's eyes raced around the table, looking for a logical explanation.

"I know it was them, not just because nothing was taken," she paused to grab something from her bra, she flung it on the table. A matte black business card with the golden lettering of 'FORTUNE LIMITED' slid to a stop in front of Lance. "They left that there."

Lance's eyes widened, and his mouth dropped open. Any sane person with Lance's extreme distrust of Fortune wouldn't truly be shocked by this revelation. Even so, he was shocked. A multi-national, multi-billion credit enterprise blatantly sending goons to a small-time whistle-blower's apartment as a scare tactic, and not even trying to hide it was them? Lance's stomach churned. It signalled something to him. It meant there was something to uncover. They wouldn't go to these lengths for nothing. That worried him. Lance snapped back to reality.

"Shit, are you okay?"

Grace shrugged the question off, "I'm fine, but excuse me if I want to be a little more discreet from now on."

"Uh, sure, yeah"

"Not that that's necessary right now," she glanced around the bar, "everyone here's either too drunk to notice or have noticed and have already sent a report to their masters. In which case, it wouldn't hurt to speak plainly now that the secret's out," she paused, "Not that their break-in was a secret, really."

Lance glanced around the room, but saw no guns being pulled out. And no side-eyes pointing in their direction.

His military training had been activated, though for the life of him he could not make out anyone present as a bad actor. He focused his attention back on Grace, who seemed to be itching to tell him something.

"So?" she questioned.

"Yes?"

"Not going to ask me about the show I was watching?"

"Uh, what show were you watching?"

"Wasn't a show, I was just cleaning up and had the TV on," all subterfuge gone, "news and what not when a general broadcast came on. One from Fortune themselves."

Lance checked the date on his device, "Okay so? They usually have a broadcast this time of year. What's it called, the-"

"Twilight Message, yes."

Lance was again getting agitated with Grace's less-than-stellar cryptic words. She was looking at Lance with intent, as if he was meant to say something. He had no idea what she wanted him to say.

"Okay, so?"

Grace let her hands fly up in defeat, "Jesus Lance, do you need me to give you a map?"

"Please do."

"Do you even listen to those broadcasts?"

"No."

This was not true. Lance knew there was no way not to listen to the broadcast when it came on and he was near a device. He just stopped paying much attention to it. Something about being reminded of thousands of peoples' imminent death put him off it.

"Well, lucky for you, I found a recording online," Grace fumbled in her pockets to find her device. She eventually found it and scanned it for the specific video file she wanted to play. She slid it to Lance and tapped 'play'.

"Good afternoon to everyone in the Southern African Sector." The recording began. Grace clicked her tongue and motioned to fast forward a bit. The cool voice skipped and continued, "This includes any complicated funeral arrangements and personal wills. Please keep in mind that there are local Fortune Limited Offices all over your respective countries, should you require any assistance with your affairs. Remember to keep healthy, and have a wonderful rest of your twilight year. Thank you."

The recording ended, and Grace again looked at Lance for approval. Lance gazed back at her. In the back of his mind, he thought maybe she was losing it. Everything that seemed obvious to her was not seeming the same to him. So what? Arrigo Meyer did the same address every year. What of it? What was so special? Lance shifted uncomfortably in his seat and chose then to sip his beer.

"Well? Did you hear what I heard?" questioned Grace, "Please tell me you heard it."

"I heard the same address he gives every year."

"It's the wording, Lance, anything odd?" Lance's expression was not what Grace wanted, "Really? Nothing?"

Lance shrugged. What could he say, he didn't know what he was meant to hear. What wording?

"What do you mean?" he asked.

"Listen again, really listen this time." And Grace played it again. And this time Lance listened. He listened as best he could, but the cadence of the evil voice was just as monotonous and eerie as before, and the words just the same as every other time he had heard them.

"Jesus, Lance," said Grace, clearly exasperated, "he tells people to be healthy!"

"Yeah, so?" questioned Lance.

"Please, Lancy, please just think about it," begged Grace.

"Okay so, Fortune Limited sends out a broadcast."

"Yes"

"Every year-"

"Correct."

"To all the expirees-"

"Yeeeees"

"To wrap up their affairs and stay healthy?"

"Yes!"

Then it hit him like an anvil.

"He tells them to be healthy," repeated Lance.

Grace punched the air a few times and let out her cliched, "Ding ding ding!"

Lance took a second to let his racing thoughts process into an articulate sentence. Something hit him like an anvil, but he was not entirely sure what that thing really was; all he knew was that something clicked into place, and that he had to make it make sense. Grace was clearly eager to tell him, but he needed to parse it himself before being told. Arrigo Meyer had effectively told the expiring population to stay healthy. To someone on the ground doing their usual thing, that would not be something that would raise an eyebrow. But to Grace... they were dying. The Expireds were being told about their Twilight year. Their last year. Why would they need to be healthy? Lance ruminated on the thought. Well, the donors were being used for scientific research. It was the whole point of the new clause. People had the option, it wasn't just forced upon their dead bodies.

"It's not sunk in yet, has it?" asked Grace.

"Something... something," tried Lance but he couldn't put it into words. Meyer's words lit something, but he couldn't quite explain his thoughts.

"He tells everyone, Lance. Everyone," finished Grace, "He tells all of them to stay healthy, and then he gave that ugly smile."

And there it was. The thought Lance was trying to grasp. Arrigo Meyer had not just asked the donors to stay healthy, he told all of those about to be expired. It was a choice of words, perhaps a simple slip of the tongue, but it was 'off'. And that's what didn't sit well with him.

"Which means," began Lance slowly and thoughtfully, "which means that it's all just a charade. Nothing's changed."

"Nothing's changed," concurred Grace sadly, "They slap a tick box and make people think they have a choice. I mean, whether Marc opted for the donor option or not, is irrelevant. Clearly they give no shits."

This statement gave Lance pause. For the first time since meeting Grace and talking about all of this, he realised he didn't actually know what Marc chose. He knew he opted for the closed... and then more recently, open... expiration... but had Lance just assumed that that meant he had also opted not to be harvested or experimented on? After half a second, Lance realised he felt a deep disappointment in himself. This was something he should have investigated. Why did it take meeting a random stranger for him to question which option Marc had taken? He honestly had no idea what his brother wanted. He felt like, somehow, he had let Marc down. As if, by knowing beforehand, he could have then done something about it.

"But," said Lance, "we don't know this for sure, do we? I mean, what? Arrigo Meyer wishes Fortune's clients a healthy last year, so what? That's not proof."

"No," Grace said matter-of-factly. "It's not proof, but do

a little digging, and things fall into place. Did you know, for example, that a few months after the new policy came into effect, another new, 'minor' change came about too? All bodies are to be cremated. Some faux care-about-eradicating-the-problem-of-unused-burial-land – another problem created by overpopulation and thus another problem Fortune Limited simply must deal with!"

Again, Lance didn't know. It had never occurred to him to do this kind of research. He was always concerned about releasing his brother, not what would happen to his body against his will. However, now, with his brother's time almost up, thinking about what Marc left behind – or didn't – was becoming more of a priority. Again, Lance felt a pang of guilt. He should have done more to save him, and he should have done more to protect his legacy. Or at least asked what Marc wanted.

"So, cremations means no need for 'autopsies'," continued Grace, "in other words no evidence of any wrongdoing."

"These bastards," breathed Lance into his beer glass, "they have no fucking human decency."

"We're going to take them down, Lance," decided Grace, "Someone has to."

Lance looked up from his glass, looking defeated, "What if we're wrong? What if this whole thing is just coincidence, and the donors are being used and the others are just being cremated?"

"You believe that?"

"If we are wrong, then I go down as the person who went through a whole lot of time and effort to discover essentially nothing, all while ignoring his own brother. Instead of spending what little time I have left with him, I'm the one chasing a ghost of a story."

Grace sat back and thought on that for a while. Lance could see she was probably thinking of her brother and her father. She looked out past him, and into the window.

Without breaking her gaze on the view outside, she finally said, "But if we're right, we get justice for the families, and we potentially take down Fortune Limited."

Grace leant forward and looked into Lance's eyes. There was a desperation there he hadn't clocked before.

"Lance, cards on the table, I have no proof for you. You have no reason to believe me, I could be talking a bunch of crap, I could just have my own unreasonable vendetta, and I could just be purposefully fueling your feeling of impending loss for my own gain. They haven't done anything to you except offer a service. A service which your brother willingly accepted. You have been investigating them for the past nine years and come up with nothing concrete yourself. You have nothing to base this idea upon except your own intuition. Knowing all of this, I am still going to ask: do you really think they aren't doing something bad? Boil it down to this: are you happy that Marc's body is being left to them?"

Lance stared at her. He could see it on her face, she had the same guilt for her father as he did about Marc. Their situations might have been different, their contracts vastly different, their stages in the process far apart, but what was the same was the feeling that there was something they didn't do to help. Something they'd overlooked. Lance searched his mind, and all rational thought told him that he was wrong, that Fortune Limited was doing just what they purported to do. Nevertheless, Lance met Grace's stare. The decision between their eyes was clear. Come what may, this time they would leave no stone unturned.

Chapter 11
Wolf

Wolf leaned back in his seat and stretched his arms. His back felt the tension of spending an afternoon hunched over a laptop. He gave a small grunt as he rolled his shoulders back. He looked around him. The bar was picking up a bit for the night. A quick glance at his laptop's clock told him he was late for his night shift. With a gasp, he quickly stood up, slammed his laptop screen down and shoved it into his satchel.

On the streets, a chill swept around him and he flipped up the collar of his jacket as he turned towards home. In a city that never sleeps, night shifts were not uncommon at all. In fact, most people worked jobs that required night hours. He wished he didn't, but there was very little he could do about it.

The street was packed as usual, and Wolf felt some shoves and nudges from people as they sped off in every possible direction to meet their deadlines. Wolf often wondered just how many people actually had social lives. And not just the kind of time he had to go have an occasional beer between shifts, like *actual* social lives. How many people had the time to rush to a birthday party, or a family dinner, or even just an all-nighter club? Logically, he knew there must be many. There were restaurants and clubs afterall, but the faces he saw on the street showcased a narrative of determination, not one of partying. No expression ever screamed 'happy' to him. It always just seemed people were consistently late for an appointment of some kind.

Wolf turned a corner. He could see his building in the distance. He considered hurrying up, but thought against it. Yes he was late, but he wasn't that late. LazerTech could wait.

Wolf felt a body bump against him. In his daze, he took his hand out of his pocket to indicate it was his fault – though it wasn't. The man who bumped into him returned his gesture with a slight panicked look, and took off in a run. Wolf's mind snapped back, his hand clasped his jacket pocket: empty.

"No, no, fuck!" shouted Wolf as he sped up into a run.

Some people saw or felt the commotion and gave way to the two runners, others couldn't care less. Wolf cared even less about them than they did about him. If they didn't make way, he shoved them out his path. His military training kicked into action as he tracked the wallet thief's trajectory.

The thief dashed right down another packed street, and proceeded to duck into some oncoming traffic. Wolf sped after him, vaulting over a waste bin to save on time, but he was not as lucky as the thief in traffic. As soon as he made it to the curb, a bus blocked his path. Wolf took a split second to decide his move, and chose to head around the back of the bus and over the street, dodging a very irate taxi driver. Once on the other side, Wolf continued to jog, but scanned the surroundings for his thief. There he was, heading into the back door of a building.

Wolf sprinted towards the building – a restaurant – and threw open the door. The kitchen staff looked like they were experiencing deja vu, the one chef meekly pointed towards a door on the opposite end of the kitchen that was still swinging.

"Thanks," Wolf breathed and continued his pursuit. The door led to an indoor stairwell, and since they were on the ground floor, there was only up to go. Wolf thought it odd, but did not pause to assess the logic of his opponent. He needed his wallet. It had his personal flash drive, which had all the hard-to-get, questionable programs that a hacker needed. He kept them on that flash as a form of security, rather than on his devices.

Wolf reached the third floor and looked around again. He tuned out his breathing to try and hear the thief. It took a few seconds, but he eventually heard the scramble of footsteps and the grating opening of a door. The kind of door that would only be used at the top of a building. The industrial type. Wolf glanced up the stairwell, only five stories in this building. He raced on.

When he made it to the roof, he saw a frantic young man backed up against the wall. He was looking left, right, and centre for somewhere to go, but aside from over the ledge, there was nowhere to run. Wolf sauntered, panting slightly by the time he neared the man.

"P- p- please, I'm sorry I just need-" began the thief, but

Wolf cut him off.

"I need that wallet."

The young man whimpered. He looked very young to Wolf, possibly just over eighteen. The pathetic whimper softened Wolf's heart a bit. He could see he just needed money. The problem was that Wolf really didn't have much to give. The theft of his wallet was less about his money and more about the flash drive.

"Look, boy, I know it's tough out there, that wallet just means a lot to me," continued Wolf.

He was not going to specify what in the wallet was important, lest the thief think the flash would fetch something on the black market. Wolf had thought about it on the run: any banking card he had in there could easily be blocked, and if there was any cash – which was highly unlikely – it would not be a lot. He was happy to let any of that go. In his experience, thieves this young in the city were thieving according to some gang lord's will. Wolf guessed taking something back would help him from being beaten for a job badly done.

"You can take my cards, I think there's a hundred in there, take that too. I just want the wallet. It was my father's," the last part was a lie. Wolf took a pause. He assumed that the thief's father figure was either dead, dying, or very badly off, so he added, "It's all I have left of him, please."

Wolf felt the cringe of his words, but did his best to hide it and emanate sincerity. The boy looked at the wallet. In reality, it was a shabby wallet. It was faded, brown pleather and deeply disfigured from years of use. His story could be true. Without a word, the boy fondled in the wallet, taking out all the cards he could find, and snatching a one hundred-credit note and another fifty-credit note – which both surprised and disheartened Wolf. The boy stuffed the cards and money into his pockets, and, after a pause and a short glance at Wolf, tossed the wallet in the opposite direction of the door.

The act did not seem to have the effect the boy had intended. Wolf did not jump to protect his precious, though ruddy heirloom. Wolf just stood where he was. An awkward silence ensued until Wolf took the hint and moved – slowly – towards his discarded wallet. Out of the corner of his eye, he saw a flash of tatter clothes and heard the swinging of the industrial door. The boy had left.

Wolf grabbed the wallet and searched for the secret zip. He fumbled, but eventually retrieved the tiny flash drive. He let out a sigh. He was relieved, but frustrated at the now-empty wallet in his hand. His spirits dropped again.

***

As Wolf reached the steps of his building, now nearly an hour late, he dug into his pocket for his wallet that had his-

"Fuck."

The boy had taken his access pass.

Chapter 12

Marc

Marc sat upright in the rather uncomfortable chair that was one of many in the glistening lobby of Fortune Limited's head office. He glanced around the black and gold trimmings aimlessly. The receptionist gave him a brief, shallow smile and continued her work. Marc thought she looked miniscule. Her head only just bobbed up over the high granite counter that stood in front of a very imposing dark wall that stretched to suit the high ceiling. Again, they locked eyes, and Marc swore he could see her thinking the same thing of him as he sat there alone in the void of the lobby. He could hear a pin drop. Marc cocked his head as he heard a shuffling in the room closest to him. The way it broke the silence was deafening.

For some reason, Marc always felt unhappy in this

building, despite the cafes and high-end stores in the floors below him. No aspect of this company's head office lacked curated design – even if it was a bit emotionless in some areas – like the legal area; the one area in which he found himself.

Honestly, Marc hated being summoned here. It caused a knot in his stomach every time. Sure, Fortune had made him sign away his life, but it was all for the good of his family. The company had supported him throughout his career, and now he knew his entire family was safe, and wouldn't need anything when he was gone. He owed his family's existence to Fortune Limited.

Marc himself was living his dream. He was recognised as one of the best actors of his generation. Sure, the company had funded his journey and opened doors, but the critics were the ones who made or broke his career. He had made it through their ringer unscathed. He was a natural. That said, he was always very aware that he had only been recognised by the right critics because of the help from Fortune Limited. He was proud to have made the decision he did. Even so, the head office made him queasy, and he didn't know why.

Marc slapped on a smile and sat more upright, adjusting his suit. That always helped his mood: changing his outside to kickstart his inside. It was almost like his motto for himself, that and 'the character will come'.

The next time the shuffling came from the door it resulted in it opening slightly. A high-heeled, suited woman exited into the lobby. She strode up to the counter and the shallow receptionist, who exchanged a few muffled words with her. With a double tap of her hand on the granite, the woman took off across the lobby towards the elevator. As she entered the lift, she turned to look at Marc and gave him a warm smile, uncharacteristic of the setting. The doors closed, and she was gone. Marc snapped back to reality, the brief feeling of warmth fleeing his body again.

What is it about this place? He thought to himself.

A bell chimed from the desk, which seemed to notify the receptionist that her overlord was ready for his next victim. Marc ran his hands over his knees and clenched them slightly before rising anticipatorily. The receptionist noticed his movement, and nodded slightly to let him know he had the right idea. Marc gave a weak smile and he moved towards the door nearest to him – the one from which the woman had come moments before.

She was in a good enough mood, he thought, *It shouldn't be that bad.*

Marc, however, had managed to forget that not everyone came to Legal on a summons… or for the same thing. It's likely she was a first time client, or not even a client at all, and some other employee. Marc gritted his teeth and knocked on the door politely. A dreary voice came from within.

"Enter."

Marc opened the door to reveal a very lavish office. One that didn't suit the voice it was inhabited by. Of course, most of the finishes were of the characteristic Fortune black and gold, but there were some feature pieces of furniture and accents that clearly were unique to the lawyer. And some that looked particularly expensive, Marc noted. Clearly working for the legal department had its perks.

In the centre of the office, behind a large oak desk – varnished black – sat an elderly gentleman with a face that Marc could only describe as 'old *old* Hollywood'. He had the expression of a director who had no problem recasting an actor's role if they so much as questioned his vision. As

Marc admittedly gawked, a smile spread across the man's lips that completely muddied the impression for Marc into something even more sinister.

"Mr. Mason," said the man, "what an absolute pleasure to meet you!"

Marc was taken aback by the apparent warmness of his greeting.

"Uh, thank you, um, sir," began Marc, who was suddenly at a loss for a decent reply, "you have a lovely office."

The 'director' waved his hand haphazardly, "Oh thank you, but it is nothing, just some trinkets."

"Okay, " responded Marc.

The 'director' again waved his hand in the vague direction of the chair that stood before his desk, "Please."

With the invitation clear, Marc sidled towards the chair, and sat down as delicately as possible. He felt a bit like he did at his first audition. Nervous, confused, and without the correct sides to deal with the scene. It was a feeling he had never really wanted to experience again.

"Well, I suppose I should introduce myself, shouldn't I? I mean I know all about you, the whole company knows you. My daughters simply adore you. I believe the term 'heartthrob' is coming back, if twenty-something year-old girls are to be believed. I must say I can see the appeal. Not just looks though, you really are stellar, one of Fortune's biggest success stories."

"Thank you," said Marc, feeling a tone of condescension, but also happy to be recognized. Though he did not know how to broach the fact that the 'director' had not actually introduced himself.

"It's a pleasure," came the reply. The 'director' had a momentary flash of deep thought cross his mind, "it is rather a shame. Fortune's going to miss you, Marc."

Marc shifted uncomfortably. Took a steadying breath.

I knew this was coming.

"But that's the contract, isn't it?!" the 'director' seemed to be back to his faux friendly nature again. Then, after a beat, he added, "Oh yes, I am Mr. Topheles."

He held out his hand for Marc to shake. After a second, Marc stood up and leaned over to shake his hand before returning to his seat. Mr. Topheles immediately moved towards his device, and pulled up Marc's file.

"Right. Now, do you know why you are here, Mr. Mason – Marc, if I may?"

Marc stared at the file, "Uh, actually I don't know."

"Mr. Mason then?"

"Oh no, Marc is fine," said Marc, still glaring at the file.

Was that all he was to them? A singular document? Surely not. He was Marc Mason! One of the greatest actors of all time. Mr. Topheles had just said so himself.

He managed to tear his eyes away, "I mean, I don't know why I'm here."

Mr. Topheles seemed genuinely upset by this admission.

"You mean it did not mention anything in the email?"

An email? What email?

"No, uh sir."

"Typical," replied Mr. Topheles, who tapped a button on his desk top, "Janet?"

The receptionist's voice drawled through a speaker system Marc had not yet located, "Yes, Mr. Topheles?"

"Mr. Mason was not given the details of his visit with us."

"No, sir, I *am* sure I-"

"-this is the fourth time this has happened. You are on thin ice, Ms. Pinkel."

"I'm sorry sir I-" Mr. Topheles cut her off before she

could finish her sentence.

Mr. Topheles sighed very audibly, and rubbed his temples. He stood up and moved towards the window to pour a glass of some alcohol. From where Marc sat, it looked like whiskey.

March shuffled in his seat. Did he really need to draw this out?

Mr. Topheles took a swig, and then turned to Marc.

"My deepest apologies, Mr Mason," he began, "I hope you know this is not the calibre of employees we usually employ. She is a friend of the family, and all."

Marc nodded, as if it mattered to him.

"In any case, we cannot continue our meeting today as, frankly, it would take too long. You were meant to have been given a comprehensive guide and suggestions. This was merely meant to be the finalisation process. A signature or two."

"I'm sorry," Marc began, "but what was I meant to do?"

"Of course, yes, apologies," said Mr. Topheles, "this was meant to be your will and testament finalisation meeting," Marc's heart skipped a beat, "All outgoing clients have this meeting in their twilight year. Janet was supposed to have sent you a breakdown of the process, and suggestions for asset assignment, et cetera."

Will and testament? This *was supposed to be my will and testament meeting?* Marc found himself utterly speechless. He had not thought about a will and testament – at least not in any great detail. He had drawn one up with Lance and his mother, but that was years ago already, back when Anita had thought about doing one for herself. But that there was meant to be a meeting with Fortune in which he discussed it? One filled with alcohol and missed emails and stuffy business chairs? He'd not been told anything of the sort. Aside from their company assets, what business was it of theirs?

"I, uh, I already have a will," was all Marc could muster.

"Unfortunately, you do not."

"I'm sorry?"

This seemed to annoy Mr. Topheles more than Janet's lack of receptionist skills.

He strode over to his desk and device, and scrolled through that same damn file, "Mr. Mason, your contract states that 'any and all will and testaments pertaining to you and your assets must be seen to and administered by Fortune Limited or any affiliated Fortune Limited legal firms," he said, monotone, as if it wasn't life and death he was talking about, "and as we have since decided to streamline the service, we have not picked up any external legal firm. Ergo, you have no legal will and testament under your contract."

Marc gaped. He – 'the greatest actor of his generation' – hadn't been alerted of this sooner? This man couldn't take two seconds to give him a phone call, or even shoot him a message about his impending death?

Mr. Topheles, oblivious to Marc's internal crisis, checked the timer attached to his file, "Legalities are a pesky business aren't they? And you are quite literally running out of time. I will have Janet – no, on second thought, I personally will send you the documents to review. Please follow the correct procedure, and I will set up a catch-up meeting where we can do all the signing legalities. How does that sound?" at this, he looked up from his desk to see Marc staring into space.

This man was… far too calm.

He very slowly came back to himself, "Yes, sir. Thank you."

"While you are here, as you are so far into your Twilight Year, I'll just check a few things in your file," there was a gliding movement as Mr. Topheles' hands typed a few commands into his Fortune system. "Full bill of health, good, and ah, I see in your file you recently changed your plan to include the open Expiration? A wise choice, good for the family an all that.

I have taken the liberty of adding your Expiration Date to your calendar, then of course cremation will be within three business days of Expiration. Your Villa stay has already been booked; a good suite too, lucky you, Mr. Mason."

Marc barely processed what was being said to him. This all seemed so... last minute. A badly run show with a very big budget.

"I will send those documents as soon as I can. And I believe that is all for now, we will be in touch," Mr. Topheles stood up, "Go well, Mr Mason."

Automatically, Marc rose from his seat, shook Mr. Topheles' hand, and exited the room. His mind buzzed. As he left the room, the lobby and then the building itself, he thought about Mr. Topheles. His demeanour. He hadn't expected bouquets of roses when he met with his Expiration Date, but this... business-as-normal attitude was a side of Fortune he had not yet encountered. He felt like an old stage light about to be removed from service.

Chapter 13
Wolf

Wolf plodded up the last few stairs to reach his floor. Even he had to admit that his own mantra of always taking the stairs was beginning to seem more like a punishment. It was *meant* to be a sort of coping mechanism. A way of reflection. A means to some extra exercise. However, for the past year or so, he had been feeling considerably not young anymore. His military training meant he was in peak physical fitness for his age, but after fifteen flights of stairs, he reasoned he'd forgive anyone for a little shortness of breath.

He reached his door and was met immediately with a projection hovering millimetres from its surface. The projection simply read: 'PAST DUE'.

Yeah, yeah, he thought as he attempted to wave the

projection away.

It didn't budge. He tried again. And again. By the third time, he knew it was a fool's errand. Wolf grunted and fumbled around his pockets for his device. He needed it to unlock his door. Eventually, he found it and swiped the door open. In that moment, he thought about the humiliation he had gone through for him to get into the building without his access pass. A kind soul had held the lobby door open for him. This kind soul also happened to be Mr. Miles, who lived two doors down on his floor. Who had undoubtedly seen his 'past due' note. Wolf grunted again, this time in uncharacteristic embarrassment.

In Wolf's mind, everything should be on his device so that he could open his apartment door and the building door with one device. One less thing to worry about. One less way for neighbours to throw a pity party in his honour. But he would never get that luxury. His building was one of those older buildings, where the systems were quite outdated. Frankly, his apartment door *should* have had an old-school lock, but he outfitted a smart one when he moved in. For that he didn't ask permission; he didn't like the idea that anyone could have a key and come rifle through his things. Some hills he would die on.

He entered his hovel, and immediately moved towards the small fridge. He needed a drink. His desires would not be so easily met, though, as he opened it just to find a depressing site of old leftover pasta and two bottles of water. Wolf grunted again. With his prospects few, he looked over to his bed, sleep it was.

***

Wolf jerked awake to the fading sound of screaming. Again,

he was being haunted *again*. Wolf's arms quivered as he moved himself from his bed to the safety of his mirror. He took a deep breath, and out of the corner of his eye, spied his device's reflection. The competitiveness took hold of him and he turned around to check the time: three-fifteen. Worse than last night. He turned back to face himself, and attempted to forget the fact that he had made the timing of his episodes some sort of morbid competition. He closed his eyes, and when he opened them, he recited his lines.

"You survived," he told himself, "You survived and that is alright. It is not your fault."

The next part of his ritual was cut short when he was plunged into total darkness. For a split second, all rationality left his body, and he was back in Europe, deafened by enemy explosions and blinded by pain. He felt sweat begin to form on his brow, and a chill ran down his spine. He wanted to cower, he wanted to scream. The voice of reason that usually occupied his mind was gone, and all that was left was a scared little Wolf without a pack.

As fast as it came, it went. Wolf found himself curled up on the floor. He felt like he had experienced a black out, but not the good kind. Not one you get from a night on the town with buddies. One that made you question where you were, how long you'd been out and what you had done. He scrambled to his feet and searched for his device. It lay on his bedside, and shone like a shining beacon in the darkness. He grabbed it and looked at the lock screen: three-sixteen. Relief washed over his body like a cold spell. He hadn't been out, he'd just fallen. He composed himself. He was caught off guard, he fell. *Now, to assess the situation.*

On quick inspection Wolf realised what had happened: his power had been shut off. He knew this, because he could see lights illuminating the bottom of his front door. The building wasn't out. It was just him. He hadn't paid for more electricity. He hadn't thought the units would end so soon, clearly that was a lapse in judgement. Although, lapse in judgement or not, there was no fixing this anytime soon. He had no money. He knew because he had just spent the last at the bar, and on the thief. Then, he checked the date, and, just as he had feared, it was too early in the month to be dealing with this shit. Wolf let out a groan and threw his device towards the direction of the bed. In the darkness, he'd misjudged the distance (a remarkable feat, considering the tiny dimensions of his cupboard of an apartment) and the device slammed against the wall. Wolf saw it happen, but despite seeing it with his own eyes, he still could not believe his luck. The device's screen shattered, rendering it practically useless.

"Fuck. Me."

Chapter 14
Grace

Grace shook off the impending sense of dread that seemed to creep up on her lately, and gave her locks a stylish flick. They were in her face, and she didn't like that. Her eyes were part of her face, and she needed them unobstructed so she could see. She was staring at a screen, trying to think up a plan. They knew there were shady things happening at Fortune, but how were they going to get the proof? Grace looked up from her device, and her eyes had to adjust to the darkness that surrounded her.

On her left, Thabo groaned, half in pain and half in his sleep. She was sitting at her brother's side, on his bed. Her bed? Lately, the bed was shared. Since the break-in, Grace took less time for herself and spent most of the night at his side. She knew Fortune was not technically after him, and she knew that they'd be dumb to try another home invasion so soon after the first – though another one in the future was not out of the question. The bastards had sent their message. Loud and clear. And they knew it had been received. Even knowing this, Grace felt a sense of duty to, and spent as much time as she could with, Thabo. Nothing would bother him on her watch.

Of course, Grace could only do so much, nature does what nature wants – and nature wanted to take Thabo. Grace could see his deterioration daily. And since the incident, Thabo seemed even worse. He complained of pain more frequently, and his movements were even more staccated than they had been before. It bothered Grace that she couldn't do anything but be with him. This knowledge informed her actions, so she did exactly all she could do: be with him. That was, of course, with one exception: her mission to take down Fortune Limited.

In a strange way, she rationalised that her admitted vendetta with the company was something that would help ease Thabo's suffering. If she could get revenge for what she viewed as injustices done to her father, then perhaps Thabo would rest a little easier. If it turned out that he had not been experimented on after death, but others had, then she reasoned it would have a similar effect. Thabo would see his big sis as a hero who exposed a multinational corporation in the name of their father. Surely he would rest a bit easier with that knowledge?

It's worth a try, thought Grace as she swiped up on her device. In the back of her mind, she knew full well that nothing would *actually* help her brother's condition.

She let out a sigh of almost-defeat when she suddenly had an epiphany. With a glance down at Thabo, she reasoned he was finally fast asleep, which bought her a few hours where she at least didn't need to worry about his pain. Gingerly, she stood, and tiptoed out of the room. She lifted her device to her eye line, allowed herself a grin as she realised she looked just like her mother did when she had used 'newfangled' devices, and tapped the icon that would start a chat with Lance.

***

Grace entered the now all-too-familiar Gretchen's and did a quick scan of the crowd that night.

Where is that brooding thirty-something?

Ah, she spied. There he was. *Brooding in his usual spot, in his usual way.*

Grace plucked up her courage. For a moment, reality sunk in. Lance was really still pretty much a stranger to her, and there was *still* a chance he was some super secret double agent. If not that, then he could just turn out to be a big old wimp and chicken out when the things became tough. Things were going to get tough, and she needed someone who was up for the task. She sensed it might be Lance, but she couldn't shake the feeling that she might end up alone in this. It wasn't a pleasant thought, and she didn't like to have it, but she definitely thought it, and she usually liked to heed her thoughts. She turned to the bar and requested two drafts of the cheapest beers.

It's fine, she thought, *I'm almost positive he is at least genuine. But just remember, Gracey, this is a dog eat dog world. Don't get too attached.*

She swiped her payment and headed to her acquaintance with their beers.

"You're kind of late," came Lance's greeting. Kind of rude, but Grace could make out a slight joke to it. Sort of like thirty percent was serious, and seventy percent was in jest.

"Yeah, I had to be quiet for my brother," said Grace curtly, she did not want to go into detail.

"Ah, I see," said Lance, who didn't really 'see', "So, what's the plan?"

Straight into business, Grace could work with that.

She took a swig from her pint, "Well, we can probably assume that the proof – whatever that manifests itself as – is being kept at the Fortune head office."

"Which is practically slap bang in the city centre," said Lance.

"Correct, so it goes without saying that whatever our plan is, it's going to involve breaking into that building and stealing some files. I suppose someone could hack their systems, but I'm pretty sure that is much easier said than done."

"Yeah, if they are doing something underhanded, they'd probably not keep any records on something that is connected to the wider internet," chimed in Lance.

Grace nodded at his comment, happy that he seemed to have given this some thought himself. A sign at least that he was partially invested.

"My thoughts exactly, sir," said Grace, who took a deep breath, "however, Fortune HQ is a huge frikken building, Lancy. How in the hell are we going to figure out where to go? How do we know where the main server room is? Frankly, how do we even know there is one?"

"We're flying blind," muttered Lance, "how are we going to do this if we don't even know where to look? Or if we are looking in the right place?"

"So, I suggest we hit a smaller satellite office instead," said Grace.

"Haven't you tried that already?"

Grace made a little face, to herself mostly. For all her worries of Lance being 'not a good person,' in this instance, she kind of really needed him. Perhaps for stage two or three she could lose him, but for this… she needed him.

"Well, yes," was her response, calculated, "I have tried something… similar, so they will know to look for me. You, on the other hand…" she trailed off to make time for the thought to percolate in Lance's head.

His expression barely changed when he realised what she meant.

"True. They don't suspect me, and they have you on camera," said Lance, "So then… I'm sticking my neck out?"

"Exactly," said Grace, sounding a bit too relieved, "but never fear, because I have a plan. It's highly unlikely that the juicy info at HQ would be in the cloud, but the blueprints for Fortune Limited offices might be. I mean, they'd need to access it easily somehow if audited, right?"

"It's a big assumption-"

"True, but it's the best idea we have, and you wouldn't even need to go too far in."

Lance looked off to the side, appeared to make up his mind, and looked back at Grace, "Alright then, what's the game plan?"

Chapter 15
Wolf

Wolf wiped away the sleep in his eyes as he stood in the line of other down-on-their-luck souls. The building was drab and depressing, but accented with the characteristic colours and detailing. He had not managed to sleep enough the night before, after his realisation: the solution to his dire situation. But he managed to get to sleep eventually. An annoyingly deep, peaceful sleep. He couldn't quite understand how, after all this time, being at relative peace with his financial and social situation caused him to have weak, thinly-veiled sleep, but the night he made the most difficult decision of his life, he slept like a baby.

He also found that expression annoying. In general, babies didn't sleep well through the night. Wolf grunted audibly at his mind's racing thoughts. The lady in front of him, who was already trembling, jumped a bit, and Wolf almost felt apologetic. But he didn't apologise.

The line edged forward. At a snail's pace. Why was he here? He could have done this at his apartment. They did house calls. Unfortunately, he didn't have a lot of time. If he wanted to keep his home – which he did – he would have to do this as fast as possible. Going to the main building would also take longer, that's where everyone went. If he thought this line was long… the line moved forward again. He let out a long sigh. Logically, in this day and age, he should be able to do all this online, but no, they preferred in-person meetings for the final signature. Old school pomp, ceremony and all of that. Potential clients could easily have a change of heart standing in line, waiting to sign their lives away. Wolf had thought about it a few times, changing his mind, but he would stick it out for the time being. He had a plan… of sorts. He ran his hand through his unwashed hair, and felt dirty.

A flash of blond found his eyes, he couldn't help but look. His years of tactical training and experience wouldn't let him not look. He spied an attractive, lean man with dirty blond hair in casual wear. Jeans, t-shirt, hoodie. Wolf stared on, somewhat thankful for the distraction in this boring line that led to his sentencing. The man seemed to be on his own mission. He was acting cool, but to Wolf, it was clearly just that: an act. The man made his way across the hallway towards the back. The back was occupied by a total of one door and an uninviting couch. The door was a staff-only entrance, and for some reason, Wolf didn't think the man was part of the staff. The line moved forward again.

The man had reached the doorway, and seemed to be talking to himself. His expression changed to a grimace, and then one that told Wolf he had just realised something. He pulled a card out of his pocket.

Wolf's mind started to race. What was happening? The line moved forward. What was this guy playing at? Wolf's mind came up with a million scenarios at once: he could be here to bomb the place, in which case Wolf was obligated by duty to start an evacuation, he could be hiding a small firearm in an attempt to rob the building.

Why? There is no money on the premises.

He could just be trying to send a message. Perhaps he had a family member who signed up and he was unhappy? The line moved again, and Wolf realised he had now very little time to act. He looked back at the man, who had just looked backwards himself, and then out towards the windowed walls of the building.

There was a coffee shop situated just outside, across the road. Wolf looked over and scanned the patrons as best he could. He could see a couple having an argument, an elderly gentleman sipping his beverage, a woman working on her device, a man in a suit looking down on his life – the woman happened to look in his direction and uttered something. Wolf spun his head back to the man. He suddenly seemed calm, moved to the couch, and sat down. Wolf was then shoved through the doorway by the line behind him and had no option but to comply.

As he entered the room, he assessed his surroundings. There was very likely a bomb about to go off and he needed cover, and fast. He spied a desk and a doorless archway that led to a little temporary storeroom of some kind. Either would do in a pinch, though he hoped he would be out before the chaos ensued.

The attendant at the desk looked impatient as she waved her hand at the seat. Wolf took it, opting to sit on the edge for maximum ease of motion.

"So, Mr. Goode, what brings you to Fortune Limited today?"

Even though he was anxious about impending doom, Wolf let out a scoff, "What do you think?"

"Straight to the point, I see," was the reply, "very well, I am obligated to go through with you the rules and guidelines of your package, you have opted for the Twenty Financial Stability package, correct?"

Wolf nodded and continued scanning the room. He had read the terms and conditions. He knew what he was signing up for: the relatively new package that was a twenty-year contract opposed to the usual ten years. This one basically just provided its purchasers with a reasonable salary each month – no benefits. He could live his life mostly financially free for the next twenty years. The attendant carried on with her scripted monologue of the procedures, etcetera, and the utterly life draining speech made Wolf understand (more) why someone might not worry about bombing a Fortune Limited satellite office. The staff here were arguably more far gone than the ones who established the company in the first place. They were acting like it was nothing. At least the higher-ups had some stake in the matter, and pretended like they cared. These people just saw it like any other job.

The woman's speech went on for a good few minutes, and by the end of it, Wolf found that he still had a body with which he had a hand with which he could sign his life away and get out of this godforsaken hell hole. The woman thanked him for his signature, and then motioned to the door on the opposite end of the room. Wolf had ignored the door initially, because he assumed it went deeper into the building, and thus was not the best place to hide from an explosion. He rose and moved towards the door, and out of the room.

Chapter 16

Lance

There were a lot of people in the small building. Too many people in the small building. Lance felt his palms begin to sweat as he moved as casually as he could through the bystanders; the ones waiting to complete the process of applying to die. An elderly woman was one of those people, and Lance found himself looking at her for a little too long. She had greying hair and an expression of deep sadness. She shouldn't be in this line, she should be living out her days with her family in relative comfort. Like they used to do back in the old days. Before people couldn't afford to be alive; well, at least when the idea of being able to afford to live was alive and well.

Lance sidestepped a young man and rounded another in his quest to get to the 'sweet spot,' as Grace called it.

"Take your time, dude," came Grace's voice through his earpiece, "it's not that big of a building, get to the sweet spot and we can get to work."

Lance replied affirmatively and continued.

He had to cut through the line, and finally was facing the back of the building. But it wasn't the back of the building. It just appeared that way from the line's perspective. From his view, he could clearly see a modest corridor heading off to the right, just past a dismal-looking couch.

"I'm here, now what?" said Lance as he glanced around, semi-casually.

"Just a second," there was a clink of glass and a scrape of a device on a metallic table, "Ah, now I'm comfortable. Okay, right. You just need to hang around there a little bit, just as we planned. Maybe take out the receiver, might make it quicker, you never know."

You probably should know, Grace.

Nevertheless at her command, Lance dug in his pocket to pull it out. He felt a little important, but also a little ridiculous.

"Now what?"

"I don't know, I can just make out a couch from here, sit down."

Lance huffed and moved to the couch. He still felt suddenly very conspicuous, "Grace, you have that code ready, don't you?"

"Don't stress my man, I've got you," was her casual reply, it was layered with a certain sense of self-importance, "Self-taught you know, well, a little from my brother, but mostly self-taught."

Lance glanced around again, this time, a little more nervously. Grace was not a hacker. She knew some tricks, but that didn't qualify the level of a hacker. Hearing her say that she was self-taught was not reassuring in the slightest. She was safe and sound across the street, while he was in the lion's den. He curled his free hand around his knee. A man in a green hoodie passed him by and Lance gave him an awkward smile. *What was that for? Did the army teach you nothing?* The nerves were getting to him alright. He took a deep breath. All he could do was hope for the best: that the plan would work out smoothly. It was a simple plan, really. Get in, stay long enough to make a connection, sift through the cloud for blueprints, get them, and get out. As far as mitigating any issues, Grace said she had a few tricks up her sleeve. She couldn't quite get control of their cameras, but she said she could 'flicker' some of them – again, her words, not his. She was convinced a 'flicker' could help to distract the poor soul watching the feeds from looking at the one attached to him.

She could get into the internal comms system. At least, she said she could. She could get into their text channels and set up a bot to report false info, further distracting the possible troops on the ground. Of course, all of this depended on her having a connection to their server, which purposefully had a very small range. So Lance sat on the couch nervously as people watched him.

Lance had never felt this nervous on a mission, perhaps because the outcome really meant something for him. It would determine whether or not he proceeded on their main mission of taking down Fortune Limited. And if they were successful, there was a chance Marc could be saved. The fact that he had made a promise to his brother didn't help his nerves either. All Lance could hope for in that moment was that the receiver would do its thing in no time flat, and he'd be able to walk out of the building with no Fortune security personnel the wiser.

"Okay, so the connection is giving me grief in stabilising," came Grace's voice from the nether, "shouldn't take much longer though, and then it's just a case of finding a needle in a haystack." Grace chuckled a bit, but Lance remained deadpan. This was not the best start.

"So I just sit here indefinitely?"

"Yes Lancey, like we discussed," said Grace.

"What if they get suspicious? I mean, a simple review of the camera feeds would show that I literally walked in and sat down. That's a little questionable don't you think? Something like that would not do a defendant well in, say, court-"

"Let's not be dramatic, we have some failsafes, remember? Perhaps talk less, though, you don't want them to record a guy talking to himself, that certainly wouldn't hold up well in cour- ah! I'm in."

Lance let out a sigh of relief, Grace was in – they were one step closer. Now, she just needed to find a very specific blueprint of a very important building. Assuming it was even in this building's database to begin with. So, basically, a piece of cake.

"Shit."

"Grace-"

"Shut it, Lance," snapped Grace, "the system has made a tiny flag of my unauthorised entry. Just act normal; there's no reason for anyone to suspect it's you. Now, where's this database?"

Lance's eyes danced around. Back in Europe, he knew when he'd been discovered during a raid. Everything there was in-person, there were usually sirens, and there would be an overlord who had real-time aerial footage of the complex he was raiding. They would be able to alert him of hostiles, how many and from which direction they came. But he wasn't in Europe anymore. He was in a Fortune Limited satellite office, not a military complex, and the analogue he had of an overlord was Grace. And she couldn't even hack into the security feeds.

"Okay, haven't found our print yet, but I have the comms system up on my other screen and there's started to be some chatter. They're instructions to look for someone."

Great, thought Lance, *we're done for*.

"Hold tight, act normal, just identify someone. Don't talk a lot, remember? Big brother is watching, brief description, quick."

Lance's mind raced, there were so many people here, who would he choose? What would happen to them?

"Green hoody... Black hair... Male." *Sorry, guy*.

"Gotcha," came Grace's voice, he heard some typing in the background, "okay, I just dropped a description of a possible suspect. That should keep security busy a little while longer. I'll keep looking now."

From another door across the crowded hall came a lone ranger. He tried to appear casual, looking for his mark. Clearly, he was scouting the scene in the lobby, looking for the man with black hair in a green hoodie. Lance smiled to himself. Thankfully the green hoodie guy had long since left. He had seen him leave during his awkward wait. It would take some time before the guard realised the man wasn't here.

"There's so much information here," chimed Grace, "nothing damning though – as far as I can tell-"

"Print," reminded Lance, stealthily.

"Yes, yes."

The guard completed his round, and seemed to call for back-up as another guard entered through the same door. They exchanged a few words and pulled out their devices to inspect. They were going to catch on sooner or later. Lance could just sense it. He had to think of something else. He spied a camera that was pointed down the hall to his left, the right of the couch. His keen eyes searched for some sort of identification for the corridor. Nothing, nothing, nothing – there! 'Corridor B' was written on the wall. A tiny sign that he could just make it out. He knew he had to start setting things up.

"Corridor B," muttered Lance casually, brokenly, "flicker."

"What?"

Lance huffed to himself and tried again, trying desperately not to move his lips too much. At the same time he, casually as possible, returned the receiver to his pocket, "Corridor B... *flicker*."

"Oooh! Gotcha!" responded Grace, catching on, "gimme a sec... and we're flickering. I feel like I've almost found the print by the way, must be in this folder somewhere."

Lance was barely listening, a bead of sweat slid from his forehead, and he breathed shallowly. There were three guards out now, right in the way of the main exit. Ideally, he wanted no guards in his way, besides, of course, the one that was, and had been this whole time, stationed at the door. He wanted his entrance and exit to be captured, and to be as unremarkable as possible. Nothing the higher-ups might want to flag.

Phase two of his make-shift plan hinged on two things: that Grace found the blueprint and he could go, and someone being in Corridor B. The latter shouldn't be too much of an issue, he saw people exit into the corridor from a concealed door.

It must be the exit of the room most all those poor souls are lining up to go into, he thought.

He looked around again to appear casual, perhaps he was just waiting for a relative. He made eye contact with a middle-aged woman who appeared to be bored of the sales pitch the clerk was making to her in the further end of the lobby. Lance played it cool, and slowly pretended that his mind was wandering off from her piercing gaze.

The original two security guards had by now been alerted to the 'flickering' and were moving to Corridor B to investigate, but were doing so slowly, so as not to draw suspicion. Lance almost chuckled: too many people were trying to act calmly in this lobby.

"Got it!" shouted Grace in his ear, which gave him a slight jump scare, "I've got it Lancey, get out of there."

Now, Lance had to make his final move. He shot another look at the door in the corridor and his heart skipped a beat when he realised his luck. The door opened and a man stepped out. He was tall and built. He looked like he could handle himself in a fight, which was good, because Lance was about to identify him as the suspect. He was holding a device and everything, he looked the part…

"Corridor B… frizzy black hair… device… male," instructed Lance to Grace who thankfully knew what he was on about this time. Lance shot another glance in the corridor's direction only to be met with the man's gaze. He was looking at him as if he knew something. In fact, he looked… concerned? Lance didn't have time to dwell on the stranger as Grace announced her success in sending the tip to their comms.

The three guards looked at their communicators and immediately made their move. Less stealthily, but still as calmly as possible. The stranger watched as Lance stood up, and began walking casually yet swiftly as possible to the exit. Lance tried not to think of the stranger who was about to have an unpleasant confrontation. Hopefully, they'd do a quick device check and conclude he was not an issue. By then, Lance would be well clear of that building.

All Lance *knew* was that their mission, despite some hiccups, had been a success. He walked through the glass doors and into the throng of pedestrians triumphantly as the midday sun beat down on him.

Chapter 17
Grace

The coffee shop was a perfect base of operations. It was strategically situated to provide an unfiltered view of the Fortune Limited office. The office façade itself was one of large windows.

Fitting, Grace made a mental note, *the façade is a façade itself.*

She supposed corporate wanted to exude a sense of transparency, and the architect had gone a little literal with the interpretation. Either that, or it was just cheaper to build with glass? Grace had no idea, she wasn't a contractor. Whatever the reason, it worked for their purposes.

A live waiter brought her her coffee. Another reason she liked this coffee shop, it had human waitrons; not the mechanical kind that was becoming all the rage in the city bowl and the fancier suburbs. She liked to know she was being helped by people, but perhaps, more importantly, she liked to know that, even in these times, a human was chosen over a machine for a job. She thanked him quickly, and he moved on to his next customer. She didn't touch her coffee. She was focused on something a teeny tiny bit more important.

"Corridor B... frizzy black hair... device... male," came Lance's halted voice in her ear. She knew exactly what he meant this time – even the device part. Clearly, he wanted her to mention this on the security guards' comms, creating a proper diversion so that Lance would be able to exit the building without anyone batting an eye. Grace's hands scrambled over the keyboard that she made appear. She knew what she was doing now, sort of, she had just done it a few minutes ago. And done! Message sent and received, loud and clear.

Grace brought her head up and squinted through her sunglasses. She was trying to discern between Lance and the other Fortune patrons and the guards. Trying to see a movement that meant she had done the right thing – that Lance's quick thinking had worked. Sure enough, after a minute, the automated glass entrance slid open and Grace could make out the blond hair and jeans of her partner in crime. He seemed extremely casual, she almost hoped he would hurry up a little. However, she remembered that Lance was an army guy. He knew how to act in operations like these, and the less attention he drew towards himself, the better. So she waited for him to get closer. He made it to the road, looked both ways, and then crossed with a group of people onto her side of the road. Grace's gaze followed as he moved towards the coffee shop and through the main entrance, until he was almost on top of her.

"Success," Lance muttered as he sat down next to her.

"Now, we just need to appear normal, no device play, just two friends meeting for coffee. Smooth."

"Except," Lance retorted, "except that one of the friends has been sitting here for ages talking to herself and staring at Fortune Limited."

Grace waved a hand, "Please Lancey, plausible deniability: I was doing work and on a call. It's easier to focus on the job when I stare into the distance."

"Airtight, that," scoffed Lance, but he seemed content, and somewhat relieved. He motioned for the waiter kindly and ordered a cappuccino, "How long should we have our pretend date? I'm kind of eager to have a look at the prints."

"Calm down, Lancey, good things come to those who wait," said Grace as she sipped her beverage. She leaned back, happy with their success. They were one step closer to justice. Justice for Marc, for the millions of people before him, and most of all, justice for her father.

Something drew Grace's attention back across the street. Something that seemed familiar, but was, at the same time, almost completely new to her eyes. It was a man, walking towards the shop. Grace stared some more and suddenly realised that he seemed to be heading towards them. Though confusing, no alarm bells went off inside her head; he was not dressed as security, so he couldn't be one of the guards. And if he wasn't one of the guards, then he couldn't be anyone involved with what they had just pulled off.

He was closer now.

"Friend of yours?" said Grace casually as she nodded in the man's direction.

Lance appeared confused, and turned to look at the man.

He snapped back to Grace, his eyes wide with shock. Immediately, he started scanning the shop for an exit, but the man was practically upon them.

"Shit," said Lance and he froze.

Grace was confused as all hell, she leant a bit forward, attempting to begin a witty round of questioning. She had clearly not noticed just how close to their table the man had become. He was definitely within earshot, and only a feeble row of bushes stood between them. The man spoke, and Grace's fight or flight instincts perked up as soon as she realised he was there for them both.

"You two should be glad Fortune hires such poor security," said the man matter-of-factly, "and not people like me. Stay here, you owe me."

With that, the man left both Grace, who was now quaking in her literal boots, and Lance.

I have the prints, I could make a dash.

The man walked around the perimeter of the coffee shop and in through the main entrance. Grace managed to cock her head to follow his movements. Did he have a gun? Was he going to call for back-up? Was he roping in the waitstaff to his grand take down of the both of them?

No. He seemed to be ordering an espresso.

This did not calm Grace, however. She was still racing through scenarios in her head, cooking up exit strategies. Most of them did not include Lance; she had the file she needed on her device. Sure, a part of her wanted to be loyal. But if it were to come down to her life or his, she wouldn't think twice.

The man sauntered smugly up to their table, snatched a steel chair from the table adjacent, and scraped it into position between Grace and Lance.

"My coffee's on you two, by the way," he said casually,

and then, "so what are you two playing at? Domestic terrorism, or what?"

Chapter 18
Marc

The Proscenium arch of Marc's resident theatre had never looked so big. It loomed over him, like a lion about to pounce on a mouse. Lately, Marc was feeling like the mouse. He played at being self-assured and a go-getter. He played at being a 'big man', someone who accepted his choices and stuck with them. He played at being the person who understood the terms and conditions of any situation, and was the first to let others know that they were in breach of contract, social or otherwise. But in that moment, looking up at the intricate details of the stonework that led all the way to the greek-style capstone, Marc felt weak, miniscule, and most of all, powerless.

It wasn't all his fault. Had no one mentioned the impending forever sleep, he might have forgotten until the very last days. But people knew, and people talked, and worst of all, people pitied. His co-stars had begun to be less jovial around him, they stopped joking about death and destruction – the kind of dark humour that was funny until it actually happened. They had started hanging out with him more, though in a shallow way, never quite genuine. Marc thought that, perhaps they wanted to be there for him, but to become less attached, and make the inevitable a little easier. Marc also suspected it was because some of them were beginning to realise their own mortality had a timer. Even so, how people acted around him affected his own performance, and the way he looked at the world. Marc could not help but feel like one of the men Dylan Thomas wrote about in his poem.

Grave men, near death, who see with blinding sight.

Except he was not old, frail or sickly: his timer was simply on its last legs, and everything and everyone around him started to remind him of that fact.

The director announced another final run-through of their play. Act one, Scene one. First positions. Marc moved automatically to his mark: downstage, centre. Years of talent and experience told him that he belonged in that position, but all he could think about was the transience of his role. He was about to die, and very soon one of his sponsored co-stars would take his place. He was a place-holder; they all were. That thought went macro in his mind, and he imagined that after his death life would go on as normal for most people he knew.

Marc felt his chest tighten. These were thoughts he had never allowed himself to think. Never allowed himself to feel. It was an inescapable truth he had spent the last nine and half years trying to evade.

I have no one to blame but myself, he'd think – when he

allowed himself.

Now, standing there on the empty stage with a director whose show would run for years after his death, Marc could do nothing but reflect. The words of his character were not coming to him, he was trapped in his own mind. It was no one's fault but his own. No one made him sign the documents, no one gave him the ambition to become successful at all costs. He had been living a life of luxury, he had provided for his family. He had got them all on track. They were his legacy, nothing to scoff at.

He had done something good and yet…

I don't, his breathing started to double, *I don't*, Marc could barely see properly, the arch seemed to be shrinking around him,

I don't want-

The darkness of the dimmed auditorium seemed to grow.

I don't want to-

The slap of the stage mat against his cheek echoed throughout the hall as Marc struggled to breathe, to see, to live.

I don't want to go.

Then, it all faded quickly to black.

Chapter 19
Wolf

The two characters in front of him gawked in silence. Wolf was enjoying himself immensely. It had been the first time in a while he was actually smiling. It was at someone else's expense, but they had just tried to dump a cyber attack on him, so he figured that they were even. He grunted, amused.

"So what's the angle?" Wolf reiterated. The two continued to stare motionless – their eyes darted towards each other and the exits. Eventually, one of them spoke – the blond guy.

"Uh, well-"

"Look, blondie, save your excuses. I know you two are up to something, and quite frankly, I think I am the only one from that damned building that does. Do you know what that means?" interrupted Wolf, not keen on the bullshit blondie was about to spew. He did not wait for an answer, "it means that I kinda have the power in this little," he waved a hand around the table, at their basic equipment and their coffees, "... whatever this is."

This time, is was the woman's turn to stammer, "We, uh I was... look, it's nothing bad really, we were hired to check their security. It's our job, sir."

The 'sir' was a nice touch, though a poor attempt to add a layer of professionalism to what was clearly *not* a professional gig. Wolf spied her subpar tablet and some old school paper with scribbled notes. No one used paper anymore. Those who did used it because they didn't want what they *had* uploaded to any clouds. The perfect digital data protection: analog.

"Look, Locks," Wolf had decided on nicknaming the pair based on their hair, since they hadn't had the decency to introduce themselves yet. Though, neither had he, "my name's Wolf, and I can spot a grift a mile away. This is a grift. A poorly executed one, but a grift nonetheless."

"Mr. Wolf," began Blondie.

"Just Wolf, it's my name."

"Fine, *Wolf*. Fine, you've got us. Clearly up to something. We're obvious, okay," continued Blondie, suddenly with a sense of entitlement and confidence that Wolf kind of appreciated. He had 'cut the crap', so to speak, "Why haven't you alerted the authorities? Why isn't there a Fortune security detail descending on us right now?"

"Yeah," piped up Locks, "if you were so sure, that we – two random people just minding our own business after a day at a dreary Fortune office – were actually some sort of cyber security hacker extraordinaires, then why aren't we in cuffs right now? Oh I know, because you have no proof and a hunch. Frankly, its insulting you would just assume this of two perfect strangers-"

"Oh shut up." Clearly these two had not cut the crap, but were wading even deeper into it, "First of all, extraordinaires? Please. Secondly, I know a hacker, however pathetic, when I see one. Or two."

"What makes you so sure?" responded Blondie.

"Because I am a hacker, a pretty good one in fact," Wolf's espresso appeared, and he quieted as the waitress set it down on the table. She asked if there was anything else she could get them, and all three shook their heads, rather suspiciously. Wolf groaned internally. These really were amateurs, why had he bothered?

"So, Mr. Hacker," Locks continued, "you're what, here to judge our skills and then head off? Why are you here?"

This was a question Wolf had not really thought about fully. He kind of knew his reasoning, his thoughts were logical, however, he felt that he had perhaps made a mistake. A lapse in judgement. Would they prove useful at all? He had thought that they might be able to help him in his own endeavour, but sitting with them now, he felt more like a primary school teacher with seven-year-olds after he had just caught them doing something naughty. However, he was someone who stuck something out until its conclusion.

"Well, to be honest, I thought you could help me," came Wolf's response. The pair simultaneously pulled back in shock. Clearly, this had not been the response they had expected.

"You want our help?" asked the man with the bleach-blond hair.

Still Blondie, until you introduce yourself thought Wolf.

"That's what I said, Blondie," but every second that

passed made him doubt his initial rationalisations. Finally, he opted to go all in, "I have no love for Fortune, as I'm sure you two don't. I was planning to do something for myself, but when I saw you, I thought you might have a more solid plan than I do at this point in time and... logically... as the saying goes: many hands make light work."

The two of them seemed just as perplexed as a moment before. Clearly, nothing had prepared them for this. Wolf imagined them leaving their home earlier today with the confidence of a tweenager about to fact-check their teacher. Just two souls eager to do a little bit of hacking, have brunch and get away with it having no one be the wiser. They never would have imagined that someone would clock them, insult their methods, out himself as a superior hacker, and then ask for their help. As Wolf mulled this over, he realised how strange a situation it really was. He didn't need a whole big team, however hacking Fortune Limited was not going to be an easy feat; he needed people dumb enough to join him in his crusade. He had only applied for the 'Twenty Financial Stability' package after promising to himself that he would find a way to get out of it. And being himself, he preferred doing things in the moment; there was, after all no time like the present. Especially with this big of a shadow looming over him. Procrastination was just not his thing. He liked getting things done, or at least to have everything he needed.

These two could help him reach his goal: financial stability, without the whole 'looming death' part.

"So, what are you guys, a part of the Anti-Faust Movement or something?" pushed Wolf, though by their skillset and the look of them, he could guess they were not a part of the 'official' movement against Fortune Limited.

'Official' was a loose term when it came to The Anti-Fausts. They were merely a dormant group of freedom fighters. Once in a while, they would anonymously post a referendum or a damning message, but because there was never any real substance to what they were 'exposing', people just viewed them as one would a child complaining about chores. Wolf was one of those people. A resistance of some kind may be necessary, but with a corporation as far reaching as Fortune Limited, they needed to be a little more 'on the offensive' than they were.

"No," came Blondie's reply. Finally, a reply Wolf could take at face value. He hoped this would keep up, "no, we actually want to make a difference."

There it was, that was the spirit that had drawn Wolf to Blondie in the satellite office. He may have seemed out of his element, but Blondie had at least looked like he was on a mission.

"Great, I want to make a difference too," said Wolf. This was not entirely accurate or inaccurate. He wanted to make a difference, yes. To his own circumstances. To his own contract. He couldn't care less about the other two. However, he sensed that he would need to play along a bit if he was going to get a team together – or at least get them to spill their plan. Assuming they had one more substantial than a coffee date outside their target's headquarters.

Maybe this was a bad idea?

"Oh, really?" said Locks, her dark eyes narrowing. She did not like Wolf, that much was apparent, and could he really blame her? She was sceptical, they both were. He'd have to give them something. So he did.

Wolf took a deep breath and, over the course of another espresso and a round of beers, told them his story. He made it emotional as well, just to get them on his side.

He went all the way back: to the days in the army, to the accident. He told them how it had affected him, and made him act out-of-character. He layered the feelings as much as he could for their benefit, but as he told his story, he found himself feeling less burdened. He told them about his financial struggles and what had led him to coming to this branch to sign his life away. He told them how he hated Fortune Limited (which was true) and that he planned to take them down (this was a little less true, he still needed money. But they didn't need to know all his intentions right away).

Blondie seemed particularly affected by his story; he even introduced the both of them. Even Locks had softened a little. Wolf was amazed by the power he could have from spewing his feelings to strangers. Blondie was, in fact, called Lance, a name that Wolf agreed suited his stature and personality. Locks was called Grace, but Wolf decided that Locks sounded better, and made a mental note to keep calling her that for the time being. Mostly because it seemed to annoy her and she annoyed him. So they were even.

"Thank you for sharing," said Lance, "I'm ex-military too, I know how strong a bond you must have had with your company," those words hit Wolf a little harder than he thought they would.

"It is hard."

"So, if you're a master hacker, why do you need us?" pushed Locks, "I mean, we still haven't agreed. I feel for you, but we're in a rough situation, here."

Wolf appreciated their situation. It was tough for them. They had not planned on gaining a third, especially a talented third. Especially someone they had just met who could easily have been recording their conversation with the intent on ratting them out.

"I need a team, I can't do everything from my device, I mean your... operation... required at least two. And honestly, I don't even really have a plan yet."

"So, you want us to trust you with our plan, and you'll help us take down Fortune? Just like that?" said Locks, "Dude, you don't even know why we want to take them down, and here you are, ready to shack up with us?"

This was all true. They knew his story, he knew nothing about theirs. He understood her reservation.

"I have time, tell me your story. I knew when I saw you working earlier that we have mutual goals; namely to wreak havoc on Fortune," again, not entirely accurate, but a necessary white lie, "but if you would prefer to get absolutely everything out in the open, then so be it."

Locks looked Wolf up and down, but eventually sighed and looked over to Lance, who looked at her. Their eyes seemed to communicate. Wolf hoped it was something along the lines of agreeing to trust him.

"You want to go first, or should I?"

Lance took the stand first, detailed his aims, his mission, his reason, and Wolf found himself impressed by his devotion to his brother and family. It was a feeling Wolf had not had himself. His family had not been the best. In fact, where they were now was a mystery to him. A mystery he didn't really care to solve.

As the afternoon progressed, Wolf felt a strange sense of camaraderie building between the three of them. They all had reasons to hate Fortune. They all sounded, he assumed, like they believed each other. Plus he was having beers on their tab. It was almost like three long lost friends had just made up after a feud that none of them knew who had started. Wolf sat back while Locks spoke about her father, and then both of them took turns offering their conspiracies regarding the post mortem experimentation. Wolf was not entirely sold on that part of their story, but he could tell they were. In any case, it did not matter much to him, he had his own agenda, and he needed their help.

"Fine," said Lance, eventually, as the waning sun set on their backs, "you're in, we actually could use a proper techie, and you seem just as determined as we are. And-"

"-And, even if that isn't true," butted Locks in, "you probably have a recording of us from earlier admitting everything. So, playing along with your charade is likely our best move at this point." She shot Lance a look that said: *what?*

Well Locks is clearly in the camp of 'I have no choice but to do what you want'. Wolf didn't mind her reservations, he understood them, but at the same time, he didn't quite like her. At least they had that in common. Regardless of their trust, it seemed she would do what he needed.

"Send me your contact, we'll have a proper planning meeting at mine tomorrow, when we're sober," came Lance's logical ending to the coffee-turned-beer throuple date. Wolf tapped his device with Lance's so their contacts would share.

"Right then, see you both tomorrow, will message you bright and early," said Wolf as he stood up. He could hold his alcohol, and so did not so much as wobble, even though he felt a slight buzz, "Thanks for the drink."

Chapter 20
Marc

The air was cold – especially for early springtime. It felt like a physical obstacle in his path. It was as if it were something that he had to plough through, like snow, or a crowd of adoring fans. The latter would usually bring him a level of joy, but, on this day, Marc was filled with quiet dread. He did not want an adoring fanbase. At this point in his life, they seemed superfluous.

They all knew how he rose to stardom, they knew his contract was at an end, they would mourn his death, and then find a new thespian to adore until they also met the hour of their passing. It was a phenomenon Marc had not thought much about before signing his contract. But now, everything seemed clearer: celebrities went the Fortune route. Of course, they had to have talent. People still had artistic tastes. Fame had always been a fleeting commodity to possess, but in the age of Fortune Limited, it was fleeting in both the literal and figurative sense.

Marc pressed onwards against the breeze that threatened to freeze him. He was almost at his destination. He didn't quite know why he was heading here on foot, and not going to his own home. He didn't really want to think about the motivations for his actions, either. He just knew that his body, mind, and soul wanted to get *here*.

When his co-star had picked him up from the stage floor, he had had the urge to move. He did not quite know where he wanted to go, but he had wanted to move, and so move he had done. He had left the co-star's arms, said little to the director (who was a mix of confused, angry and concerned) and had headed to the auditorium's exit. He'd moved past the staff at the concession stands and out the door. He imagined he looked a bit like a zombie; in actuality, he had looked quite normal. He had looked like someone who had made up his mind. Which hadn't been true. After all, what had there been to make up his mind about? He had no choice in his future, nevertheless he had had an air of determination that a zombie could never possess.

And here he was, an e-hailing service and lengthy walk later, nearing his big brother's house. He knew where it was geographically, but he had not been the driver of a trip here in ages, so he'd given the cab the wrong address. Rather than filling in a new address, he had opted to walk the rest of the way. Perhaps to give him time to think? He really didn't know why he had done that. He had no direction; perhaps that's what was scaring him. Perhaps that's what was willing him to his older brother. He did not know; he just knew he wanted his brother.

The icy wind swept his loose, black rehearsal shirt upwards. The wind seeped through the breathable material and sent shivers all across his body. He had not taken his jacket; it was still at the theatre. He neared the front door and knocked loudly, but briefly. His hands felt like they might fall off. He waited for what seemed like an age, but eventually, the entrance flew open, and a warm light illuminated his sister, Jan.

"Marc?!" she exclaimed in surprise while ushering him into the house. The air immediately warmed his skin, and Marc felt a little at peace, but only briefly.

"Marc, what's going on? Why are you here?" questioned Jan. She was clearly concerned, she had definitely not expected visitors, let alone himself. She moved them both through the hallway and into the living room. Marc sank down into a couch, and Jan muttered something about hot chocolate and a blanket before leaving the room.

Marc surveyed the room, automatically, the way he did in a new rehearsal space or production location. He knew the exits and entrances, he had been here before, but he had always been here with his brother. And usually, they'd have a disagreement about Fortune, or become so involved in the game or movie they were playing that he hadn't taken in the room.

It was modestly furnished with comfortable chairs and couches made of a soft material. The colour scheme was grey, but a warm grey, something that made him think about being covered in a blanket on a cold, wintery day, eating soup next to the fireplace. The fireplace was simple and of the old style, cut into the wall and lined with paint-covered brick.

There were only a handful of pictures on the wall, mostly paintings of the sea or a landscape. There was a side table next to the armrest of the couch he was seated on, which held a photo of him, Jan, and Lance. Marc smiled and picked up the frame. Again, Lance had not opted for digital, unlike what Marc had in his home. The quaint fact of a still image was comforting to Marc. He felt grounded somehow, looking at that image, he felt like his character almost *had* a purpose.

Jan entered the room again with a warm blanket and a mug of hot chocolate. She offered both to Marc.

"So," said Jan after she handed him the mug and Marc had settled somewhat, "what's this about then?"

Marc couldn't answer. It wasn't that he didn't want to answer, it was more that he didn't even know the reason he was there. He had just left the theatre on instinct; it was only by luck that he had had his device with him to call a cab and get to the third street down.

"I don't know," replied Marc. rather lucidly. He surprised himself with that remark. He wasn't in a daze or anything. He was in his full senses. But there was something nagging at the back of his mind.

"Lance wasn't very happy with me last time I was here," continued Marc.

"No, he wasn't," said Jan. She was not one to rattle on unnecessarily. She said what she meant and *usually* meant what she said.

"I…" began Marc, perhaps he was closing in on his reason for being here, "I can't have him…" Marc lost his words. He had a feeling in his stomach. He had an instinct of what he needed to say, but he was finding it difficult to put it into words.

"I don't understand, Marc."

A tear started to well in Marc's eye. His mind had connected the dots, somewhat.

"I can't have him hate me."

Jan's expression changed from one of confusion to one of compassion. She reached over from her spot next to him and pulled him into a hug. Marc began to sob.

"He doesn't hate you, Marc, he loves you. You know that," reassured his sister in his ears. Her arms tightened as he convulsed, and she kept him firmly in her grasp, "He could never hate you. He hates Fortune. Fuck it, *I* hate Fortune."

"Every… time we are… together he gets… so…" sobbed Marc in Jan's arms.

"He gets so emotional, Marc. Because he loves you. He doesn't want…" it was Jan's turn to hesitate. Marc could see the tears starting to form in her eyes as well. She put on a brave face, but she was still his little sister.

"I don't want to either!" exclaimed Marc. It was the first time he had said this out loud, and the second time he had thought it. Ever. He was lost. He could do nothing, but wait to die. He had no power. Nothing he said or did would ever change the fact that, in a few weeks, he would be legally terminated. He would become a statistic.

Jan and Marc sobbed together on the couch for a while after that.

***

It was later in the evening, Marc was not sure what time, but he didn't really care. He didn't really know much anymore. He didn't know what he wanted, whether he had made the right choice or not. His fate was sealed. He had not fully realised until the eleventh hour that he was a condemned man, from the first day he had signed those papers. He had been so wrapped up in the glitz and glamour of his new life. He had been so focused on being a success. He had been so reassured that what he was doing was a benefit to his family that he had not stopped and taken stock of his life. He had lived life in the fast lane for over nine years, a continuous run with very few moments to rest.

Now, his contract was ending, and he had more time to think. He had more time to dwell on his life; his decisions. There were no new roles to sink his teeth into; to keep his mind occupied. There was only the role of victim.

Marc was wandering through the home he had never quite taken in. The house was fully furnished with some really top of the line pieces and artwork, yet the rooms still retained a very homely feel. As he walked down the passageway, which had a few modestly sized family portraits, Marc felt like he lived here, and that this was his passage. He stuck out a hand and caressed the wall; he could imagine a child or two running down the passage into the kitchen on a 'Flapjack Saturday' morning. He could imagine that he was still asleep in the master bedroom, and his wife had woken up early for the kids.

The flicker of warmth that Marc felt in his dream state was suddenly snuffed out as he came to Lance's study door. It was ajar, and Marc spied an old pinup board filled with strings and printouts. In the middle, he could just make out the word 'Fortune'. His dream future washed away like the audience at the end of an uncomfortably long play. He'd never be married, would never have kids.

He fought back the darkness that was creeping back around his vision. He would rather focus on something else, like the pinup board.

Marc pushed the door open wider, and like a naughty teenager, he gave a furtive glance in both directions sliding into the study. Marc felt like he was transported into a film noir depiction of a private investigator's office. The furniture was a mix of brown and black, there were thick curtains drawn, and a large oak desk situated roughly in the centre of the room. His inspection of the room's decor ended abruptly when he looked over at the pinup. It looked much bigger now that he was in the room. Red string filled the board. Images, names, newspaper articles, and post-its packed the board to its limit. Marc had to take a step back.

The darkness crept back again; Marc could see his vision tunnelling.

He looked away and shook his head. It took a beat or two, but eventually Marc returned his gaze to the board. Lance had never given up, Lance had never not known the severity of what Marc had signed. Marc had known but he hadn't *known*. Lance had; Lance had been on the case from day one. Some of the papers stuck on the board were yellow, faded from the length of time they had been pinned there. Lance had been working. It appeared that he had investigated every angle.

Marc took a deep breath. Was this Lance's idea of free time? Is this why he hadn't found someone? Had he also missed out on love because he was too busy trying to save his little brother? A wave of guilt washed over him; it blinded him like stage lights. He looked away again.

Lance has been stuck trying to save me.

Tears again started to form. He at least had lived a life up until now, his brother, on the other hand, had not. By the looks of it, Lance had spent all his time focusing on one thing at the expense of his own happiness. Marc would die, and while he didn't want to go, he knew that when he was gone he would not be feeling anything because he'd be dead. But Lance, he would beat himself up for years to come, perhaps until *he* died. He would refuse to live. Marc had lived a life, a short one, but a life with friends and success; Lance had not, and would not.

Through the blurry vision of his tears, Marc spotted a single post-it with a number written on it. Only one number, nothing else. Marc wiped his tears, sniffed and closed in on the post-it. Something about the number seemed familiar. He ripped the note from its spot; a few sprinkles of dust floated to the floor. Marc stared at the number, willing his brain to remember it. Where had he seen it? He was so focused on the post-it that he didn't hear someone enter the room.

"Marc?"

Chapter 21

Lance

Lance arrived home later than he had expected. He and Grace had sat at the coffee shop for what seemed like an age longer, after their new acquaintance had left. He was glad that Grace shared his level of uncertainty about Wolf, but in the end, they had decided that it was all really academic either way. He was a much better hacker than any of them, and if he wanted to, he could easily turn them in and cook up some proof of their recent exploit.

So, Lance had caught himself contemplating, *work with Wolf or risk jail?*

After a long discussion, they decided on the former.

Lance kind of liked Wolf. He had an interesting personality, and they could both relate to being in service. There was something about him, he felt he knew where

Wolf was coming from. That is, if his story was real. Again, that was all academic. Whether he believed Wolf or not was irrelevant, their best option was to work with him, and hopefully his skills would prove useful.

Lance reached the front door, fumbled for his keys and let himself inside. It was mostly quiet, save the snoring coming from Jan's room. Lance chuckled to himself. Despite the drama of today, they were successful. He was happy. He decided he would have a glass of wine and headed straight for the fridge. Inside, he noticed a half-empty bottle of Sauvignon. He thought that was odd, but not too odd. He supposed Jan had simply helped herself to his stock. Something she did regularly.

He swiped the bottle and moved over to pick up a glass when he noticed two empty ones in the sink. Lance's mind thought through the logic. Perhaps Jan had had a friend over.

As Lance poured himself a glass, he let his mind wander a bit. Grace and he had taken a look at the blueprints briefly. They were seemingly endless, and as a result, daunting, but to navigate them seemed simple enough. They had decided to start work on their master plan in the morning. With Wolf. It was going to be a long day, but he was determined to come out the other side of it with a fully-realised plan. There was no time to sit around. Marc didn't have that luxury. In a strange way, the magnitude of what they were going to attempt dawned on him. It wasn't just Marc they would be helping, it could potentially take down Fortune Limited. Lance scoffed to himself. On second thought, that was unlikely, but he might be able to leverage something for Marc.

"Crap!" said Lance as his glass overflowed and cascaded onto the counter. Lance flapped his hands in an attempt to make them dry and moved over to the sink.

What was that?

Lance noticed a movement in the reflection of the kitchen window. It was so subtle, but it was definitely a movement. Jan's snoring still resonated through the house. If it wasn't Jan, then who was in his home?

Lance's military instinct went into overdrive. All he could think about was Grace's story. He swivelled around silently and expertly, plucking a large pan off the drip tray and bending over slightly. He moved cautiously towards the area of concern: his study. Typical of Fortune's thugs, they must know he had all manner of leads and ideas plotted out on his board. The easiest way to discombobulate him would be to destroy his entire visual thought process.

Lance glided against the walls of the kitchen into the passageway. There was little sound, perhaps a sniff. Jan's call to the high heavens was drowning out any silence he had to work with. His eyes glanced towards her room, and saw that the door was closed. And there was no light seeping out the bottom of the door. Thankfully, the intruder had not entered her space.

Lance stood against the wall next to the slightly ajar doorway, he swapped the pan between hands so that his right hand could palm the door while his left could strike any assailant, should they suddenly stick a limb over the threshold. Lance took a breath and slowly pushed the door open.

Lance let out a sigh, both of relief and confusion. He had swung the door open on his brother, Marc. Marc had never been in his study. He looked odd in the room, as if he didn't fit. Lance's demeanour softened considerably, and he straightened himself up. Still holding the pan, he stepped into the room. Marc's back was turned, and he seemed engrossed in something on the far right side of Lance's board.

"Marc?"

Marc started with a gasp. He spun around, bewildered, and when he met Lance's eyes, he looked so much like the nine year-old Lance used to tease so much. A boy who had been caught doing something naughty. It was almost comical.

"What are you doing here?" asked Lance, meaning his home, though Marc's response told him he thought Lance meant his study.

"Um uh, I was just wandering, couldn't sleep-"

"No, I mean he-" Lance stopped, he noticed what was in Marc's hand. His heart skipped a beat. He beelined straight for Marc, snatched the post-it from his hand and chose his words as carefully as possible, "I meant, here, in my home."

Lance stuffed the post-it in his pants pocket and attempted to pretend he had not. He just started taking random, unimportant notes off of the board, trying to look like he was cleaning up obsolete information. It appeared that Marc was too stunned to really notice.

The last time he had seen his brother, Lance had been rude and flippant, and Marc had been confident and steadfast. Now, as Lance took a look at him, he could see his brother was different. He was less. He was not wearing his tailored and pressed suit, he clearly had not arrived in his chauffered car, and his face... it was so... scared. Lance threw the last bit of 'cleaning' in the bin and gave his brother a hug. He didn't know what had happened; he didn't care. His brother was in distress, and all he knew to do was to hug him. They stood there for a while in their silent embrace until Marc cleared his throat and pulled back a bit.

"Is it alright if I stay for a bit?" he asked, as if he thought the answer would be a 'no'. Lance would never say 'no', "I just don't really want to be alone right now. I can take the couch-"

"Of course you can stay," said Lance, "I'll take the couch, I have a busy day tomorrow, anyway."

Lance wanted to tell his brother that he would be busy plotting the takedown of Fortune Limited. He wanted to let his brother go to sleep with a sprinkle of hope that, at least in death, he would not suffer. He knew that the odds of Marc's execution being halted were stacked against him. But, at the very least, he could ensure the beginning of the end of Fortune. And ensure that his brother would not suffer any post mortem indignities. He wanted to tell Marc this, but decided against it. All he had was a blueprint, not even a plan. His brother was here, clearly upset about something. He would bet a lot of money it had to do with what was on his investigation board. Bringing up Fortune now would just upset him even more. Besides, he would be there tomorrow. He'd find out sooner or later.

"Come," said Lance, "let's get you to bed."

Chapter 22
Grace

The sun crept over Grace's duvet, warming the foot of the bed. A welcome feeling in the lower temperatures. Grace roused and rubbed her eyes; she hadn't been sleeping with a curtain drawn. Why? Because Fortune's goons had decided they didn't like the colour, and removed them for her when they'd done their rearranging the last time they'd stopped by to visit. Grace being Grace, did not have the time nor money to bother replacing them; she already had to replace most things in her home, some blinds were the last on her list. Besides, they acted as a perfect, tech-free alarm clock.

She rolled out of bed, flopped to the floor, let out a groan, and spread her weight onto all fours before hoisting herself up. Thank goodness she had stumbled into *her* room the night before. She had perhaps had a bit too much to drink the night before. She had rationalised it as both drinks of celebration, but also the possibility of everything going south.

That oaf has us by the balls, thought Grace as she stumbled to the tiny little ensuite, *we'll see if he comes or not.*

As she brushed her teeth, she imagined the police and Fortune Limited storming her apartment building without warning, then locking her up for illegal hacking or whatever the technical name was for what she and Lance had done. Technically, only she had executed it. That was the annoying thing, she had been so stupid. If this thing with this new guy, Wolf, went south, then Lance could very easily pin everything on her. They were her devices, she had done the actual hacking, she had pretended to be Fortune security staff over their private channels. She had the blueprints. Lance could easily cut his losses and try another approach, and what would she do then?

Seems I have to rely on the word of a man.

She liked Lance, but time and again she came back to the fact that they hardly knew each other, and truly had very little in common. He seemed decent and genuine, but what about with a gun to his head? It was an eerie feeling Grace couldn't shake.

She shoved some clothes on. The weather looked as if it was going to be warm, so she removed her hoodie. She was fumbling around, looking for essentials for the day, when a faint voice called her name.

"Morning, Thabo!" called Grace as she slid her device into her pants pocket. She did a final pat down, looking around her room. It seemed almost alien to her in this light. She had not slept here in a long while. Usually, she stayed with her brother, but last night she'd come home rather late, and decided in her drunken state that it was best not to disturb him. Of course, that only delayed the disturbance. Thabo had just awoken to find his usual sentry not on duty.

"You want some coffee? I have the fake stuff!" asked Grace as she exited her room and went towards the kitchen. She waved the kettle on and tapped the glass of the fridge to see what food they had for breakfast. Ah yes, nothing. Unless she counted four-day-old pie. She moaned audibly and sighed.

"Yes, please!" came Thabo's reply.

Grace pulled out a mug and smiled. She knew his answer would be yes; it always was. She waited for the water to boil and reflected on her situation a little more. Mostly on her brother's. She struggled to imagine what it must be like for him to know his whole body was fighting against him: to know it would never be lethal, but it would feel that way. Thabo could barely do anything himself anymore; the pain was too much. He could lift a small cup of coffee to drink, type for an hour or so at a time on his device if he was angled the right way (usually, Grace helped him with that), otherwise, his days were largely uneventful.

A tear began to form in Grace's eye, but she fought the emotion back. This was not the time, she had to remain strong for him. And besides, if all went to plan (a plan she didn't really know yet), she'd be bringing some comforting news to her brother soon. Well, it would certainly free *her* mind so she could focus more on him.

Grace poured water into the fake coffee granules, stirred in some milk, and took it to Thabo's room. There he was, in his perpetual half-lying half-sitting position. Grace placed the mug on his makeshift side table near his left hand. The table was really just a thick, sturdy board on the bed. It just meant Thabo didn't have to lean across himself to put down things he held in his hands.

"Anything need changing?" said Grace in her nurse's tone.

"All clear," was Thabo's curt reply.

"Small miracles," said Grace with a chuckle, "where's your device? Ah here, did you fall asleep reading again?" Grace bent down and collected the device from the floor.

"Yes, where were you last night?"

Grace was expecting that kind of a question. She had not thought about what kind of answer she should give. She could be flippant, and say it was none of his business, but that would be rude. She could be completely honest and tell him she had just been with a co-conspirator to plot their takedown of Fortune Limited and expose it for the human right's violations she and said accomplice both believed it to perpetrate... but that would be a little too much information, and still a little bit flippant. So she decided to lie.

"I... met a guy."

"Really?"

"Yes, don't act so surprised, I'm a catch, you know," said Grace with a convincingly casual chuckle. She laid the device on Thabo's table next to his coffee.

"I am surprised," said Thabo, "I didn't know you had a social life outside of work, and well, me. It's nice though, you go do the things."

"I was not *doing any things*, thank you very much, I am a lady," said Grace, happy for two things. Firstly, that the conversation had easily become about her social life (regardless of the legitimacy of it) and, secondly, that Thabo noticed her hard work and wanted her to live a life too. The latter touched her soul a little, because it meant that her brother loved her just as much as she did him. But it also stung a little, because it meant he thought of himself as an unnecessary burden. Grace had never seen it that way.

"I came home a bit late. And I didn't want to wake you. That's all."

"Thanks sis," said Thabo, "but really, wake me up next time, you know I like to hear what's happening out there in social land."

Grace smiled, and without missing a beat, said, "Sure thing."

***

The morning was only just upon her, but the rest of the city, much like Grace felt, had not slept. As soon as Grace stepped out of her building, she was met with a throng of people, all with places to be and people to meet. Grace felt like one of them, albeit briefly. She had a purpose, she had a reason for being, she had a destination, and she sure as hell was going to show up for all of it. She knew at least one of her compatriots would be there, and the other was practically unimportant. She had reasoned on her elevator ride that, since she was not in custody, she was safe. Wolf would have reported them by now, and since he had not, it meant he wasn't a threat. At most, he was a willing accomplice, which would help her and Lance in the long run. By no means did she trust the man (hell no), but the fact that she was still a free bird spoke volumes.

She made her way down the street. A taxi was too traceable; she had to use public transport. She reached the underground's entrance and descended the steps. The stone finishes were annoyingly reminiscent of the London

Underground, and always gave Grace the feeling that colonisation was not quite so much a thing of the past.

She shunned the disgust away from her thoughts, and put them on more pressing matters. What exactly was their plan going to look like? Was she to be an agent on the ground this time? She quite liked the job of being the overlord safely in a coffee shop across the road. Her escape plans were so much easier when they worked out like that. She sighed, this time to herself. She had to give Lance a little more credit. Nothing he had done had actually given her any reason for pause. Even so, she could not help how she felt.

She hopped on the first train heading her direction. The carriage was packed to the brim, and Grace felt almost like her presence was the one that would cause the packed can to burst. Fortunately, this was a common occurrence and the feeling remained simply that: a feeling. In reality, the trains were designed to support an over-capacity, despite the warning signs. After all, how would the corporations make money if their products didn't do at least what was required? For many corporations in the world, overpopulation was just a way of life, and to imagine a world without it was a world fit for fairytales.

A man coughed next to her, and a pregnant woman groaned in pain. Either she was in labour or the little shit was kicking. Grace hoped it was the latter, she had a good half hour left of her trip.

***

Grace finally arrived at her station, which was modestly packed for the time of day. Shift changes had already happened, and it was likely that the souls boarding and exiting the trains were those who had the luxury of social engagements. Unlike her. Grace was boarding and unboarding the trains with a very specific, non-sociable reason. She was heading to a meeting that would ideally be the beginning of the end of Fortune Limited. She chuckled to herself when she thought of that notion. Even she was not so blinded by the ways of the world that she would think she would ever succeed. The thing is, she just wanted to try. The little ray of hope like sunlight in a harsh winter was all she needed. She would give it her all, but in the end, she had backup plans. She wouldn't stop going after Fortune, but she would change tactics if needed. That was a promise she had made to herself, and to Thabo.

She exited the underground to a strangely pretty suburb. There were buildings (obviously), but there was also a decent amount of well-kept foliage. Grace had to take a second to remember that, even in a world with too many people to bear, there was still such a thing as class. And, in that, there were the 'haves' and the 'have nots'. Grace steadied her mind; perhaps this was what her instincts were hinting at: Lance was a 'have', and she was effectively a 'have not', though she chose not to think of herself in that light. Lance may have had his quarrels with Fortune Limited, but through his brother and his own lot in life, he had managed to land very well on his feet.

Yes, Grace had to admit that it wasn't until her father was gone that her life had started its decline, but it was also true that unlike Lance, Grace was not quite financially independent at the time of the execution. Sure, she had some of her trust fund, and so did Thabo, but she had only been able to save so much over ten years, and Thabo's sudden condition had used up a lot of their money. Therefore, Grace had not had her own life step up like

Lance apparently had. They were not the same.

Not incompatible, reasoned Grace to herself, *but not the same.*

Grace shook off the feeling for the moment, and turned to the right, in the direction of her and Lance's meeting place.

Chapter 23
Lance

The electronic drone of the front door bell told Lance that he had a visitor. He was already up and about, unlike his two siblings. They were both fast asleep in their beds, Lance had made use of the lounge. And so, in his need to remain orderly and tidy, had woken at the crack of dawn to ensure the living room was, in fact, no longer a bedroom.

Currently, he was making breakfast for a town. He had to rest his spatula on a bubbling pan of lab-grown bacon. Lance grabbed a dishcloth on his way to the door, drying his hands as he went. He swung the front door open and there was Grace. He greeted her with a friendly smile, while she greeted him with a gawking expression.

"Nice digs, man," were Grace's first words as she crossed the threshold into the hallway.

"Uh, thanks," he did not quite know how to respond to this, clearly she was not used to being in a modestly sized standalone home. To be fair, very few people were. Lance remembered she had had a large home while growing up with her father during his Fortune Years, but he also remembered what they did to her financially. All this made Lance think about the short conversation he had had with Marc the night before, about his will and the fact that he had to do one through Fortune. Perhaps that had been a recent development, them insisting on it. It made sense, less legal battles from those who could afford it, disputing the seizure of property and assets from Expireds without a will. Fortune was greedy, but if Lance and Grace knew anything, they knew that Fortune tried (on the surface, at least) to cover their tracks. They had only *just* called Marc and thrown a curveball calling him to finalise his will through their methods, giving him hardly enough time to truly think about it.

Grace made her way towards the direction of the kitchen, dropping her bag in the hall against the wall as if she lived there. Lance did not mind much, but also thought it very familiar.

"Do I smell bacon?"

"Uh, yes," said Lance, realising he still had food cooking. It smelled like it was burning, actually, "speaking of," he whipped past Grace and into the kitchen to continue his breakfast prep.

"In all seriousness, you do have a beautiful home," said Grace. She appeared to be trying to sound friendly. Which was nice, "Got any juice, coffee, soda, water?"

Lance nodded at the coffee pot he had just brewed, steaming across the kitchen. Next to the pot were five simple, yet sophisticated looking coffee mugs.

"Great!" said Grace, and she went to work pouring herself one. Lance noted her pause as she thought about pouring one for him. She seemed to decide, and poured an almost-full cup, "Sugar, milk?"

"Milk, please, thanks."

Grace did so, and soon was by Lance's side, placing his mug on the marble counter beside the stove, and leaning next to it, sipping her own mug.

"My, uh, siblings are both here," said Lance. He felt like this should be announced, given their reason for meeting, "They're still in bed, I'll introduce you all later."

"Is Wolf coming?" asked Grace, almost as if she did not care for his siblings. Didn't care or didn't think it was something Lance needed to announce? Lance couldn't tell.

"I messaged him, no reply."

Grace sipped her coffee again, her eyes narrowed and she let out a barely audible, "Hmm."

Lance could guess the reason for her hesitation. Wolf was an unknown, he had not stopped calling her Locks, and she had not been the most friendly person to him the night before. That, and of course the fact that he had the power to rat them out made it clear to Lance that Grace did not like him.

"I've been doing some thinking, Lancey," began Grace, "I don't trust that douchebag, but we have little choice. So, I suggest we use him and lose him. Deal?"

Lance was glad she was not going to put up a fight. The last thing he needed was to pick sides between the two of them. All three of them needed something from Fortune, therefore they all needed each other. Lance was not about to not go ahead with their plan, so had Grace had a huge problem with Wolf, he would either have to continue alone, or go with Wolf.

"Deal."

"Great," said Grace, who then looked at the fake bacon and eggs, ready and waiting to be fried, "You making for all of us?"

"Yeah, how do you like your eggs?"

"Soft," said Grace, who then chuckled. Lance knew it was a chuckle at his expense.

"What?"

"Nothing, it's just there's a man wanting to blackmail you to help him do something illegal... and you're making him breakfast."

"I like being hospitable. Besides, would it not be better to win him over?"

"I'm just saying you didn't make me breakfast the second time you met me, and I'm not threatening you with life in prison, or worse."

Grace chuckled again, her smile revealing bright teeth. She shoved Lance on the shoulder. She was joking, it was all in jest. Small talk.

***

The bacon and eggs were prepared, the coffee was reheated, and fresh mugs were poured between Lance and Grace. Grace helped Lance set the dining table. The domesticity of what they were doing was not lost on Lance, but he had his brother and sister here, together, for the first time in a while. He wanted them to feel at home. Grace was here, and Wolf would be too, but that was superfluous.

Jan was the first to exit her room. Luckily, she was fully clothed and showered. Her face lit up when she saw Grace. Ever the socialite, Jan ran over to her and introduced herself right away. Grace seemed a bit taken aback by her eagerness, but Lance was happy to see a smile spread across her face as they started chatting about some viral internet sensation they both knew. Sometimes, Lance forgot, not everyone with a cause was like him: super fixated to the point that it affects your social life. He knew no internet sensations, none of the current memes, his form of entertainment was drowning his sorrows at Gretchen's every so often, and of course, digging into Fortune Limited. His demeanour had changed slightly since meeting Grace, but not drastically. He was, in fact, still the socially reserved older brother who hardly ever had visitors.

Jan moved over to Lance, eyeing the spread on the table, "To what do we owe the pleasure?" Lance was about to respond when she cut him off, "and how exactly do you two know each other?"

Grace shot a look at Lance. He had not thought about this. He did not want to keep a secret, but suddenly spewing their whole meeting and subsequent exploits seemed a bit... strange. Not to mention, Wolf had to be factored in. He wanted to tell her, he had to, they were going to plan the whole thing in his office, in the very house they were all in at that moment... it was foolish to think they could keep it a secret, but at the same time, he didn't want to burden Jan, or Marc.

"We, uh-"

"Hello?" came Marc's voice from down the hall.

"Oh Marc, you stayed over?" said Jan, turning to his direction.

Marc entered the dining room, he was dressed in Lance's bathrobe, clearly he had just showered. Grace did a double-take.

"Hang on, Lancey," said Grace, "this is perhaps just a

little bit of information you neglected to tell me."

Lance was perplexed. He indicated for everyone to sit down and begin breakfast. Marc slowly edged to a seat, probably feeling a bit under dressed. His eyes were fixed on Grace, though. Lance noticed they weren't harshly fixed, rather inquisitive. She returned the expression.

"What do you mean?"

"You said Marc was your brother, but you never said it was *Marc Mason*," said Grace, and Lance heard a slight layer of fan-girl in her voice, "My brother and I love your work!"

Now Marc blushed slightly, giving a little smile and nodding, "Uh, thanks."

Grace flopped down into her chair, she flicked her locks out of her way, picked up a fork and said, "Well, now we have to do this."

Lance cringed internally, *Not now Grace, can't we have a nice breakfast first?* But she continued.

"Jan, it was Jan, right? Yes, to answer your question, Lancey and I are actually friends with mutual benefits." Lance cringed again, she phrased it like that on purpose. Now, Jan would be the first to-

"Oh, I didn't know Lance was-"

"She means we have mutual interests," saved Lance. He wanted to stop that thought process before it took root. Then he took a deep sigh, "Grace and I met, via a chase down, because we are both... well, we're both looking at taking down Fortune. At least, in some capacity."

The room went silent after that. Marc looked down, continued to chew his bacon. Jan's face told Lance that she didn't quite know how to feel. Lance hated cliches, but to him the tension felt like he could cut it with a knife. He had no idea how to progress from there.

"Look, you know very well that I have been doing this for a while. Hell, you saw my board," started Lance, he was mostly speaking to Marc, "You know me, I don't give up. Even when-"

"Even when I do."

This was not an accusation. Marc was not chiding Lance into an argument. It was worse. It sounded like complete and utter defeat. Lance's stomach turned. It's funny how the energy from those closest to him could affect his resolve and belief in his own thoughts. Should he just give up? Was anything good going to come of it? The post-it note flashed across his mind's eye, briefly.

Grace broke the silence again, "You may have given up, and we get why, Marc, but that doesn't mean that we have. Shit, my father's long gone, and I haven't given up. In any case, for me it's become more than just revenge. It's the principle of the whole thing. That's what I am fighting for, and I think that's what Lance is also fighting for," she paused, then added, "As well as you."

"I've not given up on you, Marc, I promise," began Lance, "And Grace is right. I'm doing everything I can, because I made you a promise. But if I can't... if I can't save you, then at least I might help others."

"There's more to it than the executions, Marc, we need to make Fortune pay."

"More?" replied Jan, Marc also had a puzzled look in his eyes.

Lance went into damage control. This was tough enough for his brother to hear, given his very recent return to his senses, and the inevitable end he was about to face. He had just had to consider what he had given up all those years ago, and Lance didn't think adding the notion of past Expireds' cadavers being experimented on would be of any use to him at all. If nothing else, it would not do well for his dwindling mental health. Lance grabbed Marc's hand.

"All that you need to know is that I am still here for you. I'm not going to stop, no matter what."

Marc looked at his brother. Lance saw a glimmer of acceptance in his eyes, as if Marc finally understood what he meant to Lance. All the fights of the past seemed so petty, yet, in his eyes now, Lance could see Marc reliving them, and seeing them for what they really were: a brother hellbent on helping the other. Time was almost up for Marc, but Lance was still not going to stop, because that's what family did.

"Thank you," said Marc meekly. He then returned to his food.

Lance let out a sigh and tucked into his own, now cold plate. He and Marc had finally made peace. In the grand scheme of things, it meant very little but for Lance, it meant everything. In a way, he finally had his brother back. Even if only for a little while.

Chapter 24
Wolf

The bright, white door reflected harshly in Wolf's face as he stood on the doorsteps of Lance's home. He raised his hand and knocked three times in sharp succession.

As he stood awaiting Lance and Locks, he took stock of his situation. He had something they needed, and they had something he needed. They needed someone who actually knew their way around the web, and he needed people to do the legwork for him. He made a great field agent, but he preferred being behind the scenes, it gave him more freedom to think and to work out the solutions they needed.

Wolf sighed as they took longer to answer the door than he thought was necessary. For a split second, he wondered if Lance had texted him the incorrect address.

I did a background search, though, he'd barely completed the thought before the door swung open.

Lance's face replaced the blinding light. He gave a strange smile before realising who was in front of him, and then his face changed to a different expression, one that said: let's get to business.

"Uh, hi," he stammered, "you came, uh, come in."

You're damn right I came, Blondie, thought Wolf as he entered Lance's home. Wolf was not sure what to expect, but for some reason, this sight was it. Clean, modest, with references to the days before technology took over everyone's life.

"I smell food," said Wolf as he sniffed the air. He had not yet received his first allowance from Fortune; the'd said it would be two to three working days. In the meantime, Wolf had had to make do with perishables in the recesses of his kitchen cupboards. He was hungry.

"Uh yes, we've just finished up, but I did make some for you. Left it all on a plate just through here."

Wolf followed his host, wondering why he was being so generous. They entered a kitchen, and Locks was there leaning against the counter with a mug of coffee in her hands. She gave him the stink eye as he picked up his plate, and found a seat by the breakfast bar.

"So, you didn't rat us out, I see?" said Locks in a not-too-welcoming tone.

"Not yet," replied Wolf curtly.

Locks scoffed and took a sip of coffee.

"Can we just agree to work together? No ratting out anyone, please," Lance was packing the dishwasher, an attempt to seem nonchalant in the face of a strange situation, "we all have something to gain and lose here, don't we? So, best to just work together; we all get what we want, and then we can part ways."

Spoken like a true lawyer. Cutting to the chase, trying to make all parties agree to a proposition. He was right about one thing, though: they all wanted something. Whether or not they all had something equal to lose was another thing entirely.

Whether he needed them or not, Wolf was not going to put their interests above his own.

"Yeah, sure. No ratting out," Wolf said, choosing to acquiesce.

"Great, then, when you're done, we can move to the study. We have work to do; some of us were on time," Grace placed the mug on the counter and shoved off in the direction of the doorway. Towards the hall, and, presumably, the study.

"Make yourself comfortable," said Lance as he continued tidying up, "don't mind her, I haven't known her for too long, but she's good people. She's just a bit on edge, I mean, what we're doing isn't exactly the safest thing in the world."

"Sure," said Wolf as he glugged down his orange juice. He collected his cutlery and crockery in military fashion and brought it to the dishwasher. Lance made to take it from him, but Wolf gently dodged his hands, pausing slightly so that Lance could get the picture, and then packed the dishwasher with his dirty dishes. Lance had taken a while, but he must have understood. In the military, they were taught a certain level of discipline and respect for their hosts. A good soldier treated his equals with that said respect. Wolf was not about to let Lance deal with his dirty plate when *he* had been late and *he* had dirtied it. Also, he did not want to feel like he owed anyone anything. His dishes were dirty; he packed them away. It was bad enough he had just eaten the meal unnecessarily prepared for him, so he already owed this man something.

Lance told Wolf to follow him and Wolf did so. They left the kitchen, briefly walked through the passage, then entered a study. Its main feature was a board full of notes. Clearly, Lance had been at this a while. Wolf felt a strange feeling in his gut. Lance wasn't just a chancer, it seemed. He knew Lance had some noble fight for his brother in mind, but when he was told about it, he admired his spirit in the same way he would admire someone talking about their grandfather's bravery or misfortune in the Second Cold War. But seeing the board up made it all seem… real… now. Lance was not just talking the talk, clearly he had been walking the walk for some years. For a moment, Wolf wondered what he had stumbled upon.

"Just admiring your board, Lancey," said Locks, "I had an idea to do something similar for my dad, but it just seemed like too much effort."

"Yeah, I'm a visual learner. Anyway, shall we get started?" Lance really meant business.

"Well first of all, guys, what are we doing once we have the intel? Whatever the intel is?" Locks posed a good question.

Lance looked at Wolf for insight, but Wolf was not yet ready to make a comment. He wanted to see what they came up with; he saw himself more as a consultant.

"Well, perhaps we should take it to the police? Right?" was Lance's response.

"Oh sure, Lancey, let's just hand the intel back to Fortune on a silver platter and offer ourselves up in the process."

"You know what I mean, Grace," countered Lance, "Of course we don't give it in ourselves but surely we could… I don't know… hack into their databases and then do an anonymous tip off?"

"Really, Lance?" said Grace, she looked as though she couldn't believe his stupidity.

A bit harsh, thought Wolf, *but not altogether unwarranted.*

"She's right," said Wolf and the two looked to him, "she's right, the police are undoubtedly in league with Fortune somehow. Giving it to them is as good as giving it back to that psychopath Marlowe, himself."

"So, then?"

"Press?" said Grace, "I know there are stations sympathetic to the mission, but there are a lot of stations who don't quite agree with Fortune and its methods."

"Who's to say they don't just quash the story for fear of what Fortune might do to them? At least the police are a government force, they won't need to worry about-"

"Press is equally shit, Locks," said Wolf, cutting Lance off, "What we need to do is hack a broadcasting router somewhere and broadcast it to all the devices we can at once."

Lance and Locks let the idea sink in. Wolf could see the cogs turning in their heads.

"Is that possible?" asked Locks after a short while.

"I'll make it possible," replied Wolf with a finality that took the other two by surprise.

"Uh, right then, I suppose then we move on to the plan?" said Lance.

"Bring up the blueprints," said Wolf.

***

The discussions took ages. There were times Wolf thought he might die of sheer boredom. He felt like he was hearing the same thing again and again. Locks and Lance were going around in circles. He was starting to regret his decision to team up with them in the first place.

The plan's beginning was simple enough. They would approach it almost like they did the satellite office, only better, because now Wolf was there to shed some logical light. Their plan was to have Locks stationed in the foyer cafe. It would be packed, so she would blend in, and be able to be the 'in-person' eyes on the ground. Lance would be the footman on the ground, Locks claimed he was great at thinking on his feet, and Wolf noted that Lance did not disagree with her, in fact, when she'd said that, he'd puffed his chest a little. It was then decided that Wolf would be in a vehicle, parked in a getaway spot closeby. He would do all the necessary hacking in the back, covered by… something the team had not thought about yet. Because they were too busy arguing about how Locks would be relaying information to them both without looking suspicious.

Wolf sighed, stood up from his oak chair, and paced the room. The other two barely noticed his movement. Wolf went to the board and examined it in more detail. While the others squabbled over everything but a very obvious solution, Wolf was trying to get into the mind of Lance who (despite his present bickering), he was growing more intrigued by as the day went on. When they had met the day before, Lance had made a positive impression on the hacker and ex-officer. Now, in his home, the hacker and ex-officer had a chance to investigate why.

The board was plastered with red string and paper. In the centre was the creature everyone (even the Fortune staff if they dared to admit it) hated. Wolf followed a few branch-offs. There was a branch to the communications officer, obviously; another to a small cloud of postings and printed, blurry images that seemed to make up a comprehensive understanding of the Twilight Year. In the cloud, anyone could see glimpses of the lives that were taken away by the corporation. It was hard to think that, willing or otherwise, everyone whose photo resided in the cloud had, in fact, consented to their own death. Wolf shivered again.

A chilling thought, he reasoned to himself, as he read a few news headlines.

The headlines detailed the 'highlights' of one's Twilight Year. It seemed that, no matter what profession or path in life Fortune had granted people, they all seemed squeezed into the same clinical structure during their final year on Earth.

First things first, the client had to go out with a bang. As such they were given preference over any big, showy, gaudy, unnecessary yet lauded accomplishment or activity that suited their current situation. They could be put at the helm of a big research project, or cast as the limited lead in a big blockbuster franchise or perhaps given an honourable title or degree of some kind. Sometimes they might get a combination of a few things. Something flashy, for sure. Anything and everything to make them feel special.

From then on the client's life would focus on family. Fortune would take them to their family, or simply give them time off to do so as they please. On occasions they would outright tell the client to make peace with loved ones, to start their rounds of goodbyes. On others it would just be a hint.

Thirdly they would get the client to wrap up their legal life – this is where Lance's pinboard was lacking somewhat, Wolf noticed. Wolf knew of the third stage well. His neighbour. He had had no one at all left alive to bequeath anything to – and indeed nothing left to bequeath.

He had attempted to dump his one or two furniture items on Wolf. Wolf grimaced to himself and let out a grunt. The neighbour had not reacted well to his Twilight Year and had gone on a full nine month bender ending with him living alone in relative squalor next to Wolf.

Not all are suited to the throws of the end of days, Wolf thought.

The final stage was of course the weekend away. The final trip before the client's final trip. Fortune had a number of beautiful villas across the countries in which they held their bases of operation. Each of them ran on a mix of taxpayer money and Fortune Limited stocks. Each villa had multiple presidential suites with all the amenities one could ask for. A final going away present, as it were. All Expireds, as they were thus soon to be known as, received a long weekend stay at 'The Villa' before being escorted in equal style to their selected local Expiration centre. And well, the rest is obvious.

Wolf's eyes moved away from the cloud and found another one similarly littered with post-its and images. Only, in this branch, there was not a multitude of different people; there was only one person's image: Lance's brother, Marc. Sprouting from the epicentre like a virus multiplying were short, brainstormed escape plans: 'fake identity', 'international travel for immunity – France?', 'anti-Faust network smuggle', 'haven cities? – farms?'. The ideas seemed to spring up like annoying dialogue boxes on a glitching machine. Wolf imagined this was the part of the board Lance both cherished and hated. Cherished, because he seemed invested in saving his brother, but hated because all of his ideas were lacking in logical follow-through. In essence, they were shit.

Still, as Wolf turned back to Lance and Locks, he felt that

feeling bubble in his stomach again. He could not quite put his finger on it, but it definitely was not pleasant. Lance was passionately detailing what he thought was a good plan and Wolf could see his determination. For a moment Wolf forgot he was there for selfish reasons. Lance – and Locks – were a means to an end.

"Locks will walk into the building on a call," said Wolf, cutting the two of them off mid-sentence, "Locks will come in and be on a call the whole time, she just needs to look like she knows what she's doing. If she enters on a call, and plays it right, it will look less suspicious than if she sits down, looks around, and then starts one. Also, use your brains, idiots. I'll code a signal-bouncing algorithm on her device so her call can actually be to us; then there's no need to conceal an earpiece. Also, less to buy beforehand," then, he concluded, "you're welcome."

Lance's face turned from confusion, presumably of the fact that he forgot Wolf was even in the room, to a face of awe.

Wolf scoffed. It wasn't rocket science.

Lance's eyes danced from Wolf to the escape plan cloud of notes on his board. It looked as though Lance was both scared that Wolf had seen something, and had also remembered something unrelated. This awkward eye dance was, once again, intriguing. Wolf made a mental note to have another squizz at the board when next he could, but ultimately decided that whatever the motive was for Lance's sudden nerves Wolf concluded that it was none of his business. Had it been Locks, he might have said something. Lance was allowed his secrets.

"Next order of business, then," continued Wolf, "I don't have a van."

"I do," came a confident voice from the doorway.

Chapter 25
Grace

Grace had not expected Marc's surprisingly deep voice, but when it came, she didn't jump. Grace found Marc's voice strangely soothing; she could listen to it for hours. Plus, it wasn't truly unexpected for him to be there. Unlike a lot of people who butt into a conversation, this particular conversation was quite literally Marc's business. He was the catalyst for the whole thing. If it hadn't been for him, Lance would not be this deep into wanting to take down Fortune Limited, and Grace wouldn't be here. Nor would Wolf.

Marc was standing by the doorway, leaning on the doorframe. He looked a bit too casual to Grace, even though she'd only seen him once before in person. He was wearing Lance's clothing, and looked like a little child in his father's clothes. The thin jersey draped over his slim physique, and his pants seemed a bit too baggy. Even so, Grace could not help but smile, genuinely. Marc had 'the look' about him; it was not hard to see how he'd become so successful as an actor. Despite recent events, he was confident, and carried himself well. Frankly, Grace was a bit starstruck.

She glanced at Lance, who had a smile on his face too. But his was a smile of pride. Grace stared at the brothers for a moment. It's amazing what one can discover about people simply by their facial expressions. Very few people had good poker faces; Grace liked to think she was one of the few, but Lance was not. His smile told a story. A story that said there had recently been tension between him and his brother, but now, all that was left was an understanding. An understanding that had never quite been there before. A sense of camaraderie, like they were in something together. Fighting the same fight, on the same team. Which of course they were.

And then there was Wolf, who looked like he couldn't give a crap about Marc's butting in.

"Great, when can I get my hands on it?" was Wolf's response. It broke the warm scene.

"Hang on, what do you mean you have a van? Since when?" Lance seemed sceptical. Marc Mason owning a van of any kind seemed a bit out of character, it seemed too... domesticated.

"My theatre company has one, we use it for prop, set, costume deliveries, and pick-ups," said Marc, "I could borrow it and lend you the fob."

Now that tracked a bit better. Marc Mason, who owned a theatre company, had a van at his disposal. It wasn't his personal van.

"I don't want to spoil your heroic entry, but won't it be just a little conspicuous?" retorted Wolf, "A branded van ain't going to cut it, especially if it leads back to you, and therefore back to Lance."

"He has a point," said Lance.

Marc clocked Grace and smirked. Clearly, he liked being the centre of attention.

"I'm not an idiot, you two," said Marc, he walked over to the chair previously occupied by Wolf and sat down casually, "I've had a good think about the whole thing, and I've decided I want to help in any way I can," Marc's show of confidence slipped slightly. Grace felt his waver as it reminded her of her father in his final days, "It may be too late for me, even if you blow the whole company wide open on national broadcast. The legal system has a way of taking its time, I get that, but if what you guys are doing has any effect on the next… batch of us, then it will be worth it."

Grace smiled, Just like dad.

"My theatre company is new, one of Fortune's final 'legacy' projects for me. We have no branding at this point in time. The van is completely blank and," this time he clocked Wolf, as if to try and equal him, "it's currently still being registered. It's technically not roadworthy, but with the current backlog I was told a few weeks-"

"So a van that is, as yet, untraceable," concluded Wolf, "At least to us. Good, that will do just fine. Of course, there are ways to decipher whose it is, but that would take some days, and by then, the jig is up, right?"

"Best case scenario," said Lance, nodding, "at the very least, some damage will have been done that any repercussion to us will be worth it."

"Here, here!" chimed Grace, who was feeling a bit left

out. Marc chuckled a bit at her outburst, which made Grace chuckle herself. However sweet the interaction was, Grace was almost immediately pulled out of it by the thought of the fact that Marc was due for his Villa stay in just a few weeks. In a few weeks, he would no longer be here. He was right. There was little hope for him. Grace couldn't help but wonder what Marc and every other soon to be Expired might be thinking at this point in their Twilight Year. She didn't think she would be as strong as Marc appeared to be, sitting in that chair.

Chapter 26
Lance

Days passed by like lightning. Lance found it unnerving, the speed. It seemed as though they had so little time, yet they had so much still to do. The meetings were held primarily at his place. On paper, it was for size purposes, but if he was being honest, it was because he had the most stability. Wolf had a one bedroom apartment in town with noisy neighbours. Not to mention nosey. And Grace had her brother to take care of. They had met there once or twice, but she was reluctant to talk much about the plans at all, for fear of him listening in. Lance had gathered she did not want him knowing of their plans, both for plausible deniability and simply to shelter him from the truth… at least for now. Lance could understand that need, he had had it before with his own siblings. The only difference was that neither of them were diagnosed with an incurable disease. Adding emotional pain into his physical pain just seemed… cruel. So, they met at Lance's, and he didn't mind it much at all. He liked being home; he always had. It also gave Marc an excuse to stay over more often.

Marc had changed a lot since that night a few moons ago when all had seemed lost with him. He seemed more confident, but not in the previous arrogant sense of muddled duty and resignation. Now, he had a cause to fight for before the end. Lance would often catch him staring out a window with a look of acknowledgement, as if Marc were thinking about all the things he needed to do before he left this world. Whenever Marc returned his focus back to the people in the room with him it would appear as if he had once again made up his mind to fight.

Every time that Lance saw this, or even thought about it, he would get a pull in his stomach. He was happy Marc was feeling the proper feelings. The feelings Lance thought were proper, at least: upset, sadness, defiance, determination. Lance was proud of his brother, but at the same time, the pull in his stomach would come: a feeling of sadness and guilt on his part. A feeling that reminded him that he had not managed to do what he had promised his little brother. He had not saved him… yet, that is. There was still time.

There's still…

No, the mission was the priority. He couldn't let himself dwell too long on what may or may not happen to Marc.

Despite being in the latter part of the year, the day before the plan was to be set in motion, it was pouring hard with rain. Lance sat at his breakfast bar, staring out the window at the falling rain pummeling against the glass. He liked the rain, it was calming to his thoughts. He could sit there for hours and not even notice.

Wolf entered the kitchen wearing grey sleeping shorts and a tank top. He mumbled a good morning to Lance, who quickly looked from the window to his guest and back to the window. He'd seen Wolf, and decided it would be awkward to stare.

Wolf helped himself to the contents of the fridge. To an onlooker, it might've seemed like the kitchen was a little too familiar to him, but Lance had given him the permission to take what he wanted and needed. And Lance knew that Wolf held people to their word. Wolf had been crashing occasionally at Lance's ever since Jan left to stay with their mother. They had thought it best for her to be with Anita for the next few weeks. So, when she had left, and there was a spacious empty room with an ensuite and a fully stocked kitchen just down the hall, Wolf had had no shame in asking Lance if he could crash there every now and then. Lance had agreed, out of common hospitality, the knowledge of Wolf's current financial situation, and also because Wolf was growing on him.

They shared so much in common, and in their conversations, Lance found himself learning so much. He was getting the hang of some basic techno mambo jumbo, and had been taught a delightful new soup recipe. Despite his apprehension to get attached to anyone, Lance had developed a friendship with Wolf. Whether it was reciprocated was another thing entirely. In any case, Lance reasoned that he might as well live his life to the fullest, despite the dark times in which he found himself. He found that he now rebelled against the notion that people should cut themselves off from happiness, friendship, and relationships just because of some inevitable, life-changing event. He was trying to see the positives and not only the negatives. In a strange way, Marc had helped him realised this.

And so, Lance embraced Wolf and Grace. He found that he trusted them. They all had different motives, but they wanted the same thing. Wolf and he had talked for hours the previous night, and Lance had learnt a lot about his past, and his reasoning for being here. He was out on his luck, effectively. He had no family, no real friends, but he had a will to live, which Lance admired. He had so little that some might claim he had nothing to live for, but even so, Wolf didn't want to give up. He was a fighter, a survivor, and Lance liked him for it. Again he caught himself staring as Wolf retrieved a carton of milk from the fridge.

"Today's the big day," said Wolf as he poured himself a glass and came to sit at the breakfast bar with Lance.

Lance had reverted quickly to his window staring, "Is this going to be a problem, I wonder?" He was referring to the rain, mostly. He was a bit worried. What if it all went wrong? What if they made no difference at all? Worse, what if they were caught? He could deal with the repercussions, he had mentally prepared himself for it, but his mother and Jan had not. And if Grace's story about the break-in was anything to go by, Fortune Limited cared very little for the sanctity of the innocent.

"Not for me," said Wolf mid gulp, "I'll be in the van. But not for you, either. You're inside the building, remember?"

"Yeah, I know," he said. He looked out into the rain yet again. The rapping on the pane soothed him a little. Rain wasn't the harbinger of death; rain was just the weather.

"Well, we better get ready. Locks will be waiting impatiently."

Wolf pushed off from his perch and headed to Jan's room.

Lance took a few moments at the window until he took a deep breath, and headed to his own room.

***

They had decided on a location that would not appear strange, given that they were about to hop into a van. While there was undoubtedly a camera set up somewhere around the dingy parking lot of a costume warehouse on the outskirts of town, all it would see were two tall, hoodied men entering the van, and then driving away. Wolf and Lance had taken precautions on their commute to the destination. Nothing was left to chance in their venture to be as anonymous as they could be in a time where surveillance was second only to gluten-free bread.

The two had left Lance's home in very different outfits, and had gone their separate ways. Wolf had taken a brisk walk to the train station while Lance had hailed a cab. Both parties had decided to take very unusual routes to reach the dingy parking lot. Lance had not been entirely sure of Wolf's travels, and Wolf would not have been entirely sure of Lance's.

This was a part of their plan: plausible deniability.

If Lance knew anything about the law (which he did), he knew that, at times, technicalities could make or break a case. Therefore, he'd suggested that, aside from the most important aspects of the mission, neither Wolf, Grace, Marc, nor himself should know everything that any of them were doing.

Lance had taken a cab initially in the opposite direction to his destination. He had gone a little into town, in fact. He had stopped by a deli stand and had purchased himself a breakfast wrap, making a concerted effort to both appear casual and also as though he was stuffy (despite the rain, the air was warm and humid). He had known there were cameras in the far left corner of the room, honed in on the stall he was at. Again, he had wanted a plausible explanation for his wardrobe change, should he need it in court. He then had moved towards the public restroom.

The dank smell of misused toilets and urine had destroyed his sense of smell, but no matter. He had thought twice about actually eating his breakfast wrap, since by then it had most certainly been contaminated. He'd shoved past a man who had been heading out, and had entered a cubicle. Throwing off his jacket revealed a red shirt underneath, and from his bag, he had produced a blue cap and had slapped it on. He'd done a superfluous final check on his outfit, and had made to head out of the stall when he'd heard a groan. It was the kind of groan that he knew all too well; it had not been dissimilar to his own after he had had a bit too many beers. As Lance's mind had raced to make calculations, his plan had suddenly become even more solid. He'd packaged his wrap in his jacket, and had thrown it over the stall before hastily exiting. It would have been just another layer of camo that he could use. He might've been going overboard, but Lance would rather be called overly cautious than overly confident. The man (presumably someone living on the street) would have benefitted from a breakfast, but also (if he wore the jacket) he would appear to be Lance when he finally left his stall, throwing potential onlookers off his scent.

Lance had exited the public bathroom alleyway and had made a casual yet deliberate turn in order to avoid the camera's view. He'd walked as fast as he could without drawing attention to himself through the streets and throngs of people. Luckily, the rain had decided to let up a bit, so he had not enjoyed the feeling of being utterly drenched. He'd spied the underground station sign, and had beelined towards it. The station was a mixture of new and grime. The entire underground had only been a few years in service, yet, with the current government upkeep, it appeared like it had been left alone for years upon years. Lance had paid for a ticket with a generic fob from some staff wellness seminar his company had hosted. He'd then waited patiently for the train to arrive.

The train had arrived in true fashion, ten minutes late, though Lance thanked his lucky stars it was only ten minutes late. He'd boarded and found a seat. He then had taken a second to process his morning; he felt like he had run a marathon even though the real task of the day hadn't even started. There had been a number of passengers around him, but they had been too glued to their screens to bother about a new person on the train.

Plus, Lance had reasoned, *why would they think I'm special at all?*

Then, he'd realised his outfit actually made him stand out quite clearly. Without disturbing the other commuters, Lance had carefully stood up and had made his way to the bathroom. Luckily, the one at the end of the compartment had been vacant, and a quick glance had confirmed that no one had actually seen him enter. Lance had made a point of coming to this station because he had known that the cameras in the trains on this line had been either wrecked or stolen for parts. The minute he'd entered this train, his trail would have gone dark, and now all he had needed to do was change into something completely different, and get off at the station, which was a two-minute walk from their rendezvous point.

He had made his final costume change and had exited

the toilet. Wanting to be as cautious as possible, Lance had decided not to go back to his seat next to a very nice looking elderly woman, but instead he'd moved up a compartment. He had found some standing space near the exit. And so he had just had to wait fifteen or so minutes depending on the stops and he would be in the final stretch.

***

Lance hopped off the train at his stop, immediately drew his hood over his head, and headed in the direction of the van. Luckily, the weather seemed to be on his side; the rain had just restarted. On his walk, he could not help but wonder what Grace's travel plans had been, or Wolf's, for that matter. Lance knew that he was pedantic, and liked to cover his tracks, but he did not know whether the other two would be as calculated as he had been. At least in this sphere. Of course, they had all discussed being cautious, but Lance had taken it to heart. Had the others done the same? Grace seemed to Lance to be a bit reckless at times. Perhaps she had just put on a hoodie and went straight to Fortune's head office? She would probably not mean anything by it, but she *did* already try something, and that had been caught on camera. Sure, it was a fuzzy image, but Fortune had figured her out and stormed her apartment... were a new hair do and glasses going to fool them?

And what if Wolf had done something similar? Gone to the train station and headed to the rendezvous point without anything in between? After all, he had been staying at Lance's place... not his own. If anyone tracked him, it would lead them to Lance, not Wolf. It was entirely possible that Wolf's cautiousness would only come into effect after the mission, when he returned home. The thought of this possibility took Lance by surprise. He did not want to think that Wolf might do something like that to him. Aside from anything else, Lance had placed a certain amount of trust in him. He really didn't trust a lot of people. Yes, his trust in Grace and Wolf had come quickly, but it had also come out of necessity and mutual understanding. Lance did not want his trust to be broken, especially because he had gone out on a limb to give it.

Lance turned a corner, and his rain infused view was that of a parking lot with a few cars, and one van. Lance had the keys, and there was no sign of Wolf yet. Lance's spirits raised slightly. He crossed the streeting into the lot and headed for the driver's side of the van. The van beeped open and Lance clambered in, rather sick of the rain. He was careful not to throw off the hood, though the wet cloth made him feel like he had been dunked under water as part of an interrogation tactic. Nevertheless, he persevered.

He swung his head to look into the back to take stock of everything. It had been a risk leaving all their possessions here overnight. Wolf had put up a hell of a fight when it came to his old laptop. Lance understood sentimentality, but in the larger scheme of things, he thought the argument had been a bit unnecessary. Regardless, Wolf had agreed, and there on the floor of the van was his laptop, various cables and outdated (but still working) modems, some concealed earpieces, a security contractor uniform for Lance, and various other gadgets and clothing accessories that the group had thought they might possibly need.

Lance's assessment of the gear was interrupted by a rapping on the back of the van. It startled him so much that he jumped and gave a little yelp. Clearly, he was on edge. Lance glanced at the wing mirror and saw Wolf's chin and nose stick out from under a black hoodie at the rear of the van. With a sigh, Lance flipped a switch near the steering wheel, and the back door unlocked. With a hiss, the door glided open, and Wolf's sopping figure climbed into the back, uttering profanities as it did.

"Fucking rain," he mumbled as he flicked his hands free of the rainwater that soaked him, "I suppose it's my fault getting off the next station over." Wolf wiped his face, threw back his hoodie, and smoothed his hair, letting out an exhausted huff. His chest was heaving, clearly, he had been running.

"What happened to you?" said Lance, trying to lighten the mood as he went to start the engine.

"Was going to have a nice little jog down, fifteen minutes or so, then the bloody rain started again. But when I looked at the clouds before I got off, ag… " he trailed off, perhaps he thought it was a boring story or he didn't quite know what to say; either way, he dropped it. Lance held his gaze for a moment and then turned quickly to the wheel. The van lurched suddenly, as Lance remembered how to kick off an automatic set to manual. Wolf almost toppled completely back as he had been on his haunches.

"Urgh, you're the getaway driver too, aren't you?" moaned Wolf as he steadied himself on the ride out of the parking lot.

Lance chuckled, he knew how to drive, this was just a new type of vehicle to him. He was still getting the hang of it. He dared not use autopilot, and some cars set to automatic transmission were also set to autopilot. On his own car, he knew exactly how to calibrate the driving options, however, on this make, he was less of a pro. So, he set it to fully manual so that he could understand it.

"You'd better get set up back there," said Lance, looking left and right as he turned onto a thin street headed towards the centre of town, "it's not a long journey."

Wolf grunted an affirmative.

Chapter 27
Grace

Being cautious was not something hardwired into Grace's system. She was more of a go-getter. A fly by the seat of your pants kind of girl. Sure, she took some precautions, but usually she put her faith in her abilities, and Luck. However, even Grace had to admit that Luck seemed to have taken a sabbatical from granting her auspicious gift, what with her failed first attempt and the home invasion. So, she decided to heed Lance's words and be 'better safe than sorry'.

After they'd broken up their meeting the day before, she'd gone to get a whole new look. Not only had she concealed her locks, but she'd chosen a bland replacement colour that didn't really sit well. But most people saw her as the outgoing, fashion forward type of woman, so they wouldn't exactly pin her as the black haired bop at the subpar café. She also found some glasses. They made her eyes strain, but she looked business-like.

She could feel a headache coming on. But, she declared to herself: *It's all for the greater good.*

Certainly no one close to her would ever recognise her in the look she was 'serving' for this mission. Frankly, she felt like an imposter; like she looked like a boring business woman who was undoubtedly more book-smart than Grace. If anyone asked her about tax deductibles, she truly did not know what she would do. Nevertheless, it was a character, and, according to Marc, step one of a successful act was to embrace the character. She felt she achieved this, and even had a name for her new alter-ego: Quinn. She didn't go so far as a surname. That, she felt, was overkill.

Grace had taken two buses, a train, and walked the rest of the way to get to her present location: two blocks away from the Fortune Limited. building. She stood on the pavement and tried to look as inconspicuous as possible as she waited for Lance to call and say they were closing in on the building. When that happened, she'd begin her call, which Wolf had assured her would be routed through their comms. Then, she could begin her part of the plan: setting up shop in the cafe.

Grace stood under a store front cover watching the people and the rain. She was almost in a daze when her device buzzed in her pocket.

She retrieved it, and saw the text from Lance: 'ON THE MOVE'.

Grace slid the device back into her pocket and straightened out her jacket before heading out into the rain and people. She decided she would have to call them after setting up shop in the cafe, as Lance had clearly forgotten to call her. She shook her head. Not an issue at all, in fact, it would help her, as now she could order a coffee before the show began. Grace trumped through the rain, shielding her face with her arm – mostly to keep her eyes dry and open so she could see the ground beneath her feet, but also because doing so made her much less traceable.

She rounded the first block of buildings and quickly glanced down the path to make sure she'd taken the right turns, then arrived underneath the Fortune Limited building, which was practically towering over her already. She threw caution to the wind and zoomed across the road, barely looking at traffic whether it was oncoming or not, and reached the stairs to the looming building in good time. Not skipping a beat, she leapt up the stairs in her muted high heels, and barged through the automatic glass doors in moments.

Grace let out an exasperated breath of air, shook her hands as dry as she could, and fixed her hair. A man passed her and gave her a slight smile.

"No umbrella?"

"Just my luck, I forgot it!" replied Grace in as 'Quinny' a voice as she could muster. She imagined Quinn would have a strong, deep voice; something to carry all those sales pitches to upper management. The man chuckled and nodded his head goodbye and left the building, unfurling his bright yellow umbrella. Grace looked around, as casual as possible. Thankfully, it seemed like no one had seen their interaction. Her whole aim was to blend in, and she'd just bounded into the enemy base, meeting someone who noticed something odd about her immediately. And of course, he had to be carrying a bright, yellow umbrella. A very identifiable marker. Any onlooker could easily talk about their encounter to the authorities, prompting them to check camera footage, and leading them to Grace. However, everyone seemed to be minding their own business, so at least for that moment, she was safe.

She sidled towards the cafe. The decor was not unlike the rest of the building: shiny marbled black with gold trimmings. The interior designers at Fortune Limited were nothing if not consistent. Grace wished they weren't, though, a pop of another colour somewhere might just lift the company's PR. Everything just looked a mix between stately and morbid. Grace found herself a table on the outskirts of the cafe. She felt a bit out in the open, but she liked the spot because she could see the exits to the left, and she had a completely unobstructed view of the lobby floor. Her job was minimal, but important. She was to function as the initial eyes in the lobby, and she had the final say in the situation when Lance left. If there was a situation, like a mob of guards coming down the stairs, she could clock them and direct Lance where needed. Grace leaned over, again, casual (always casual), to see how far down the passage to her right went. From her point of view, it seemed to go deeper into the building. She saw the side of an elevator entrance along the concealed wall. Of course, after pouring over the blueprints for days on end, she knew where everything was, but being there in person was a whole other feeling. She had to acclimate to her surroundings.

Lance would take the stairs. It was more work, but it gave him more options to take cover on the fifth floor if needed. Floor five was labelled as the server level, and Wolf was positive that if there were any incriminating files, it would be stored in a local cloud in an analogue server disconnected from the internet entirely. The only way Wolf thought it possible to gain access to those dark files was to be there in-person with an access fob of some kind. Lance had his work cut out for him. There were many steps in their plan, and they all had to go smoothly, otherwise, it was game over.

Grace called over a waiter, ordered herself the coffiest coffee on the menu, and started working, making it look like she was just doing her job. She hauled out her laptop and powered it on, placing it to the side. Quinn was the type of person to still want to use paper when jotting down notes (screw the trees), so Grace pulled out a notepad and pen, and scribbled some nonsensical notes. She placed her cell on the table next to her in anticipation, and then went to actual work, taking actual notes of her surroundings so that she could report back to the boys.

So far, it looked busy, but clear of obstructions. Grace counted two security personnel, about three receptionists (two of whom were very involved in gossip and the other very involved in work), and a large number of civilians. Grace noted that the guards carried the new standard assault pistol in holsters. Although they had expected this, since it had been in the news the last year – Fortune's security upgrade – it still made Grace uneasy. If something went wrong… Grace shook her head clean of disaster. Nothing would go wrong. They had put a lot of thought into this. Lance would get in and out smoothly.

Grace's cell lit up. She froze for a moment. It was showtime. Lance was calling; they were close. Grace closed her eyes, took a deep breath, and answered.

"We've parked," came Lance's voice. Grace noted a twinge of nervousness and fear.

"Okay," replied Grace, "the café's lovely," code for letting him know she was all set up, "Menu's quite diverse, but good. Two strong coffees, but they are at the top, once you get past them there are some lattes that seem like they might not be a problem on the stomach."

"What?" said Lance.

He wasn't getting it. She'd have to change tactics.

"Such a lovely day, though there are some storm clouds closer to you, and a few just to the west. Doubt they will rain too much, just make sure to avoid the storm on your way into the city."

"For fuck's sake, Locks," interrupted Wolf, "you can speak normally, Fortune's system only captures video."

Why had he not mentioned this in the meetings?

"Well, you could have told me!" said Grace before she sighed and looked around to see if anyone had heard her little outburst, "Fine, two guards, packing at the entrance, three receptionists in today, too involved in their own thing, good number of civilians for coverage. There, get it now?"

"Alright, thanks, just getting changed. I'll be in soon."

"Great, I'll just stay on the line, then."

Chapter 28

Lance

Lance hoisted himself from the driver's seat into the back of the van with Wolf. He removed his hoodie, which revealed a white vest. He noticed Wolf's eyes, and suddenly became slightly abashed. He jostled around so that his back was towards the techy, and heard Wolf start to type something on his laptop. But he never heard him turn around.

Lance chose to focus on the mission rather than fall into some teenage locker room cliche. There were bigger things to worry about.

He quickly pulled on the dark blue overalls they'd purchased at a hefty price on the black market. Thanks to their resident criminal-adjacent techspert, they'd managed to procure an authentic overall worn by maintenance officers at the company Fortune outsourced from. Lance would blend right in, just a few moments ago, he'd seen someone wearing the same outfit enter the service entrance to the side of the building. Lance zipped up his garment.

Turning around to face Wolf, who immediately looked back at his screen, Lance fumbled around on the floor of the van to locate his forged access fob. Eventually, he found it, the back of which was (again) authentic Fortune Limited black and gold plastic, and the other side sported a microchip with Lance's grifter name: John Mathers. What had spurred him to choose that name was beyond him, it was simply the first two names that came into his head when Wolf set up his ID. He just went with it; it wasn't as if it were his actual name anyway. Lance slipped the small fob into a sleeve that clipped to his breast pocket, then he went to work on his hair.

Lance had the strangely perfect privilege of being at one point described as 'handsome in a John Smith kind of way'. Though he had not taken it as a compliment, rather more as a backhanded one at the time, it was at this point in his life that he appreciated his relative anonymity. Truly, most people he met and then met again a few days or weeks later rarely ever recognised him. He just had that sort of face that was not unattractive, but also unremarkable. Few discerning features came to mind even to Jan or his mother. The only thing that might be identifiable was his blond hair, and even that wasn't quite the tell-tale distinguishing sign. However, given that he was on-camera invading the satellite office a few weeks ago, the group had thought it prudent to dye his hair a natural brunette shade. When Lance looked at himself in the mirror, of course he knew it was him, but he also knew that he looked like any other random guy in the street, especially with brunette hair.

Marc had also suggested a bit of dark make-up around the eyes, which Lance now applied as instructed. Just enough to appear sleep deprived. Marc had said that people who met him as John Mathers would immediately remember that instead of his facial structure, giving Lance an advantage should a sketch artist be brought in… for whatever reason.

"How do I look?" asked Lance to Wolf, who looked up from his work.

"Average and dead inside," said Wolf.

"Just what we're going for," said Lance as he made final adjustments to his outfit.

Wolf nodded and reached over to grab an earpiece, which was also authentic. He brought it to his station of gadgets and held it to a sensor of some kind. There was a dull beep, and a tap of a few keys before he beckoned for Lance to come nearer so he could put the earpiece in securely. Wolf's free hand gently held Lance's head as he fitted the earpiece. Wolf's eyes met his and he gave a short Wolf grunt and he pulled away awkwardly.

"Notoriously loose unless you fit them properly, those things. Testing, testing," said Wolf into a mic on his left. Wolf's deep voice carried through the mic, through the air on frequencies and wavelengths and probably a bunch of other technical things that Lance had no idea about, and reached his ear. Crisp and clear. It felt like Wolf was inside his head. Lance gave a thumbs up and nodded.

"Testing, testing," said Lance, and he immediately heard his voice on blast through Wolf's speaker setup.

They both jumped at the sound, and Wolf leapt to fix it. Lance nervously sent a look out the front tinted window to see if anyone passing by had heard anything. A few seconds told Lance that even if someone had, they didn't care one bit. Lance let out a sigh of relief.

"If you two are done getting pretty and 'testing testing' Lance's earpiece, might we get on with the job? It is closing in on ten, you know."

Lance had completely forgotten Grace was still on the line. But she was right: they were slaves to a time frame. Besides the fact that the company executives often started their day's work in the afternoons, around two o'clock, which the trio desperately wanted to avoid, their mark was scheduled to arrive any minute now.

"True, Locks," said Wolf who then faced Lance, "remember, get him to the far corner before you swipe his card, that's the only deadzone they have."

"I know the plan, just keep an eye out for me."

"I'll do my best."

"Let's hope your best is perfection, Wolf," interjected Grace, "all I can see is the lobby, are you into the cameras yet?"

"Hold your horses, Locks," said Wolf, with slight irritation in his voice, "we want to infiltrate as little as possible, there's no telling what kind of failsafes are in their system. I don't want to hack into the feed now while we're doing the preflight checks. What if they clock us before we're even in?"

The last sentiment made Lance's stomach turn. Why did he have to say that? He'd been feeling so confident up until then. Wolf apparently saw the uncertainty flooding Lance's face, and Wolf's own went from annoyed to... kind of caring... which was an unusual look for him.

"Don't stress, I know what I'm doing. It's always better to be safe than sorry, right? You'll be fine in there, and if not, I'll get you out."

"'Us'," piped Grace, "I'm in here too, remember?"

"Yes, both of you," said Wolf with a smile to himself.

With Lance's mind made up that he was going to do this no matter what, he snatched their mark's replacement card and started to scoot back over the seats to exit the van. Wolf let out a low grunt and threw a small device at Lance who caught it rather skillfully.

"How were you planning on downloading the records, hm?"

Lance chuckled nervously and hoped that that was the first and only moment of stupidity from himself on this mission. There was too much at stake to make rookie errors. Lance faced the windowed door and held the handle latch. He paused for a moment, and took a few deep breaths. This was new terrain, but not something new to him. He had been involved in operations before, but he had had the government backing him, and a much larger team behind him. Nevertheless, this would work. It had to. With a final exhale, Lance jerked the door open and exited onto the damp pavement. His mission had begun.

The rain had died down. Now, only the gloomy after-drizzle was softly falling down over the heads of people, the hoods of vehicles, and gently misting up windows. Lance ruffled his overalls. They weren't sitting right. He tapped gently on all the places he knew were holding mission-critical objects. When he was certain he had everything, he started on his faked casual walk to the entrance of the looming skyscraper. The height of the building struck him more and more as he closed in on the entrance; it seemed to tower over him, as if it had a mind of its own and knew exactly what he was attempting. It was like he was being watched.

"I see you, Lance," came Grace's voice in his ear, "act natural, casual as always, you've been here a hundred times, you're a maintenance man, you've got this."

Lance knew she was just trying to make him less nervous and more confident in his abilities, but she was actually making him feel less confident. He actually felt like he could do this. Sure, there were nerves and the occasional heart flutter, but above that, a feeling kept on pressing down on him: the knowledge that he was trained for this sort of thing, and that he was, in fact, in the right. He didn't quite need the odd pep talk from his watcher on the ground; he needed her to do the watching. If she and Wolf did their jobs well, he was confident he could do his, too.

Lance walked in through the automated doors and entered the dreary lobby. He scanned his surroundings; everything was just like the blueprints had described, save for one or two aesthetic enhancements. He saw the stairs, the small discrete passage leading to the elevator, the receptionists, the security, and of course, Grace – or should he say Quinn? But Lance didn't see something that he was meant to see. Or rather, *someone* he was meant to see. Their target: Justin Cops.

Cops was one of Fortune Limited's Archivists. Fortune had only a few of them, most worked in the Headquarters, presumably because most of the archives were stored and coded there on their island server. But also to keep them closer to the higher-ups. Theirs was both a revered and unenviable job. Though most did not question Fortune's possible underground… habits, most people would back away from being made the keeper of any multimillion credit company's archives. Because every company had its secrets: tax evasion, tiny typos that went unchecked, or large-scale mismanagement. If anything happened to a company as a result of these typos, their archivists would take the brunt of the fall, rather than the higher-ups.

Lance almost felt sorry for Cops. He knew that, if they were successful in their mission both today and in the long-run, that he would be that man to lose his job for it. The three of them were very likely condemning a perfect stranger to a difficult next few years. *If* they were to uncover anything that spoke to the nefarious actions of the company, Fortune would not simply reprimand Cops. Lance didn't think it would go as far as assassination, but he could think of a few tactics Fortune might employ to make Cops' life a living hell. Lance and Grace had debated whether they should be going down this route in the first place.

Surely there was another way.

Wolf had decided that there wasn't.

They needed access to the server room, and only Archivists had such access and were touchable. Anyone higher would be severely more difficult to lift from.

So, Cops was the one they planned to use. He had had a few minor mishaps in both his personal life – dug up thanks to Wolf – and professional life – again, thanks to Wolf, making them believe Cops was a bit of a clutz. He was smart when he needed to be, but on the whole, kind of a clumsy person. If they should lift from any of the Archivists employed at the Headquarters, they should lift from Cops. But right now, Cops was nowhere to be seen.

"Where's the target?" chimed Lance impatiently, "Grace?"

"He didn't come in, at least not while I've been here, and I've been here a while-"

"Wolf?" interrupted Lance.

"Tracking his device, hold on."

Lance shuffled around and decided to busy himself with a snack. He moved over towards the cafe, and eyed a bland looking muffin, he pointed to it in front of the server, and she nodded before packaging it up for him. He paid in cash, and decided to find a table far from Grace, but still in eyesight of the door.

"He's around the corner, must have just been held up."

Lance signed in relief, if Cops was somehow inside the building already, their plan had failed before it had even begun. He sat there, mindlessly eating his bran muffin. Eventually, a tall, spindly man in an ill-fitting suit entered the lobby. He looked rushed, and wet and upset. To Lance, he looked like an easy, distracted target.

"Looks like you're up. Just be careful, security is right there. Change in plans, Lance, I would head for the elevator, that's where he'll be going, especially if he's late," said Grace.

Good call. From scrolling through random camera footage they stole from other buildings and businesses frequented by Cops, they knew that he usually preferred stairs. Perhaps he was keen on fitness; his stature sure indicated as much. Lance nodded to let Grace know he understood. He stood up, disposing of the rest of his muffin in the bin on his way out of the shop. Cops was already starting to head for the elevators. Grace had been right. Lance followed.

A change of plan, but still a simple and easy lift. All Lance needed to know was where his access fob was on his person, and then he could make up an excuse to bump into him and do the switch.

"You're going in blind until I have confirmation of the switch," warned Wolf.

This was planned, just a reminder for Lance and Grace. Again, Wolf was weary of entering Fortune's most monitored systems too early. If Lance stuffed up the switch and EMP, then there was little camera surveillance that could help them, really. He'd be caught red-handed.

The two men entered the elevator passage, and Cops impatiently tapped the gesture-indicated button. Lance smiled on the inside, clearly Cops was flustered, which meant he would be an easy target indeed. Cops attempted a few more times before Lance stepped forward and waved over the motion sensor gently. Cops let out an exasperated thanks. Cops' right hand caught Lance's attention. It was curled in a fist, clutching something. Lance stared until it opened up slightly, and Cops deposited a clear access fob into his right suit pants pocket. Lance breathed an exasperated sigh of relief. He had his target, plus he had seen the outline of Cops' personal device in his other pocket. He formulated a manoeuvre in his head. He dug into his breast pocket without Cops' noticing, and retrieved his own forged fob. It had been conveniently ID'd with Cops' company code. Hopefully, Cops would never know the difference.

The elevator pinged open, and Lance was relieved to see it was empty, but did not think about it too much as his short window of opportunity was already shrinking. The following few seconds went by in a blur. Lance's tactical training and Cops' state of mind played a dance in the still-opening door of the elevator. Cops, in a hurry, stepped into the doorway, just as Lance had anticipated and had also done, causing the two of them to bump bodies and mumble their own forms of apologies. The statements turned into underhanded annoyed expletives as a mini-struggle ensued. Who would actually get in the elevator first? Of course, while all this happened, Lance discreetly transplanted Cops' fob with his fake. This took only a second, and once he knew it had been a success, he muttered another apology and stepped back a bit in faux chivalry. Cops nodded, and entered the elevator. To keep up his act, Lance did the same almost instantly afterwards, this time making sure to stand on Cops' left. Phase one was a success. Time for phase two.

Cops leant over and tapped the ninth floor, where his office was located. Lance noted this with another sense of relief; at least he was still going to his desk. That part of his routine hadn't changed due to the weather. Lance reached into his overall's right leg pocket, and his hands found the small, electromagnetic pulse emitter. Wolf had suggested the action. It was wise to assume all movements on his access fob would be sent to the staff's devices in the form of a notification. So, to keep poor Cops off their scent, his device would have to die. A precaution. Lance now casually positioned his body so that his thigh was close to Cops' left side (and his device). He took a silent deep breath and hoped it was close enough. The emitter was incredibly short ranged and very sensitive. It had to be. They couldn't risk a general short range EMP blast, because then the fob wouldn't work, and then, again, their mission would be over. Lance pressed the button and felt the short buzz of performance from the device, but otherwise, nothing happened. Lance decided to not waste this one and only opportunity, and so over the course of the elevator ride he pulsed Cops' pocket in varying angles about three more times. One of those had to have been successful.

The elevator pinged again, and the ninth floor opened up to the two of them. This time, Cops stood back, clearly indicating for Lance to head out first. Unsure of what to do, Lance did so, finding himself on a floor that was just a maze of cubicles; some had desktop devices with humans at the helm, others appeared to have automated robots. They weren't quite smart enough to plan world domination – their main purposes were to scan files to be uploaded and bring coffee from downstairs. Essentially, they were automated personal assistants doing the boring tasks Fortune Limited had chosen not to dump on its human employees.

Cops left the elevator without a word, and headed to the turnstyle that gave him access to the floor. Lance waited with baited breath as Cops took out 'his' fob and scanned it. The turnstile took a while, but it granted access. Another innovative addition from Wolf: he could mimic the low-level signal required for most of the floors. Cops could make use of any and all floors he usually would need to, just not floor five.

Lance decided not to overstay his welcome, and retrieved his device surreptitiously. He had made sure it forgot all data signals and public connections before he entered the vicinity of the building, making certain that he couldn't be tracked by his device. He was in offline mode, and had uploaded the blueprints manually via an old school wired connection. He pulled the blueprints up and confirmed the direction of the stairs from floor nine. With his destination locked he pocketed his device and headed off.

"We are a go," said Lance to the others.

Chapter 29
Wolf

Wolf cracked his fingers and adjusted his neck in anticipation. Locks had done her part – her beginner's part, her eyes on the ground in the lobby part – but now it was time for the professional to show them how it was done.

Wolf pulled his laptop to his, well, lap and began the orchestra of hand gestures and finger taps. He was an old hat with this sort of system hack, luckily he had had enough experience with high grade security that Fortune's (though higher still) was very doable. Wolf grunted as he encountered an extra firewall or two, but it took him mere seconds to decipher a coded packet or find a backdoor through another system that it was hardly something to worry him. If Wolf had taken the time to think about it, he would probably realise that it wasn't even much of a challenge. However, he would not let his emotional fanfare, gloating at the ease he felt in the situation, get in the way of his mission. Their mission. Piggybacking off a camera feed was a simple enough job even on governmental systems. However he was quite sure the rest of his job would not be as smooth. With that thought, he quickly routed into the Fortune security comms, so that he had both eyes and ears on the location.

Now, the tedious work began. He had to find a moving target in a wealth of camera angles from each floor. And Lance was not going to be dumb enough to stand around for long. Luckily, he had anticipated this search and written a short code to help him out. He had taken a few images of Lance's head from various angles, and worked them into a simple app that searched the database for matches. Simple and effective, but also risky. Fortune would surely have a detection protocol or two to identify when their systems were being used externally. So first, Wolf had to attempt this search old-school, by just looking for Lance. If he felt as though he was wasting time, he would use the app he'd made – and hope he didn't trip any alarm bells in the process.

"Got me?" came Lance's low voice over their comms.

He sounded quite professional; Wolf was impressed. Meanwhile, Locks kept bursting out random phrases every now and then. His annoyance was irrelevant. But, he couldn't help but think that it was nice Lance only spoke when he needed to. It made Wolf like him even more.

No, stick to your job, Wolf thought to himself, *no time to fraternise.*

Wolf scanned the feeds frantically.

"Come on Blondie, where are you?" mumbled Wolf to

himself, a bit too loud.

"Blondie?" that was Locks, the tone of needing to be the centre of attention was unmistakable, "Finally, I'm not the only one with a nickname from the great Wolfred."

"Shut up, I'm concentrating," said Wolf, and he muted Locks from his ears.

Suddenly Lance's hair flashed across his screen. Wolf had to go back a few feeds again, just to make sure. The figure he found turned slightly, and Wolf instantly recognised the profile.

A bit too easily, Lance.

Wolf hoped Lance's recognisable stature was purely from spending a lot of time with him lately. And not something Fortune techno-goons could easily identify too.

"Got you," said Wolf, and begrudgingly unmuted Locks.

"Did you just mute me?"

"Yes," replied Wolf and then, "I see you, Lance. Corridor seven, the stairs are straight ahead to your left."

Wolf watched as Lance grinned on his screen and nodded an affirmative. He never looked at the screens, because he was well aware that Wolf was not the only Watcher of Feeds. Something apparently Locks had no conception of as she stared directly at the camera nearest to her in incredulity. Yet, the mere thought of someone muting her was apparently inconceivable.

"Locks, stop looking at the camera, please?" Wolf felt like he was babysitting the two of them, despite at least *one* of them being an adult.

Locks complied.

"Don't you dare mute me again, Wolfie, you little-" and Locks was muted again.

This time, he could see her very conspicuously mumbling profanities towards a pot plant.

It's lucky she has her cell, Wolf thought, *so at least she looks a little less ridiculous.*

Wolf turned his gaze to more pressing issues. Lance, the man in the field, the one who depended on his keen guidance. Lance was walking swiftly yet unremarkably down the stairs by now. He had the forethought to do a few diversion tactics, instead of heading down the stairs directly to floor five. Again, Lance's tactical brain impressed Wolf. Wolf was following Lance because he had to, but a security agent might have lost interest after flagging him, because it appeared he was just doing a maintenance walkthrough of the building. Cops' key card was working wonders for Lance, allowing him into all areas he needed; something Wolf was unsure his jerry-rigged-fake-access-card would be able to do. Wolf glanced at the feed of Cops at his desk. He looked worse for wear, but very much like he was going to stay put in his chair.

For a split second, Wolf allowed a thought to enter his mind.

A simple thought of: *It's actually going well.*

However, it was followed in his head very quickly with: *But it could turn at any moment. Be on your guard.*

Sometimes, Wolf disliked his rational brain. It kept him from living in the moment. He had hardly ever had a life event that he'd just enjoyed (if it had been objectively enjoyable), or mourned (if it had been objectively sad). His mind always took him back to his first principles: assess, create a strategy, deal. It was how he had dealt with his accident from the army, and the subsequent, persisting, annoying trauma. Trauma… evolution beat him in that area, although he would never admit it. But he had his ways of coping in the waking world. The sleeping world, though, was nature's realm, and he reluctantly relinquished his hold over his mind.

Lance side-stepped some office clerks in a hallway and entered the staircase, going down for the last time. Floor five approached.

"I'm almost at the target level, path?"

Wolf grinned and pulled up the floor plan that he could see Lance viewing on his own device.

"Enter, take a right for a few metres, not far, then take a left. There's a turnstyle, and you'll be in the general archive room. I'll direct you from there as far as I can."

Just as Wolf had anticipated, but not desired.

"As far as you can?"

"There are no cameras on the general comms beyond the third archive corridor. Our target destination is just past the sixth. According to the plans, I can't hack into something that isn't connected to the network," Wolf felt a strange pang in his stomach.

Was it guilt? Or was it something else? Did he feel... worried?

"Well, we knew it wouldn't be easy," confirmed Lance, ever the professional.

"You'll do fine, just follow the plans. It seems like a direct approach, from what I can see there are no archivists in archive corridors one to three, so probably safe to assume the same for the other three."

Lance nodded on the screen in front of Wolf. Suddenly, Wolf was transported back to the EU territory conflict all those years ago, ordering a subordinate to go into a danger zone. Alone. Hoping that he would return unscathed. Lance hesitated, only a second, possibly Locks had said something to him, she was still muted on Wolf's end.

"Thanks, Grace," Lance briefly looked into the camera lens at Wolf, and entered floor five.

Chapter 30

Lance

The corridor Lance entered was starkly different to the ones he'd been trudging and weaving through up until this point. The hall was brightly lit with white panelling, very clinical, and very pristine. There were a number of doorways dotted down the long corridor. To the right, Lance spied an opening on the left which must have been the turnstyle section Wolf had mentioned. From there on, Lance was on his own.

Lance checked up and down the passage as carefully as he could. He did not want to appear out of place, but the occasional suited staff member (the ones who were supposed to be there) did note his presence with a slight look of concern. However, the concern was short-lived. When they read his overalls, they realised he was beneath them, and probably there to fix some broken pipe or something.

Not a threat.

A renewed sense of confidence washed over Lance, and he started down the passage towards the turnstiles. All he needed to ensure was that none of the suits noticed him entering the Archives. Once he was inside, he just had to worry about the people looking at him through the glass eyes above. People watching him like Wolf had been, but who Lance deemed decidedly less welcome to view him.

He approached the alcove with the turnstiles.

"Alright, there's an attendant at the entrance. Probably there to verify entrants," came Wolf's voice, oddly calm, considering everything, "I forgot to mention her before. Hang on before you come into her line of sight. I can work some magic from my side."

Lance did as instructed, feeling a bit like he was stuck on the courtroom floor, waiting for his associate to come bursting through the doors with some magical new evidence that would blow the defence out of the water. In his earpiece, he could hear some typing, and then an exclamation of success.

"Okay, you're free to go. It should work," said Wolf, "I just did a simple identity swap. Your face should come up on the fob when you scan it now."

"*Should?*" goaded Grace.

"Don't make me mute you *again*," said Wolf with a hint of agitation.

Lance nodded to himself (and Wolf). He understood the message and the risks. He turned the corner and met the attendant.

"Good morning," greeted Lance.

"Morning," the woman barely looked up from her

display.

Clearly, she did not want to be there.

Lance lifted his fob and scanned it, feeling a bead of sweat forming on his brow. If this did not do what Wolf said it would, then he would be caught, or at least the person in front of him would become suspicious. He'd never be able to get inside, then.

"Reason for entering?" inquired the woman with a drawl that could put anything to sleep.

The image had not yet popped up on her screen, she was looking at Lance now.

"Uh, routine maintenance, on uh-"

"Server B, I saw something about server A, B, C etc on the plans," said Grace, coming to his rescue, "tell her it's causing problems upstairs."

"Routine maintenance on Server B, it's causing management some problems on level ten," said Lance, trying to sound as if he knew what he meant.

"Always a problem with the servers in this place, you'd think a company like Fortune... anyway, your tag checks out, don't stay too long or I'll have to come and find you, and I don't feel like it."

Lance nodded and pushed through the turnstile, just glad the woman was too bored with her job to have read the occupation listed under Cops' name. It certainly was not maintenance. Once through, he came into a room with roughly six rows of what Lance could only presume to be servers. The pale green lights flickered on and off as new information was added or updated or deleted. The rows were split down the middle to allow for a walkway between the centre of the room, right at the back, there was a sign that pointed to the left: 'SECURE SERVER: AUTHORISED PERSONNEL ONLY'.

Lance advanced down the archive corridors, which seemed to spring from the ground and rise towards the heavens. In his head, he wondered how anyone was supposed to do maintenance on the server modules that made a home at the very top of the towering corridors. But it was irrelevant to him whether or not Fortune Limited built their buildings with efficiency of space. Honestly, Lance imagined the opposite was the case: that Fortune built their offices purely with an eye to seem imposing on the Everyman. Tall and overpowering.

Lance eventually reached the end of the walkway, beyond the sixth archive corridor. This was now unchartered territory. He had no eyes, and he suspected once he entered the secured server room, he would lose audio too. A veritable external signal blackhole.

"Lance, if you're hearing me, I have a bit of bad news," Grace came over the comms, "well, it *could* be nothing…"

Great, thought Lance, *just as I thought. Things are not going to go perfectly smoothly.*

"Mmm?" he intoned so that he didn't have to speak out loud.

"So the lovely guards out front here just had a lovely chat with a few other guards that seemed to come from nowhere. And then they left. One stayed to keep watch on the entrance, but he looks fidgety. I don't know, man, I could just be reading into things."

"Locks, did the guards leave the building or head up the stairs, or the elevator?" Wolf's voice joined them.

In the background, Lance could hear the clack of some furious typing.

"Three went up the stairs, two to the elevator," said Grace, "but they didn't seem in a hurry, I just thought I'd men-"

"I am picking up some chatter on their comms," Wolf cut in, "I think they've clocked an irregularity or something," there was a tension-baked pause, "They are on low alert, but alert nonetheless."

"So do the thing we came here for and let's get out," said Grace.

"Mm," responded Lance.

He was glad it was only a low alert, but still, he felt a little less confident now, as a low alert could easily become a high alert, given the right variables.

"You'll be going completely dark when you enter. The upload should not take a long time, the uplink I gave you is one of the best, just make sure you search for the right kind of files. We don't need *everything*," said Wolf, his tone one of encouragement.

"Roger," said Lance as he headed towards the secured door.

On the left side was an electronic identification pad. Lance wasted little time retrieving his fob again and swiping it over the pad. A few pained seconds crept past, and Lance held his breath. The pad blipped, a green light emitted from its side, and the seal to the door hissed. He was in.

"Good lu-" Grace was cut off by the sound of silence as Lance entered the server room.

As far as grand rooms for storing the evil deeds of a corrupt company goes, this one was a little lacklustre. Also like the server room: clinically white with a sort of desk and console in the centre. The room was small, and, in various sections of the walling that didn't have the white panelling, there was a server node. It looked like it was meant to be added to when the need arose.

The plan was simple enough. All Lance had to do was

take the potentially incriminating files outside of the signal deadzone using the uplink drive that Wolf had provided. Once that was done, Wolf could connect to the uplink and download the files onto his own device in the van. Then, Lance could get out of there.

Lance sat down at the console and thought about inserting the drive immediately, but chose to wait a bit. He didn't want to set off any system alerts before finding the batch of files he thought best to steal. And so, instead, he took out his trusty fob, and scanned himself into the system.

The words: 'WELCOME MR. COPS' appeared in dark lettering, and moments later, he was on a desktop screen. Lance set to work, calling up the search box and beginning his search. It was not an easy task, not being a tech genius and not *really* knowing what categories and subcategories to investigate to find his mark, Lance decided on the 'look everywhere and pray it's here' method. He began opening folders and files at random. He would continue doing so until he found something related to The Expireds, at which point he would insert the uplink and copy the entire folder's contents. He could go through the data dump at home, not here.

It took what seemed like ages, but eventually his luck kicked in. He opened a document and was confronted with an image of a pale blue face. Its eyes were closed, and it looked... peaceful. The image might have shocked someone else, but it was something Lance was not unfamiliar with. At times in his career (both in the military and his current legal profession), he had witnessed autopsy files. This face was that of a young, mid-twenties male, and it was exactly the kind of file he was looking for. Despite the ticking timer playing in his head, he opened a few other files. He did not take the time to read, but he saw what were unmistakably medical reports, and other forensic images. Everything watermarked with the Fortune Limited logo. This was the folder he needed.

Lance fumbled in his pocket for the uplink, found it, and shoved it into a port. It opened its drive for him to see visually where to copy files, and for a split second, Lance saw one file already on the device. He was sure it had said something to the effect of 'sleeper', but he could not be certain because as quickly as he saw it, so did it disappear. Lance chalked it up to the system file errors, and returned to his task. He had to copy this huge folder, and he had to do it fast.

Lance dragged the folder into the drive, and then sat back in faux relaxation. There was little else to do in this case. The progress bar of the upload started slowly, but it seemed to pick up speed. Wolf wasn't lying when he said it wouldn't take long. Clearly, this device had state of the art copying software. Within a minute or two, the copying was complete, and Lance made a quick check to ensure it had indeed uploaded onto the removable drive successfully. It was, so he could head out.

Lance lifted himself from his seated position, and headed towards the door. He opened it, and was immediately confronted by the sound of a wailing siren.

I'm found out. It's over.

Chapter 31
Wolf

Wolf dabbed away a bead of sweat that had begun forming and reforming for the past few minutes. At first, he regarded the bead with slight incredulity, as he hardly ever felt anxious or stressed in that way – aside from his uncharacteristic outbursts late at night. That was different. After the fourth and fifth dab, Wolf had ventured from mild curiosity about his mental condition to plain annoyance. How was he to do his job if he constantly had a distraction like this? Again, he swiped the bead away.

Lance had just entered the dead zone, so now, Wolf had to wait and monitor. His mind wandered briefly to things he knew to be true: what he was meant to do. Things known to only himself, and of which Locks, Marc, and Lance had zero knowledge. He had his own plan. He had his own needs and his subterfuge – which seemed necessary and understandable at the time. But now, it just seemed... wrong. Even so, he had maintained his commitment. He had to watch out for himself, but still...

"Wolf," said Locks, interrupting Wolf's many thoughts, "two more guards entered the lobby, it seems they came from the service entrance."

"Copy that," confirmed Wolf as he called up the lobby cameras.

Sure enough, Locks was right. 'Two extra bogeys on the map', as his former sergeant would say.

"Locks, there's a high probability that Lance is going to trip a wire somewhere in that server room. It would be foolish to believe otherwise."

"So, what's the plan?"

Wolf clacked his keys and surveyed the building, "Can you have a look at your blueprints? I'm looking at live footage. Try and see if you can find some place that might also have some extreme importance to Fortune."

"Will do," confirmed Locks and Wolf saw her, in the camera he had trained on her constantly, taking out her device to do what she was told.

It's so nice when your team just takes instruction and doesn't backchat, thought Wolf.

It was the first time Locks had just done what she was told.

Wolf continued parsing through the camera feeds, looking for something. He found a great many empty hallways and lobbies, a few bored receptionists per floor, and vast call centres and office floors teeming with employees. Nothing was out of the ordinary, nothing that he could use as an excuse to call the SWAT team.

Then, Locks came through.

"Uh, there's Dr. Marlowe's private office suite?"

Wolf grunted, mostly to himself, but also as an affirmation that that was a good lead.

"I'll check the logs to see if he bothered to show up to work today," said Wolf, as a log list found its way into view.

He scanned the entries a few times over. There were a lot of employees, but few doctorates and fewer Marlowes. It seemed to Wolf that the good doctor was taking a personal day, or was just tardy.

"Negative," Wolf confirmed, "that means we can try and direct traffic that way instead of Lance-" Wolf was suddenly distracted by the text comms popping up on the dashboard to his right, "Shit, I was right."

"What?" probed Locks.

"Lance must've triggered a silent alarm."

"Crap."

"Luckily, given how long he was in there before the alarm triggered, I think we can safely assume it was triggered by the files copying to an external source. Which means that he will be out very soon."

"So, what are we going to do? The two extras down here look like they're going up to investigate."

Wolf scanned the cameras again and confirmed Locks' suspicions. It seemed a few – not all, but a few – security personnel were making their way slowly but determinedly towards floor five. He had to act now. It was a simple manoeuvre, but it was a big one, too.

Distracting the enemy with something more tantalising.

Wolf sprung to work, feeding in some hints via a bot on the security comms system, implying there was someone spotted on the top floor: Dr. Marlowe's office's floor. He let a few security employees chat a little about that possibility as he opened up a console to the cameras. Now, he wanted to make a splash in their system. He needed to let them know someone was tampering with it, but he had to be good enough to leave no trace of it being him. He called up the private office suite's cameras.

Of course the Good Doctor doesn't have surveillance in his rooms, he agonised for a second, before finding enough cameras around the offices' entrances to work with.

Systematically, he began shutting them down, and as he did so, he glanced back at the text comms. It was slowly starting to buzz with confusion, mentions of getting eyes upstairs, and questions about where the boss was.

Very little mention of the slight disturbance on floor five, now.

Wolf keyed up his final play, and his finger hovered over it. He was waiting. Any second now. He needed to play his final discombobulating move. Lance had to be done by now. He grunted and pressed the button.

Loud sirens immediately sounded, the lobby camera became flushed with people looking worried and scared, and very quickly heading for the exit in panic. Wolf had set off the sirens on the top few floors, hopefully diverting all security personnel up there. After all, that was where *all* of the higher ups sat, and kept Fortune up and running. It *had* to warrant a good sweep by the guards.

Suddenly, the team's shared folder on his system started up, and hundreds of files began popping into existence. Lance had returned, the uplink had connected to his receiver – and bounced a few times across the city, of course, for privacy reasons.

"Leave guys, the files will get to Wolf and you can finish the job. Let them-" Lance began his exit speech, but Locks was having none of it.

"We set off the alarms, Lance, get your ass out of there. Now!"

Lance seemed to understand because he said nothing, but very soon, Wolf saw his disguised body flash across the cameras. In and out of the server corridors, past the entrance where the bored woman had apparently left her post and down the passageway, into the stairwell.

Now, was his next mission. Wolf's hands flew onto the keys once again as he began to hack their surveillance all out, doing his best to manually delete all camera footage from that day, starting with the most incriminating, and working backwards.

"Locks, you better-"

"It was chaos in there guys, I made my exit. Lance, I'm just across the street, no more guards seem to be entering from the main entrance, it's a pretty frenzied, but straight line out."

"Roger that," said Lance, and Wolf could hear him panting from his hurried gait, "Grace, get out of there, I'm already in the lobby, I can see the exit. Meet you at home, remember-"

"Take the back roads, got it, see you two back at base!" Locks sounded.

Moments later, Wolf had a mild jump scare as Lance ripped open the van driver side door and hopped in. He sighed deeply and quickly, and began fiddling with the controls. Wolf felt the van lurch. He had to stay on the system just a little longer; the last few camera feeds had to be wiped.

"Got the files?" queried Lance, almost aggressively.

"Yes, yes."

"Then we go," Lance shifted the van and peeled off into the busy street that was very soon going to be flooded with traffic from the commotion at headquarters.

Wolf knew they needed to get out but he was not quite done… his connection was lost.

"Shit," said Wolf. Lance glanced briefly back as he drove, shooting Wolf a quick questioning look, "I can't tell if I got all the cameras, I got most of them, but not all. At least I think-"

"There's little we can do now," said Lance, committed, "if we get caught, I'll take the fall. At least we have the files. We might not even need to worry about being caught!"

Wolf just grunted. Lance drove home.

**

Wolf knew he had to act fast, but, even so, he hesitated. Should he really do this?

Lance and he had arrived back home before Locks. Lance, still rather high on adrenaline, had flitted to the kitchen, saying something about him needing a drink… and a shower. Wolf had found a seat in the lounge, his laptop perched atop his lap.

He was looking at the data dump they had just recovered. Stolen, rather. He knew what this meant for Lance, what it meant for Marc, and what it meant for Locks. He knew it, but, even so, he had to look out for himself.

Lance and Grace both had lives and livelihoods. He had neither. And, although he had started to like Lance, less so Locks, he still had an evolutionary craving, desire, a raw need to put himself first. He knew what the consequences of his actions would be. Marc would become one of The Expired. Wolf knew he would have Marc's blood on his hands. Even so, his baser instincts came into play. He needed to survive, and although he didn't mind Marc's company, if it was a choice between himself or Marc to stand in front of the firing squad, Wolf would choose Marc every time.

The stage was already set. His uplink had planted the tiniest of codes into the main server at Fortune with a very simple command and execution protocol. In his Twilight Year, it would activate, search the server for all records of Wolfgang Ashley Goode, and permanently delete them. He would be wiped from the system, and move countries. He would escape expiration, because there would be no records of him ever having been a client. Over the years, he would plant similar trojans into the simpler systems to truly wipe his slate clean when the time came. But his application would be the most secure, and he had needed a team to get into the server room. He hadn't even thought of this plan much before meeting Lance and Locks.

The plan, unfortunately, hinged on a very simple variable. If Wolf wanted to continue receiving cheques in the mail, if he wanted to live a relatively comfortable life, Fortune Limited would have to continue to operate. Lance and Locks were determined to stop that from happening, and so their plan had to fail. And the only foolproof way to do that was staring Wolf right in the face.

The dull blue light of his laptop illuminated his torn face. He heard Lance clinging some glasses in the kitchen. Wolf's gaze returned to his screen, his pointer hovering over a prompt waiting to be executed: 'PERMANENTLY DELETE'.

Wolf knew what he was doing, he knew the implications, he knew it would haunt him in the future, even if only a little, but even so, his mind was made up. He had to choose himself, friends were not always forever, and he had already condemned many to death in the past. What was one more?

For the first time, Wolf *allowed* a few lone tears to escape his otherwise barren ducts. He knew he was being a monster, but it was his life or Marc's. He took a deep breath, and sentenced Marc to death.

Chapter 32

Lance

The morning creeped in slowly over the rolling hills that occupied the outskirts of the Villa's eastern boundary. From the balcony of his luxury suite, Marc could see quite a few other occupants doing something similar to what he was. He counted at least twenty-four people of varying age and apparent social status standing on terraces, balconies, and in gardens, all looking out into the distance. They were waiting for the sunrise; living each day to the fullest, because, for some of them, it would be their last chance.

Marc held his coffee mug in one hand and tightened his silk robe with the other; there was a strangely cold gust of wind picking up. He spotted a man. He could not see him in great detail, but he assumed it must have been someone quite important, or famous, because he too resided in one of the presidential luxury suites. The man was wearing a similar robe, and Marc could make out a glass of red wine in his hands. Some people lived life to the fullest in different ways, apparently. Marc sidled back a bit, now suddenly very conscious that he was probably being watched by someone in the wings of his own stage. Over the past few days, he had become more of a recluse to the public, whereas in the past he'd been quite the people person. His impending and inevitable dreamless sleep made him take stock of his life. It altered his behaviour slightly, and the motivation for what he did on a day-to-day basis.

Marc sipped his coffee and caught the first glimpse of the rays of the rising sun. They illuminated the roofs of the Villa apartments closest to the boundary first, but not before they cast a beautiful halo-like glow through the grass of the hills beyond the Villa. Marc smiled in admiration of nature. In a world so polluted and overrun, seeing a scene like this was extremely rare. He had only seen it himself but a few times. He was glad to be able to see it every morning during his stay here.

After all, enjoying and taking in the beauty of life was the point of your Final Stay at the Villa. All apartments were luxurious, however, in true 'Animal Farm' style, some apartments were more luxurious than others. While Fortune claimed to care about all its clients, everyone knew that, regardless of looming death, everyone wanted the chance to be one of 'The Guests' at the Villa, not just someone who was given one of the smaller luxury apartments because it was their Twilight Year and there was an obligation to be fulfilled. Certain clients wanted to go out with a bang, like they were royalty and even paid extra to be upgraded. Everyone else was sorted according to an in-depth algorithmic list from most famous to least. They were then housed accordingly. Marc was lucky enough that, with his natural talent and the Fortune boost, he had done well in the public eye.

Marc's body suddenly went cold, and his vision dimmed slightly as his consciousness attempted to recede somewhere else. It was a peculiar feeling; one with which he was now all too familiar. As far as he understood, it was a culminating feeling of stress, fear, anxiety, and the idea of the fast approaching unknown. This feeling had been coming regularly, ever since he learnt his fate really was sealed. Though, he knew how to treat himself: he just had to talk himself back out of the hole his mind wanted him to fall into.

I'm here, this is how it is, he thought methodically, *there's nothing to be done. I'd rather focus on the here and now.*

Marc felt that attempting rational thoughts while in this cloud of emotion was the best remedy. Very soon, the feeling subsided, but he knew it would be back.

Marc moved over to a deck chair and took a seat; the sun was now fully visible. He looked around. Nothing seemed able to upstage the bright rays peeking up over the horizon. Everyone around – whether they be holding alcoholic drinks or morning brews – sat, watching the sun's performance. Entranced. Marc found himself planning a hike later that day, after his visitors came and went. When he was alone with his thoughts again.

***

Marc had just finished his shower and was climbing into his casual clothes for the day when there was a knock on the door. Marc took a deep breath and slipped on some sandals as he hurried from his ensuite, through the bedroom, through the lounge, into the atrium of his penthouse, towards the door. Though he knew who it was, he instinctively used the peep hole to make sure. Sure enough, there were three bodies on the other side of the mahogany door: two women and a man. His family.

He put on a smile and unlocked the door, swinging it open with a bit too much gusto. Anita, Jan, and Lance looked at him a little confused with his flourish, but said nothing about it, though Jan did manage a small smile at the silliness of her brother.

"Hi guys, come in."

Jan entered first and proceeded to give Marc the biggest hug of his life. He could hardly breathe. Anita entered next and gave him a similar one, but it felt different. Not that it felt bad, or lacking love, just that, unlike Jan's, which seemed filled with some strange sense of false optimism, his mother's was filled with a heavy feeling of dread. Marc understood why, naturally. She was hugging a dead person walking, and not just any dead person walking. It was her youngest son. Marc returned the heartfelt hug.

Lance entered last, and hugged Marc too, but his embrace felt the strangest of all. Almost empty, as if Lance was not really there with them. Indeed, when Marc pulled away, he noted that Lance had the look of someone who was deep in thought, but desperately trying to hide it. Marc knew better than to press his brother, so instead, he showed them all around the penthouse, culminating with a tea made by the staff downstairs.

They all sat around the coffee table, mugs in hand, a vast spread of pastries and cakes largely untouched before them. They barely spoke, and when they did, it was nothing but mere pleasantries. What did Marc expect, really? He was at the end of the script. There was not much more to say. Everything that needed to be said was being said through glances and facial expressions: they had lost. And they were here to witness the consequences of that loss.

Marc looked to Lance again, who was staring off into the distance. A pool of tears formed in his eyes. Marc fought hard not to show he was affected. He didn't want to show his family how scared he really was. He knew there was no hope, and that they had lost. They knew that he was scared, but he would not let them think it would get the best of him. He wanted to be strong for them, just like he had been when he'd signed up in the first place, all those years ago.

He could have easily spiralled when he'd learned of Lance's defeat. When his brother had shown up at his door a few days earlier, balling his eyes out. He could have spiralled when he was told that they'd had the files, that they *could* have made a dent, it *could* all have been for something, but Fortune had encrypted a final failsafe that latched on to all copied files from the server, causing them to be deleted forever. He could have spiralled when he learnt that all the planning had been for nothing, when he learnt that he would die without making an impact on future Expirations. He could have spiralled, but he didn't.

He had made a conscious decision to fight that urge. He did this because, if he didn't, it meant that Fortune had won this outright game he had once been so eager to play. He knew better now, he knew who the bad guys were, and he knew that they expected him and the others sentenced to death to be wallowing in self-pity.

Marc would not give them the satisfaction.

Fortune played at being a humane company with only the longevity of the human race and Earth in mind, but in reality, Marc had finally come to see it for what it really was: a power hungry enterprise that fed and profited on the desperation of the very population it claimed to love so much.

Marc may have hardened his resolve, but his family apparently had not, and as he led them back out the door, wished them a safe journey home, and reminded them of his date in two days time, he could not shake the feeling that the farewell hug Lance gave him was less of a farewell *from* him, but rather *to* him, from *Marc*. As they stood there in that strange embrace, Lance whispered, very quietly, for only Marc to hear:

"Please don't blame yourself."

And with that, Lance disengaged, and pulled himself back over the threshold of the doorway. Marc could see the face of a man whose mind was suddenly made up as the door shut. Marc was left staring at it closed for a very long time, wondering what on earth he'd just witnessed. He knew his brother's faces very well, and Marc was convinced that he had just seen Lance make a decision.

Chapter 33

Grace

Grace sat on her couch staring into the void. She still could not believe it. They had done everything right, everything had gone so well, until it didn't. She could not help but replay that afternoon in her head over and over again, trying to make sense of something that, quite plainly, would never make sense. At least, not in the way Grace would like. She would like it to be some strange twist in fate that meant something else would bring down Fortune Limited. But of course, that was nothing other than wishful thinking. In reality, they'd been defeated. They had lost all the data they put so much effort into retrieving. That they'd lost for some silly little failsafe. One tiny program that no one, not even the great hacker Wolf, had detected. One tiny program had left them with nothing to work with, thus ensuring the survival of the company.

She was past crying. She was over it. She felt like nothing she could ever do would make any sort of impact any more. She felt like she had let her family down; let her father down. She hadn't avenged his death. She had not stopped any further Expirations. She had failed, and eventually, Thabo would catch on and realise she was a failure. She would be a failure in everyone's eyes.

The TV played some dated old sitcom while she ruminated in her self pity, and if she was being honest, loneliness. She had not spoken to Lance since the ordeal. What was there to say?

Sorry I couldn't help save your brother from being murdered?

It didn't quite have the best ring to it. In any case, why would he want to chat with her now? He had bigger things to think about, he had to spend the time he had left with Marc. Grace understood that. She understood the assignment from the get go: they were a mutually beneficial arrangement, friendly but not friends. At best, they would meet up once a year and laugh about how they took down a multi-millionaire murderous enterprise, at worst (which incidentally, was the current situation) they would go their separate ways, defeated with no thoughts about how to fix it.

Grace found herself falling asleep in her stupor. Normally, she'd fight it, but she had no fight left in her, so she let the sleep come. She welcomed the silence from her own thoughts. Thabo was asleep himself. He would call if he needed her. She hoped he wouldn't tonight. Right now, she just wanted to sleep.

***

It was the crunching of the front door that awakened her, then the screaming from Thabo. Grace leapt from her seat in a daze, not fully awake yet, but fully aware of the need to help her brother. She had almost forgotten the first sound until it came again. A loud crunch and cracking from the door, then a sharp, metallic, pop told Grace that her door was no longer an effective barrier to the outside world. Caught between two base instincts, Grace had no idea what to do. Should she go and check on her little brother, or should she investigate what was trying to get into her home, her (until very recently) safespace?

Fortunately, the decision was made for Grace when she was suddenly surrounded by a Fortune security detail, armed with weapons, all trained on her. They were dressed in all black, with masks. She couldn't tell what their faces looked like. For a split second, she wondered if they were even human. They encircled her like she was an infection to be rooted out, a danger to all she came into contact with. It didn't matter that she was in her light pink pyjamas and slippers.

Grace lifted her hands up slowly, knowing full well that a sudden movement might warrant a barrage of bullets from a trigger-happy guard. As she raised her hands, she felt and saw her chest light up with red laser points. Her heart rate picked up. Her breathing shallowed, and fear began to settle in. She would have to do whatever they wanted her to do.

"Grace?!" called Thabo from his room, alone and helpless, "What's going on? Grace?!"

Grace looked at the detail around her, trying to find the ringleader. She wanted confirmation that she could call out to her brother. She wanted to calm him down, if she

could. But none of the foot soldiers gave any indication
that they had any authority. Grace was about to throw
caution to the wind when a man in a suit overlaid with
tactical wear walked into her living room with the all the
poise of someone who loved his power but hated his job
– rounding up riff-raff, as it were. He was a tall man, with
a pale face and eyes that looked like they were already
bored. Clearly, he was the one in charge.

"Ag," the man exclaimed in frustration, "How is one to
breathe in this thing?" he tugged on his bulletproof vest,
and let the clasp go, "Stand down, she's no threat to us."

At his order, the detail lowered their weapons, and
switched off their pointers, but Grace was quick to notice
that none of them went to the 'at ease' position. They all
stood around her with rifles in both hands, ready to bring
them into position again at the slightest nod from their
commanding... pencil pusher? The man had removed his
vest entirely, and flung it over the shoulder of one of the
guards. He meticulously straightened his suit and gave a
sinisterly triumphant smile that was aimed at Grace.

"Grace Makeba, I presume?"

"That's me."

The smile widened.

"You are under company arrest by order of Fortune
Limited, and sanctioned by the Province Police in
accordance with section two hundred of the New
Constitution. I am obliged to tell you that you have the
right to remain silent, and that anything you say could be
held against you in a court of law. Also, urgh," he really
was bored, "You get the picture, Ms Makeba, I don't need
to read out all the lines do I?"

A long pause sat between them as Grace slowly realised
that his question was not actually rhetorical, he truly

wanted her permission to not have to read them all to her.

"Uh, no, whatever, read them later?" Grace felt like this was not his job, and that he had just been chosen at random to bring her in. Perhaps the 'bringing her in' part was the fun part, the part that warranted that evil smile finding its home on his face again.

"Excellent, well then, come with us," the man turned to leave, but Grace stopped him.

"Under what grounds? You can't just take me."

The man, who had turned his back, ready to exit the door that didn't exist anymore, sighed, and with his back still turned, he flicked his hand. Clearly, this was a move interpreted by one of his goons, because the one closest to Grace produced a device with a still-image displayed on it. He shoved it in Grace's face.

The image was unmistakable to her. It was her. Sitting, on the phone, at the Fortune Limited Headquarters' subpar coffee shop. Grace made a mental punch towards wherever Wolf was at that moment in time. Clearly, he had been sloppy. But at least she was disguised in the photo, so there was something she could fight.

"Who is this?"

Now the man turned on his heels, frustrated with how long this was taking. He clearly had hoped to come back successful much sooner than he was going to.

"Don't play dumb, Ms. Makeba," he said, "a change of clothes and hairstyle is not going to fool us. Who do you think we are? Perhaps, had the rest of the camera footage not been deleted, we would have all your buddies, but Fortune is happy to settle for you. We have been waiting for a good reason to take you in, in any case."

"I could be there for a drink," started Grace, she was grasping at straws.

"It's possible," conceded the man, "but in full disguise on the day of mass disruption? I don't think it's a coincidence, though you are free to argue as such at your trial."

And with that, Grace understood the question of her arrest was over. She was going with them, but she had another issue to worry about: Thabo.

"Please," started Grace, "my brother, he'll be all alone. He's got *Skelatis*, he's helpless."

"We know, Ms. Makeba," said the man curtly, "and we have a caretaker coming for him as well. He will be put up in one of our monitoring facilities, he will be just fine. I would worry more about yourself, if I were in your shoes."

This answer threw Grace for a loop. They weren't just taking her, they were taking Thabo as well. Who knew how they would treat him? Who knew if he would survive the agony of the journey? What sort of monitoring facilities did Fortune have?

Suddenly, all the fight that had been left in Grace dissipated. She physically slumped, and one of the guards had to catch her. The suited man in front of her smiled widely. He knew he had her. She had failed on all counts. The mission, avenging her father, protecting her family, honouring the family. Grace felt all hope drain out of her. She felt stupid and childish for ever thinking that she could make a difference.

The guards led her out of her apartment. She walked like a zombie. She took no notice of her nosey neighbours muttering to themselves what they thought about her. All she could think about was how stupid she'd been, and what the future had in store for her and her brother. Would they ever see each other again? What had she done? Why couldn't she have left the past in the past? Now that everything she had was crumbling around her, she struggled to think what the point of her escapades even were. She wished she'd never met Lance, she wished she had wallowed in the defeat of her own revenge attempt. Perhaps if she had, she would have come to terms with the past and could be making something of her life. Instead, there she was, being shoved into a Fortune fortified van, on her way to being detained, while her other two accomplices had escaped.

Chapter 34

Lance

Lance fidgeted with his shirt button as he leant back in his office chair. His face wore a forlorn and distant expression. In his other hand was the post-it note that had been on his board for nearly nine years. The same post-it note that Marc had queried only a few weeks ago. Lying on his desk was a glass tumbler filled with a rather unsophisticated amount of whiskey. A bottle of the stuff stood unceremoniously close by, and it was only one quarter full. He'd had quite a few shots already. Anyone walking into the room would be able to immediately see that Lance was spiralling.

There were salty lines streaking from his eyes, dried just in time to be wet again by a fresh, slow, trickle. Lance had an impossible decision to make. Well, to most people it would have been impossible, unfortunately for Lance, it was a simple choice for him. True, it was one he had put off for the longest time, in case another possibility emerged. In case a miracle happened, but as he was starting to realise, miracles were for the movies.

He had made his decision, he was just hesitating to pull the trigger.

Eventually, he could not stall any longer. He threw the post-it note on the table, and reached for his device. In his drunken stupor, he flailed a bit, but managed to grab onto it. It was further into the table than he'd thought. A fresh batch of silent tears began to flow as he unlocked his device, and messaged the number he'd already memorised from the third year. It was a once-off opportunity, and he didn't want to lose the number to the elements, or risk losing his brother.

His text read simply: 'LANCE MASON, I'LL DO IT, PLEASE'.

Then, he hit send.

***

Nine Years Earlier

A younger, more naive version of Lance sat in the grand foyer of the penthouse offices of the most powerful man in at least the continent, but possibly the world. He had not yet begun his journey overseas to serve in the war in the European Union. He had barely started his studies to become a lawyer. In fact, the notion he was going to do both simultaneously had not quite yet crossed his mind. He was, however, fueled with the same determination as a Lance from any other age. Whether he was sat in that penthouse or years later drinking whiskey amid tears, alone in his office.

He was waiting patiently because, for some reason, he had been granted an audience with the Overlord.

Why would I be granted such an 'honour'? His mind raced and he glanced again around the room. *Perhaps my constant pleading with Fortune had panned out in my favour?* It was possible, surely. He had been hounding Fortune every chance he had. What's one client, really? Perhaps he was summoned here for a strict talking to, but one that would result in a show of mercy and a dissolvement of Marc's contract.

Sure, Marc won't be pleased, but it'll be in his best interest. He'll see the light eventually. He'll know *why I did this. Scratch that, he knows why I am doing this.* Lance took a deep breath. He shifted uncomfortably in the armchair the receptionist had shown him to. He had almost convinced himself of his triumph, but even his young brain could feel that that line of rationalisation was probably not the right one. And if that was the case… why then was he here?

"Mr. Mason, Doctor Marlowe will see you now," the pretty but soul-wretched personal assistant said over her desk to Lance.

Lance nodded a nervous affirmative, and practically leapt up from his seat. He didn't mean to seem eager, but his adrenaline was kicking in. Now, some other scenarios were entering his mind.

What if I was summoned here to be reprimanded? A guard could come and take me away and lock me up somewhere for attempting to defy Fortune. He felt his pulse quicken. *I may be a nobody, but a mosquito is a tiny insect that people squash without thinking. Am I the mosquito buzzing around Fortune's head?*

Lance shuddered when he realised that that scenario was more believable than the one of him being let off the hook.

Lance had little choice now. He could look like a fool and make a hasty run for it, but the tall doors in front of him were slowly opening, allowing him to enter. Quite frankly, despite his racing heartbeat, his curiosity was getting the best of him. Why had he been called here?

And so, Lance took a step forward, and then another, until his movement could have been described as a stuttered walk in a straight line. He was nervous, he'd rather not be there, but at the same time, he wanted to know. His movement stopped when he heard the doors hiss as they shut behind him.

Lance was standing in the most opulent, oddly tastefully designed office he had ever seen. It was a large space, adorned with some couches to the left around a coffee table, all signature Fortune colour coding, but somehow, it worked in this room. To his right was a mini kitchen and refreshment bar, and in the centre, silhouetted by the bright daylight shining through the wall-to-ceiling windows, was a large desk where the figure of a man stood, facing the view. The man's figure was imposing, he was tall and broad shouldered. He stood with his hands crossed casually behind his back.

Dr. Marlowe spoke without turning. His voice was deep, strong, and hollow. It was as if a dead tree was speaking to him. Though Lance could sense a touch of an attempt to sound pleasant on his inflections. Just a touch.

"Mr. Mason, welcome," Dr. Marlowe began, "please have a seat."

Lance only noticed now that there were two armchairs in front of the desk before him. He did as ordered, and sat down. Dr. Marlowe remained standing. Looking like a king gazing down at the common folk.

"Mr. Mason, I have been made aware that you are a bit of a... shall we say, rabble rouser," stated Dr. Marlowe. Lance squirmed slightly in his seat, hoping that the doctor didn't notice his fear. "You have been bombarding my employees at almost every level of my organisation, in fact I believe I received an email myself. Bold, I'll admit." Dr. Marlowe then turned to meet his guest, "I do wonder how you managed that, I can only assume one of my employees had a lapse of judgement..." his voice trailed off. In the trail, Lance could almost hear the crying of an employee being told his services were no longer required.

Dr. Marlowe took this time to sit down in his own chair, and lace his fingers together. He regarded Lance as a cat might regard a mouse – or mosquito.

"In any case, your devotion to your brother I believe is commendable," said the doctor, surprising Lance so much that an utterance of disbelief left his mouth.

Dr. Marlowe's lips made the slightest of upwards turns, if only for a moment.

"Oh yes, I am capable of compassion, I'm not all stone," he said this, but still, Lance doubted it.

"As I was saying, your efforts to free your brother from his legally bound contract have been admirable, and I do commend you on your determined nature. Mr. Mason is lucky to have you as a sibling. We all would've wanted one like you," Dr. Marlowe now shifted his weight. For a brief moment he appeared uncomfortable.

"I invited you here for three reasons, mostly to as I have now, commend you on your struggles, but to also remind you that the contract your brother, uh-"

"Marc, sir," said Lance bravely.

"Marc, yes, the contract Marc signed is fully binding. It

really cannot be broken. You are aware of the nature of our business, are you not?"

Lance said nothing, but his look said everything.

"Yes, so you know that we have a duty to the human race, to the world really, to do our jobs. We offer a service and in exchange, yes, we do ask for the ultimate price. But in the end, it is the choice of The Expired. Free will, Mr. Mason, is not something to mess around with. Your brother, Marc, made the choice of his own volition, he was in sound body and mind according to two separate psychological assessments. He knew what he was doing, and he is reaping the reward as we speak. Your whole family is too, in fact."

Lance knew this would all be brought up. Legalities trussed up as morality.

"Frankly, you are interfering with Marc's free will," continued Dr. Marlowe, "Need I remind you that all access and funding he – and your whole family as a stipulation of his personalised contract – has would be lifted should his contract be up? You are starting university, are you not? I presume you would need his money to pay for it. With a contract annulled, that would end. Your sister would have to go back to the school she was at previously. I did some digging and, unfortunately, it is a terribly underfunded school and slated to be demolished in just over a year. And your mother? What would she do?"

Lance stared at the man. He had no words. Dr. Marlowe was taking them all.

"The fact of the matter, Mr. Mason, is that your brother signed up with us for a very specific reason. He wanted to help see his family prosper in the wake of your tragic loss. And yet you sit here, attempting to reverse his sacrifice? Your heart is in the right place, my boy, but for the wrong reason. You can fight Fortune as much as you want, but the contract will never be voided. We have a duty, as I said. This world is too small for us all. We need volunteers to allow the rest of us a chance at saving it let alone to live here on it as well. Your brother has chosen to be one such volunteer, and as a result, we are rewarding him as much as we can. Certainly rest assured, Mr. Mason, no holds are barred. We will do everything in our power to fulfil his contract's associated goals."

Lance felt like he was being lectured by an annoying uncle at a Sunday lunch. He was being told things he already knew, and things that had to date, not convinced him to halt his crusade. He huffed in his seat. Then he stood up.

Following his movements, Dr. Marlowe continued, "I do hope we have an understanding of how things work now."

"Understood," said Lance sourly as he turned to leave.

"Don't you want to hear the third thing?"

Lance stopped in his tracks, and slowly turned around.

"I said I had three things to tell you. One was to commend you, another was to remind you of your brother's choices and the third…"

"The third?"

Dr. Marlowe smiled properly now, though it was laced with evil intent.

"A one time offer. A direct line to my private device," Dr. Marlowe took out a pen and a post-it note, and scribbled down his number, "Keep it safe, you lose this, you lose the offer. I will not give it again. You share this contact with anyone and the offer is rescinded."

Dr. Marlowe stretched out his arm, and let the post-it hover in space for a few moments before Lance reluctantly took it from him. A chill spread across Lance's body as he held the post-it.

"What's the offer?"

Dr. Marlowe smiled with his pursed lips again, before he said casually, "Any time, before Marc's Expiration, all you need to do is text me through that number your name and accept the offer. Very few people have this number, Mr. Mason, much less this offer. I will know what the acceptance means."

"But what is the offer?"

"Why, Mr. Mason, the offer is simple. You for him. My investors are happy, Marc lives, only you… well, I'm sure you get the picture." Marlowe leaned back in his desk chair, a small grimace flashed across his steel gazed.

Lance stood frozen in place. He wouldn't be able to move even if he wanted to. He had a way to save Marc. One that was a death sentence for himself.

"Now, goodbye Mr. Mason, I have a two o'clock, and I am already late."

Lance looked at the number for what seemed an eternity before he looked abck up at the apparent judge and executioner. He look deep breath, turned on his heels and left.

***

A text came through Lance's device and read simply: 'ALL IN ORDER'.

Lance let out a long breath and flopped back down into his chair. His eyes closed shut, and he fell into a deep sleep.

Chapter 35
Lance

The next day was his last. Lance knew he had sealed his fate. No going back now. He'd been sentenced… by his own hand. However, in the clarity of the morning sun and breeze, Lance found that he was remarkably at peace with his choice. He had done his best. He had done everything he could. Nothing had succeeded besides this last ditch effort. His brother was going to live.

Moreover, the contract was not technically broken, so anything already agreed-upon would remain in place, and nothing legalised would be jeopardised. Lance had long since had a will drawn up. Perhaps not in accordance with Fortune Limited standards, but despite all evidence to the contrary, he thought of Dr. Marlowe as, at least, a principled man. He had to know Lance had made a huge commitment, and he strangely fully believed Dr. Marlowe would honour Lance's dying wishes. After all, the doctor had won – whatever that game he was playing. The least he could do was let the Masons move on from the whole affair.

Lance's day was less than ideal. He had to go into Fortune Limited headquarters, once again, this time as himself, and fill out an enormous amount of paperwork. He had to sign over his will and testament from his previous set of lawyers to Fortune's, he had to, in-effect, sign an addendum to Marc's contract, which Lance read meticulously to ensure he was not condemning them both. Eventually, the bureaucrats were satisfied, and Lance was given the rest of the afternoon to set his social affairs in order. This was where Lance faltered. He couldn't say goodbye, and he wouldn't. Not until the last minute. He could not risk Marc doing something crazy in these few hours before the execution. He confirmed with Dr. Marlowe's office that the swap would remain a secret until the very moment the execution took place. Marc could not know his contract had been edited.

Instead of doing his familial rounds, he decided to go to Gretchen's one last time. He sat at the booth where he had plotted with Grace, only a month or two before. He tried to call Grace, because, despite everything, they were friends, but he felt betrayed when all he kept getting was voicemail. Lance even tried to contact Wolf, but like Grace, he was uncontactable. He felt like he had been culled form their contact lists, like one does on their social media profiles. It felt harsh and he felt heavy when he thought too much about it. So sudden. His thoughts dwelled a lot on Wolf. Perhaps he was wrong about the connection they had had. Perhaps it was all nothing, just people slammed into a desperate situation filled with a collective hate and thirst for justice.

It mattered so little now. If they had joined him, what would they have said? Would they have tried to change his mind? Surely, he was doing them a better service by not calling. Let them think he didn't care for them, because the opposite would leave them with a murdered friend. But they had left him, so it was all academic, in any case. Lance just sat in the bar for most of the night, nursing his beer and thinking. Thinking that, even by just a little, he had succeeded.

***

Morning came and Lance was up early. He ran through his morning routine as normally as possible. But he couldn't help but think that everything he did was for the last time. He would not be coming back to the bathroom, he would not be brushing his teeth again, he would not be eating breakfast – why was he eating breakfast anyway?

Lance had not lost his resolve. He had wired his head to see it as the inevitable conclusion. He was always willing to die for his family, and now he was being called to do so. He was going to his death proud that he did what he could to protect them.

Lance drove to his mother's house; it was still morning, Expirations happened at midday, usually. His was nothing special. He collected his sister and mother, both of whom wore black in honour of him, though they didn't know. Jan muttered a hello and a consoling word or two to Anita, but, for the most part, the car ride to The Villa was silent, except for Anita's barely controlled sobbing. Lance felt it not difficult to keep his fate a secret. He knew that, no matter what, his mother would still be wailing hysterically come twelve o'clock. The shrieks just wouldn't be for Marc.

They approached The Villa, Marc was already standing outside, waiting for them to pick him up. Lance sidled up to the pavement and unlocked the doors. Marc climbed in, they had left the shotgun seat available for him. Marc and Lance exchanged weak smiles, and Lance noticed red rings under his eyes. He had been crying, but clearly made an effort to stop for his family. Lance tapped Marc's knee gently, as if to tell him he would be okay. At least Lance could feel like he told him… before.

Again, the drive from The Villa was mostly silent. Anita was holding Marc's shoulder from behind, and Lance felt a natural yet unreasonable tug of jealousy that he was not being held. Of course, for that to happen, he would have to tell them. And he wouldn't.

The beautiful rolling hills turned into industria, and soon, the lanes became congested with other Expirees and their families. It was easy to forget that Marc's situation was not isolated. Hundreds of Expirees expired per year. The dreary large building that began to loom in front of them was a stark reminder to Lance that their attempts really had been futile. In what way could they have possibly made a difference, when just the infrastructure spanned for kilometres?

Lance pulled up to the Expiration Centre, and they all reluctantly clambered out.

"Room eight, site B," said Lance as he looked at the document on his device.

For a brief moment, he was worried there would be a mixup, and the executioner would be notified of the swap too late. But Lance had to simmer down that fear, because there was nothing that could be done about that in any case.

The group of them filed down the demarcated walkways, following the signs to site B, and then the signs to room eight. They entered a room that could only be described as functional. The model from the execution chambers of old prisons in the States. A few rows of seating in front of a bullet proof, soundproof glass, which itself was in front of a rig of some kind. There appeared to have been some sick kind of attempt at humanity, because the rig was cushioned for comfort, and angled perfectly, so that the victim would be practically lying down, but able to see their family. A soundproof bolted door bridged the divide between the seat of the living and the rig of the dead. A lone, solemn employee stood by the bolted door.

"Good morning, Masons," the man said, both rehearsed and with a shred of empathy. He shot Lance a look, which confirmed at least to Lance that all would go according to plan. A small consolation.

"The Expiration Undertaker will be with you shortly. We recommend now to utilise this time for your last goodbyes. And Fortune would like to thank you on behalf of the world for you-"

"Shut up," said Jan through tears that were beginning to form.

Lance regarded her in a way he had never done before. She was his baby sister, but she was fully grown now. Sometimes, he had worried he was leaving her to the wolves, but in that moment, he knew she would be just fine.

The employee nodded, clearly not affected by the snap. He surely had been subject to a lot of abuse each passing year. He unbolted the door, entered the execution chamber and began to do some final checks.

Marc turned to Jan and hugged her goodbye, but his embrace was short lived. He had rehearsed his goodbye, and clearly did not want to fall to pieces. Lance took his hug, but forced Marc to stay longer. Lance whispered to Marc so that only he could hear.

"It's not your fault."

Marc pulled back, suddenly confused, but the moment was short-lived when Anita took her son in her arms, and collapsed into hysterical crying. Lance was secretly grateful for his mother's outburst, because it meant he didn't need to explain himself.

Suddenly, the bolted door opened again and the previous employee and another woman emerged. Lance felt his pulse quicken.

"I am Edna Swanson, I am the Expiration Undertaker assigned to your case today. Unfortunately, it is now time to complete the contract."

Through the crying of Anita, Jan, and now Marc, there was an air of tension, too. They waited for Marc to be called to the rig.

Edna Swanson held out her device and in a nonchalant tone said, "Mr. Mason, please enter the chamber."

Anita drew breath and Marc shot up as if called by a drill sergeant. He wiped his eyes and sniffed, "Alright, yes. I'm c-"

"My apologies, Mr. Mason, the other Mr. Mason."

The heaviness of the silence that followed Edna Swanson's statement could have weighed down a body in water. Marc took a moment or two to process, but by then, Lance had already stepped forward.

"What?!" the other Mason's cried in unison.

Lance turned to look at his family, now the tears welled

again, his 'strong man' pretence broken. But not his resolve.

"What?!" repeated Marc, "No, there's a mistake, this is my contract."

"Mr. Mason, I can assure you there is no mistake," was Edna's curt response.

"But, but I, I'm the-"

"Marc," said Lance, his family, in a state of shock, just stared at him, "I said I would find a way. And I did."

"Lance, wait-" Marc scrambled after the Executioner and his brother. The male employee grabbed him and held him back. Behind him, his mother and Jan collapsed into tears on the seating, eyes fixed on Lance through the glass as he was led to the rig.

Lance could see his family in distress, he was in distress too, but he attempted to hide it once more. He was silently thankful for the echoed silence of the chamber when the bolted door was sealed. Edna led him to the rig and fastened him in.

"Just a precaution," she said while he stared out at his family.

Anita's hands to her mouth, Jan's eyes wild with confusion, as were Marc's.

"Alright then, all strapped in, I'll just get the syringe."

Lance's eyes broke from his family to Edna Swanson as she diddled around for the lethal injection, as if she was a dentist. She retrieved it and flicked it to ensure it was filled with the deadly concoction. Lance's heart rate began to heighten. His evolutionary fight or flight instincts were kicking in. Whether he wanted to look scared or not was irrelevant, the look he could see from his brother told him that he was displaying fear. Though not slashing around like a deranged animal, Lance was still aware of the sick necessity of his death. If he chickened out (not that he could) they would just take Marc. All condoned from their fallacious 'save the world' argument. He had to do this, he was scared, but he was following through with it.

Despite being able to talk, Lance mouthed, "I love you," to his family.

To no one person in particular.

A cold hand felt up his strapped down forearm, looking for a vein. Edna was gearing up to do her job.

"Any last words will be recorded, should you have any, Mr. Mason," she said, then she flipped a switch, and addressed the room as a whole as she swabbed his vein with topical anaesthetic, "the Expiration is about to take place. We understand your feelings of distraught. Thank you for your service, Mr. Mason."

The words from Edna Swanson had a chillingly calming effect on the Masons beyond the glass. Still teary eyed, they suddenly all focused their attention on Lance, as if all wanted to ensure that they caught every single one of his last breaths.

Edna looked at Lance.

"I'm sorry," she whispered. And she plunged the needle in.

There was no pain. Lance chose to look at his family instead of the needle sticking into him. Again, he mouthed that he loved them. This time, he couldn't help but look more helpless and scared. His family continued to stare at him and cry, Marc had his hand on the glass, he actually seemed to be crying the most.

Lance could feel the drug taking effect, his arm started to turn numb. He suddenly remembered he had some last words. With his dying breaths, he managed to let out one last consolation to Marc.

"It's not your… fault."

Lance's eyes fluttered closed, and his head flopped down.

Lance Mason expired.

Epilogue

Edna Swanson set the glass divider of room eight in Site B to opaque. The procedure had been completed, she now had to move the body to the secure warehouse.

She unclipped Lance Mason's restraints as he had no use for them anymore, and folded the rig down, horizontally. She was not a caring person by nature, she supposed that was why she was so good at her job. She did not necessarily like her job, but at the same time, it was a solitary job and she liked that. She was just not the best person to be around, really. A mother she was, but a good one she was not. A friend she was, but a good one she was not. She was a person who preferred her own company, and who was simply not that well-suited to any social interaction. Fortune preyed on those types of people, because they knew they wouldn't mind doing the dirty work. And Edna didn't.

Edna, with the help of some other Site B staff, removed Lance Mason from the rig onto a cold gurney, and led the convoy through some back double doors into a connecting corridor. These corridors scattered the centre, each Expiration chamber exited into one of the corridors that all converged into larger warehouses per site. Site B was the largest of the warehouses.

Edna ensured her Expired was offered a white sheet. She had at least that bit of respect for her victims. However, once that was done, her job was complete. Through no choice of her own whether she wanted to see her victims' bodies go through the post injection process or not was irrelevant. She didn't really care all too much, perhaps as much as someone might care about putting down a domestic animal. She left the single-use device clamped to Lance Mason's gurney, and exited from whence she came. She would go off and administer a few late Expirations before she called it a day.

***

Some minutes after the Expiration Undertaker had exited the warehouse, lab technicians descended upon Lance Mason's gurney, as well as upon the others that had been left by other Undertakers. Two technicians were assigned to Lance Mason. A spindly man and a tough looking woman, both in pristine, white lab coats.

The technicians all followed each other with their assigned gurneys and filed through another set of doors to the opposite side of the warehouse. They marched down a long corridor towards a section of the facility that was not seen from the roadways; a section the public preferred not to think about when considering the lethal injections performed in the road facing buildings. Every now and then, a technician group would split off into a lab room. There were numerous such lab rooms all along the corridor.

Lance Mason's gurney was one of the last to be wheeled, rather sharply, into a lab. The gurney was wheeled towards the centre, and the wheels were braked so that the gurney acted like a stationery operating table.

"Just our luck, we get the boss's pet project," said the woman.

"Well Patricia," said the man, "it has to be someone, doesn't it? Luck of the draw. In any case, we're just the prep work. We aren't doing anything to him."

"Yeah, Stout, that means we aren't being paid the big bucks, idiot."

"Shit, that's right," said Stout, suddenly upset. "Well, then fuck it, the prep work can wait. The meds will last for hours, I'm going on smoke break. A long one."

Patricia pulled back the sheet and looked uninterestedly at the face of Lance Mason. He looked stoic and at peace. For some reason, it annoyed her.

"Yeah, let's go," she concurred. "The prep will be quick enough anyway. May as well at least clock in those basic hours, right? What about the-" and she motioned towards the restraints.

"Exactly, and leave them. The meds last forever and a day," said Stout and they both got up. After a few moments of shuffling and readying of medical tools for their job later, they exited the lab.

After a short while, the main light dimmed due to detecting no movement. The silence in the room was absolute. The labs were spaced out and insulated with sound proofing so that nothing from the outside could disturb the work being done inside.

If someone was paying close enough attention, they may have seen a slight rise and fall of Lance Mason's chest. Had they been in the room mere minutes after the exit of Stout and Patricia, they would have been shocked to the core, as suddenly and inexplicably, Lance Mason let out a terrific gasp of air, and his eyes flung open.